"I'm not staying here a minute longer, Lizzy snapped. **"I don't care what my brothers say. I know what I saw and I'm not going to sit here waiting around for that man to come after me again."**

Her voice had risen an octave and she folded her arms across her chest.

"I agree," Ajay said, his tone even.

"You agree?" Lizzy sounded surprised.

"I think home is the best place for you to be. You can recuperate at your family's ranch."

"I have my own home," she responded. "A very nice home. Thank you very much."

"You probably need to be where there's family to help you until you're stronger. Besides, I don't want to worry about you being alone. I also don't think your father and brothers want to be worried about you either."

"Fine," Lizzy snapped. "I'll stay at the ranch, but there's one condition."

"And what's that?" Ajay questioned.

"I'll only stay if you agree to stay there with me. Just for a few days. I'll feel better if I know you're there to protect me."

Dear Reader,

There is something formidable about the Colton family. I've come to appreciate the nuances of the many family members. The Coltons of Owl Creek bring the DRAMA with all-capital letters. When you toss in an array of bad guys who leave you clinging to the edge of your seat, there's no better experience. Lizzy Colton challenged me as much as she challenged the hero, Ajay Wright. I enjoyed breathing life into this couple. Ajay and his search and rescue partner, Pumpkin, are quite the pairing and Lizzy couldn't be in better hands when she needs to be rescued.

It has truly been an honor to be associated with the wonderful authors who comprise the Colton series team. To be included in this author's club has been enlightening in ways that were unexpected but appreciated. I continue to work at being a better writer with each and every book. I appreciate all the kindness and support shown to me. The romance community is truly a treasure!

Thank you so much for your support. I am always humbled by all the love you keep showing me, my characters and our stories. I know that none of this would be possible without you.

Until the next time, please take care and may God's blessings be with you always.

With much love,

Deborah Fletcher Mello

DeborahMello.org

COLTON'S
BLIZZARD
HIDEOUT

DEBORAH FLETCHER MELLO

ROMANTIC SUSPENSE

Special thanks and acknowledgment are given to
Deborah Fletcher Mello for her contribution to
The Coltons of Owl Creek miniseries.

Harlequin®
ROMANTIC
SUSPENSE™

Recycling programs
for this product may
not exist in your area.

ISBN-13: 978-1-335-50241-4

Colton's Blizzard Hideout

Harlequin Enterprises ULC
22 Adelaide St. West, 41st Floor
Toronto, Ontario M5H 4E3, Canada
www.Harlequin.com

Printed in Lithuania

MIX
Paper | Supporting
responsible forestry
FSC® C021394

A true Renaissance woman, **Deborah Fletcher Mello** finds joy in crafting unique storylines and memorable characters. She's received accolades from several publications, including *Publishers Weekly*, *Library Journal* and *RT Book Reviews*. Born and raised in Connecticut, Deborah now considers home to be wherever the moment moves her.

To Emma Cole

Thank you! Your patience and understanding
as I dealt with my father's illness and passing
were sincerely appreciated. You took my
challenges in stride and the many times
I fell short, you were there to
encourage and support me.
I will forever remember your kindness.

Chapter 1

"We have to find those babies! They must be here some-where," Lizzy Colton cried out. She struggled against the ties that bound her hands and feet together. "Why are you doing this?" she screamed.

The man standing above her grunted. The ski mask he wore obstructed his face, but she had memorized every detail of his dark eyes, his dismissive stare feeling like daggers of ice. He wore the same dingy slacks, red plaid jacket and brown hiking boots that he'd been in for the past few days. Lizzy wasn't certain how much time had passed since he had dragged her up this mountain, but he'd come and gone three times, throwing a bag of cold French fries and a hamburger at her feet every time he returned.

He dropped the greasy brown bag to the floor and pushed it toward her with his foot.

"I need the bathroom," Lizzy muttered, her voice drop-ping multiple decibels. "A *real* bathroom," she exclaimed as he pointed toward a large bucket positioned in the corner.

He leaned down to stare at her. His eyes danced over her face, and when he reached out his hand to draw his fingers along her profile, she flinched. Her discomfort seemed to amuse him. He grabbed her cheeks as if to kiss her, and then he let her go, his lips lifting in a wry smile. He untied her hands, then gestured with his eyes to the bucket.

Lizzy rubbed her wrists as she pulled her body upright, stretching her legs. She flexed her arms to revive the blood flow down the appendages. She pulled against the heavy, twisted nylon rope wrapped around one of her ankles, the length only giving her enough freedom to reach the far corner. With a heavy sigh, she moved slowly in that direction, tossing him a chilly glare over her shoulder.

He grunted a second time, motioning with a large butcher knife for her to hurry. Then he turned his back to her. A cell phone in his pocket suddenly chimed for his attention. As he answered the call, she noted the stress that rose in the gruffness of his voice. He swore, a litany of profanity spewing into the chilly air. Tossing her another look, he sauntered to the cabin door and stepped outside. He whispered angrily into the phone receiver as he made his exit.

Lizzy cursed as she dropped her pants and squatted above the bucket. When her bladder was empty, she straightened her clothes and moved back to the other corner, kicking the dinner bag out of her way. Her stomach grumbled with pain, but she ignored whatever lay inside the container. She didn't trust the stranger or anything he thought to serve her.

Leaning her back against the wall, Lizzy slid down the wood structure, easing herself to the floor. She pulled her knees to her chest and wrapped her arms tightly around herself. The last time she had tried to free herself from the bindings, he had caught her. His palm slamming into the side of her face had dropped her to the floor. The slap she could have handled, but his heavy boots slamming into her midsection had been brutal. She knew she couldn't risk another beating. She was still in pain from their last encounter and might not survive another. She settled in and waited for the man to return. Minutes later, Lizzy was still waiting.

It was only as the sun was beginning to set for the night

that Lizzy realized the man had gone, leaving without re-tying her hands. Her abductor had retreated back down the mountain, seeming to forget that he had left her there alone. Something had pulled his attention from her and thwarted whatever plans he'd had.

With every ounce of energy she could muster, she freed herself from the leg restraints, peered out the door to be certain no one was around, and then she ran, bolting for freedom because her life depended on it.

"The children have been found! I repeat...the children have been found! All are safe and sound!"

Ajay Wright felt a wave of relief float down his spine as he recognized his friend's voice. He took a deep breath and then another before he pressed the call button on his radio.

"Ten–four," he said to the man on the other end. "Good news is always appreciated, Malcolm."

"Happy to oblige," Malcolm Colton responded. "And thank you. I can't tell you how much your help means to me and my family."

Ajay nodded into the radio as if the other man could see him.

Malcolm, a rancher by profession, was also a highly re-spected volunteer with the police department's search and rescue team. The two had been giving a public relations dem-onstration with both their rescue dogs when the two children were snatched. Pacer, Malcolm's shepherd-and-hound mix, had been equally invested, determined to give Ajay's dog Pumpkin a run for her money.

"I'm happy to help," Ajay finally responded.

"Everyone be careful getting back," Malcolm concluded. "There's a storm brewing, and the temperature is going to drop fast."

"Will do," Ajay replied. "Over and out."

As the call disconnected, a round of cheers rang through the chilly afternoon air, the team of search-and-rescue personnel and volunteers within hearing distance surrendering to the comfort that this time, all had ended well. There were hugs and high fives as they all began to move out of the snow-covered terrain toward the line of vehicles parked on the road below.

Ajay exhaled another deep breath. They had been searching for two small children—Justin, age four, and his sister Jane, who was only fourteen months old. Three days prior, the two had been snatched by their paternal grandfather at Fall Fest, Owl Creek's annual county fair, and many had feared the worst.

Their grandfather, Winston Kraft, had not been given custody of the children after the death of his son and daughter-in-law. Kraft had vowed revenge against the Coltons when he'd discovered that Greg Colton and his new wife, Briony, were the family who had been given the responsibility to cherish and protect those babies.

Ajay knew from past experiences that a man intent on revenge was a man capable of the most heinous crimes. The children being found safe and sound made his heart sing with sheer joy and gave him comfort knowing that for once, all things could be right in the world.

He blew a loud whistle that echoed through the late afternoon air. Tilting his head, he listened for the familiar response from his four-legged companion. He whistled a second time, his gaze narrowing as his eyes darted across the landscape. He smiled when he spied Pumpkin, his five-year-old yellow Lab, bounding in his direction.

"Good girl," Ajay muttered as the dog reached his side. He leaned to tousle his pet's fur coat. "Good girl!" He gestured with his hand, pointing the dog toward the car. He followed as Pumpkin scampered ahead of him, her tail waving excitedly.

According to procedure, Ajay double-checked that all his staff and the few volunteers with them were accounted for. He paused, watching as everyone waved goodbye and disappeared toward town. He jotted a quick note onto the clipboard that had been resting in the front seat of his new Jeep Wrangler Rubicon, the ocean-blue SUV a birthday gift to himself. He noted the date and time that the last car pulled onto the road and out of sight.

Inside the vehicle, Pumpkin settled down against the back seat. She laid her head against her wet paws, her eyes looking toward him as if she had something she needed to say.

"What's up, Pumpkin?" Ajay questioned, tossing a look over his shoulder. "Why those sad eyes?"

Pumpkin lifted her head and barked, then rested herself a second time. She didn't look happy.

"Sorry, kiddo," Ajay said. He chuckled softly. "It wasn't our save to make this time. You'll get the next one."

Pumpkin groaned, seeming to understand what her friend was saying to her. She suddenly lifted herself again and barked.

"Easy, girl," Ajay responded. "There's a storm coming in, and the wind is starting to pick up. We'll be on our way as soon as I make sure everyone else is off this mountain."

Pumpkin barked a second time, the high-pitched yelp capped with a low growl and then a grunt.

Ajay smiled, thinking if anyone could translate the conversation, they would have heard Pumpkin cursing him, not at all happy that she couldn't still be outside running about. He and his furry friend had been conversing like that since she was a puppy. He talked to her as if she understood, and she answered in kind. They were inseparable, the bond between them as thick as the blackstrap molasses he hoarded during the winter months. Molasses and his grandmother's homemade biscuits were a daily staple in both their winter diets.

His name echoing out from the shortwave radio pulled his attention from Pumpkin.

"Dispatch to Lieutenant Wright. Dispatch to Lieutenant Wright."

Ajay pressed the talk button on his radio. "Go ahead, Dispatch."

There was a swift moment of static before a voice broke through the quiet. "Ajay, this is Della."

Della Winslow and Ajay were good friends. She was his first search-and-rescue partner when he'd joined the department. She'd found Pumpkin for him and had helped to train the pup. She was one of the best dog trainers in the field, and he had great respect for her. Occasionally, people questioned their relationship, but Della was engaged to be married, and he was excited for her. Her fiancé, and the love of her life, was FBI agent Max Colton, the eldest Colton son and brother to Malcolm. Ajay and Max were acquainted through Della, but the two men didn't know each other well.

"What's up, Della?"

"We're short one volunteer. You didn't pick up any strays, by chance?"

"No, ma'am. All my volunteers have been accounted for. There's no one up here."

"We need you to do a sweep of the area between Owl Creek and the Overview Pass. We're looking for a woman. It's Lizzy Colton, Max's baby sister, and she wandered away from the group she was with. They last saw her headed up toward the back ridge. That was on the first day of our search for the Kraft children, and she's been out of contact ever since. The family just realized no one had talked to her when she didn't show up to see the kids with the rest of the family. They all thought one of them had spoken to her until they were all together and realized no one had. Doppler weather radar is now predicting this storm is going to be a beast, so we need to find her before the precipitation starts coming in."

"We might be a little late for that," Ajay said, noting the flecks of snow looking like tufts of white cotton falling from the sky. "Are we sure she didn't just head home?" he asked. They often had volunteers who quit the job after discovering just how stressful it could be.

"It doesn't look promising. Her brother Malcolm is headed to her house now to double-check. But her family swears she hasn't been seen since they started searching for the missing kids. Max is nervous, so that makes me nervous."

He sensed something in her voice as she mentioned the man with whom she would soon be united in matrimony. Something that gave him pause and put him on high alert. "Ten-four," Ajay responded. "I've got my radio. Give me a shout-out if she turns up."

"Be safe, Ajay," Della said. "It looks like it's going to get nasty out there."

The radio clicked off in his ear. Ajay sighed as he shifted his gaze up the side of the mountain. The last slivers of bright light that had shone through the canopy of trees earlier in the day were beginning to disappear. The sky had gone a dull gray, and the temperature was dropping swiftly. The snow was falling steadily, settling in for the long haul. Ajay knew it wouldn't bode well for anyone caught out in the elements unprepared.

He was familiar with Lizzy Colton through her brother Malcolm. He'd seen her that first day, frantic over the children being taken. The whole family had been at their wit's end. She'd barely glanced in his direction, anxious to be searching. She'd been impatient throughout the safety talk, barreling toward the tree line as soon as it was finished. She'd been assigned to another group, and so she'd been someone else's problem. Not his. Till now.

He blew another heavy sigh. "Let's pony up, Pumpkin," he said, the baritone in his voice echoing around them. "We're still on the clock, girl!" He grabbed his backpack, checked its contents and slung it over his shoulder.

Pumpkin jumped from the Jeep, her tail waving with anticipation. She barked twice and then took off on an easy sprint through the tree line. Ajay shifted his bag against his broad shoulders and then followed after his dog.

Chapter 2

Ajay and Pumpkin backtracked to the festival area, meeting up with Della and another friend, Sebastian Cross. Sebastian owned Crosswinds Training, the dog training center over on Cross Road. The facility was about ten minutes from town, sitting on five acres of Cross family land. Della and Sebastian had worked with Ajay and Pumpkin to ensure their handler-canine partnership worked effortlessly. Often undertaking search-and-rescue missions together also allowed Pumpkin to engage with Della's black Lab, Charlie, and Sebastian's golden retriever, Oscar. Pumpkin was quite the diva in the presence of the male dogs.

After checking in with each other and establishing a search plan, Della, Sebastian and Ajay had all moved out in opposite directions.

Ajay had gone up and out through the thick forest of trees, following Owl Creek, which flowed down the mountain and into Blackbird Lake. An hour or so later, Pumpkin had discovered a cell phone, discarded just a few feet from the stream. Having missed the water, it was badly scratched from being tossed aside, but it still seemed to be functioning. It had no password protection and took Ajay no time at all to figure out it belonged to Lizzy Colton, the woman he was hoping to find.

Knowing she didn't have a way to communicate with anyone set him on edge. The weather had indeed turned, and there wasn't much time left for him to continue searching. He feared the worst but didn't want to consider what that might be.

Her inbox was inundated with messages from family and friends anxious to hear from her. He held the device out toward Pumpkin, palming it in his hand so she could get the woman's scent. The dog took off ahead of him, her tracking senses on high alert.

Minutes later, Pumpkin was barking excitedly, running in circles about fifty yards ahead of Ajay. Something rested beneath a tree, covered with a layer of freshly fallen snow. Ajay hurried to where his pooch now lay protectively near what she had discovered.

Reaching Pumpkin's side, Ajay knelt down beside her. The woman lying on the ground was out cold, and Ajay smiled wryly at the thought, which was not meant to be literal. But she *was* unconscious, wearing clothes that offered her little protection, and the outside elements had begun to take their toll. She'd been ill-prepared for the inclement weather, and he questioned what had happened that she was there with no coat or shoes. What had she gone through, he wondered.

Ajay knew he needed to get her to safe surroundings and get her warm, but there was no way he could carry her the distance back down the mountain side without endangering all three of them.

Ajay pulled a harness from his backpack and looped it around Pumpkin's torso. The dog whined and licked his face.

"I know, girl," he said, "but I'm going to need your help."

Her tail wagged back and forth in response. With swift precision, Ajay's backpack was secured across Pumpkin's back. She seemed content with the added responsibility.

After checking the Colton woman for broken bones, Ajay took his own jacket off and wrapped it around her torso. Then he lifted her up and over his shoulder like a sack of new potatoes.

Pumpkin started down the mountain, but Ajay called her back. He gestured in the other direction. "We need to find shelter, Pumpkin. We're going to have to ride out this storm. Let's see if we can find cover in one of those rental cabins that are so popular in this area. Pony up, Pumpkin!"

They had walked a good three miles when the Colton woman stirred, her arms clutching his neck tightly. Her entire body shivered beneath the shearling-lined coat he'd been wearing. Her face was buried in his chest, and she muttered something he couldn't understand.

He'd been following a map to the best of his ability. The uptick in falling snow wasn't making their trek easy, the bright white layer of precipitation blinding.

The setting sun and the requisite compass in his pocket kept him pointed in the right direction as he maneuvered forward, intent on reaching the row of rental cabins sitting on the mountain's upper ridge. He eased Lizzy higher in his arms, tightening the grip he had around her.

Her head lifted from his chest and settled against his broad shoulder. She stirred once again, but her eyes never opened. Her thin arms tightened around his neck, the hold she had on him beginning to feel like a vise grip.

He hugged her closer, hoping she sensed that he would never let her go. Not until she was safe.

The three-hundred-square-foot cabin was luxurious by mountain standards. Its modest size boasted three rooms on the lower level and a lofted sleeping area on the upper floor. It had been over an hour since Ajay had found them refuge, and he was thankful for the fire in the fireplace and the fully stocked pantry.

Pumpkin had already consumed a can of corned beef hash, and she lay beside the woman, seeming to sense a need there that she might be able to fix.

The mattress Lizzy rested against adorned the only bed in the space. Ajay had tended to her scratches and bruises with the medical kit from his backpack. He had enough emergency response training to know that she might have suffered a head injury when she fell. He'd cocooned her in a multitude of blankets to get her body temperature back up.

She had a good case of frostnip, but the color had finally begun to return to her fingers and toes. He was hopeful that he'd found her in time to have prevented her from experiencing serious aftereffects.

Ajay wrapped his large hands around a mug of hot soup that he'd nuked in the microwave. The power had been on when they arrived, but he knew it might not last. The lights flickered as if to confirm his thoughts. He was exhausted and ready for his own nap, but sleep wouldn't be coming any time soon. They'd found shelter, but he still needed to ensure they'd be safe through the storm.

He was grateful for the working radio. He'd been able to call in their location and assure the search-and-rescue team they were okay for the time being. With the storm raging outside, though, it would be hours before anyone could get to them, and there was no way he'd be able to get Lizzy back down the mountain with that thick layer of snow impeding their trek.

The fire raging in the fireplace would only last for as long as he could keep feeding it wood, and they couldn't afford for the flames to die out. For the immediate future, they were stuck with each other, and he was responsible for her care and safety. Sleep would have to wait.

Lizzy woke with a start, her entire body tensing when her eyes opened. Her gaze shifted rapidly from side to side, skating around the room. She inhaled swiftly at the sight of the man kneeling in front of the fireplace. However, he was familiar, and she relaxed, sensing he was there to help and not hurt her.

He was ruggedly handsome with a dark beard and mustache that flattered his brown complexion. His hair was closely cropped, and his body seemed muscular beneath the long-sleeved T-shirt he wore. He resembled the actor in that Shonda Rhimes medical show she occasionally watched.

There was a fire blazing, and he was tending it with a long metal poker. He was staring into the fire and seemed lost in thought.

She lifted her arms from beneath the covers tucked around her body, and when she did, a large dog moved beside her. Lizzy jumped ever so slightly as the animal lifted its head to stare up at her. Lizzy wasn't sure if she should be afraid, but something about her situation felt comfortable. This was definitely not like when she'd been tied to the beam in that abandoned cabin.

The dog suddenly barked, and the man turned swiftly. At the sight of her, his full lips lifted in the brightest smile.

"Don't sit up too fast," he said softly. "You suffered a head injury when you fell. You had me scared there for a minute. Let me get you some water."

Lizzy's hand went to her head, her fingers grazing the gauze wrapped around her skull. A wave of nausea suddenly pitched through her midsection, and she lay back down against the pillows.

The man rose from where he'd been kneeling and hurried to the kitchen. He filled a glass with water from a pitcher in the refrigerator. Rushing back, he knelt down beside her. He lifted the container to her lips and continued talking.

"You might not remember me, but I'm Lieutenant Ajay Wright. I'm with the Owl Creek Police Department. Their search-and-rescue team. My partner and I found you passed out a few miles down the mountain from here."

Lizzy took a small sip of the cool liquid he offered. "Your partner...?" she whispered.

Ajay smiled again and nodded. He gestured with his head. "That beauty queen beside you is Pumpkin. I don't go very far without her."

Pumpkin nuzzled Lizzy's neck and licked her face. Lizzy giggled.

"You had a lot of people worried. Everyone has been looking for you. But they know you're with me now, and they know you're safe. A rescue team will come for us as soon as this storm passes."

"How long have I been here?" Lizzy questioned.

"Just a few hours. We had to find shelter. The snow started rolling in faster than expected. It was safer for us to find someplace to ride it out, so I carried you here."

"You carried me?"

"You sound surprised."

Lizzy wasn't sure how she sounded. She only wanted to understand everything that happened that she didn't remember. She suddenly bolted upright. "My niece and nephew. We need to find..." she started, her tone bordering on hysteria.

Ajay's voice dropped lower, his tone soothing. "They're fine. I imagine they're tucked safely in their own beds with your brother and his wife hovering over the two of them. We found them safe and sound."

Lizzy could feel the weight of the world lifting at Ajay's words. A tear puddled in the corner of her eyes. "Thank God!" she gushed, a sigh of relief blowing past her chapped lips.

Ajay nodded. "We found *them*, then the call went out about *you* being missing. Thankfully, we can report two successful recoveries."

Lizzy swiped her hand across her face. "I was so scared," she said. "If anything had happened to those two babies, I would have been devastated." Her voice quivered, a wave of emotion wrapped around each word.

He nodded, understanding seeping from his gaze. "Can you tell me what happened out there?" he asked. "Did you get lost? I know how easy it is to get turned around in these woods."

She shook her head. There was just a moment's pause as she thought back to her last memories. "I was out searching for Jane and Justin when I spotted what I thought was the car that had taken them. It wasn't far from where they were holding the festival, so I went to see if maybe they'd been left inside. The car was empty, so I started walking around the area. Out of nowhere, someone or something hit me from behind. The next thing I knew I was in the trunk of the car, and someone was driving away. Then I passed out. When I came to, I was tied up in an abandoned cabin with someone, maybe the person who abducted me. He wouldn't speak to me or answer any of my questions. He would leave and come back, and he always wore a mask. But he was the only one who came to the cabin while I was there. The last time, he forgot to tie me back up before he disappeared—I think he was called away. When I was certain he was gone, I just took off running. At some point, I slipped and fell. That's the last thing I remember."

Ajay's brow furrowed as he seemed to process the information. Lizzy desperately wanted him to believe her. Maybe she had hallucinated after her fall, but he had to know there was something in her story that rang true. She knew she was telling the truth, but she also knew everyone else would have questions. Why had someone grabbed her? Was her being held hostage connected to the children? Clearly, she didn't have any answers. But it also seemed that something else was bothering him more.

"Why would you put yourself in danger?" Ajay queried, his question harsher than she had expected. It surprised her, and it seemed to surprise him as well. There was a wealth of emotion churning in her midsection, as she suddenly realized that he was feeling protective of her.

He drew in a deep breath, looking like his feelings had ambushed him, and then he snapped at her. "Why didn't you call for help? You could have been killed!" Her gaze never left him as he took another deep breath and held it.

Lizzy bristled at the rise in his tone. It was not how she had expected their conversation to go. There was a familiarity between them that she hadn't anticipated. It was comforting and disconcerting at the same time. Not having an answer for him that would make sense, she shifted her gaze from his and closed her eyes, pretending to fall back to sleep.

He had some nerve, she thought to herself. Besides, it wasn't like she owed Ajay Wright an explanation for anything she did.

Chapter 3

Lizzy stared up at the ceiling, counting the rows of wood beams. That man and his animal were both sleeping soundly. One snored louder than the other. He'd positioned himself in the recliner that rested in the cabin's corner by the fireplace. A blanket lay across his chest and around his shoulders. His dog, Pumpkin, was curled up on the floor at his feet. Clearly, both had been keeping a close watch over her.

Despite his assumption, Lizzy had known exactly who Ajay was when she opened her eyes, even though she had pretended otherwise. The handsome man had been at the center of more than one conversation between herself and her best friend, Vivian Maylor. As had many of the guys who'd been friends or associates of her brothers.

Besties since they were fourteen at Owl Creek Middle School, she and Vivian had often giggled and gossiped about the boys, and men, who had passed through their lives over the years. Lizzy would have given anything to get a cell phone signal so she could call Vivian and describe in glorious detail how Ajay Wright had saved her life.

Lizzy shook the cellular device in her hand. She had lost it when that stranger had grabbed her. Ajay finding and returning it to her had been sheer luck.

Truth be told, the last few days had been the fodder of nightmares, and nothing she wanted to recall. Being rescued was the stuff of fantasies and a happy ending wouldn't hurt her feelings one bit. And who better to share that with than her dearest friend in the whole wide world?

But if Lizzy knew anything at all, she knew Vivian would be less enthusiastic, focused solely on everything bad that could have happened. Lizzy was willing to bet a dime to a dollar that now that everyone knew she was safe, Vivian was home, curled up with a book and her beloved cat, Toby, contemplating all that was wrong in the world. Despite running one of the most lucrative PR agencies around, Vivian was not the outgoing, social-butterfly type. It was why Lizzy was always trying to set her BFF up on blind dates.

Over the years, the two women had met and socialized with many of her brother's friends. Lizzy had even dated a few, usually just the ones that irritated her three siblings most. Greg, the eldest, usually raised the most sand about her liaisons. Malcolm, the second oldest child, and then Max after him, rarely went ballistic over her antics. The two just never held their tongues, garnering great pleasure in telling her what they thought about her romantic liaisons.

She blew a soft sigh past her thin lips, and the dog lifted her head to stare at her. Lizzy smiled, and she would have sworn Pumpkin smiled back before lowering her bright eyes back to the floor and closing them.

Lizzy had never considered herself an animal person. She liked them well enough, especially when other people were responsible for them. Being raised on a ranch with all kinds of four-legged creatures, she had never had any burning desire to have one of her own to coddle and care for.

But Pumpkin had smiled back at her, and that had her feeling some kind of way. She chuckled softly under her breath.

"Are you hungry?" Ajay asked, his deep baritone voice cutting through the silence.

He startled Lizzy from her thoughts, and she found herself shaking ever so slightly. He seemed to sense she was unsettled, and he paused, allowing her a moment to collect herself. "I didn't mean to frighten you," Ajay said, his voice dropping an octave, his tone lower and deeper.

Lizzy shook her head. "It's fine. I'm not even sure why I reacted that way."

"You've experienced a trauma. You are entitled to not be okay. Please don't think you need to pretend everything's fine around me. I know better."

She nodded, quickly changing the subject. She had no interest in being psychoanalyzed by him, or anyone, right then. "Is it still snowing?"

"I think so." Ajay rose from his seat and moved to the front door. A chilly breeze filled the room as he pulled the door open. "Yeah," he said. "It's still coming down." He called for his dog. "Pumpkin, go do your business, girl, and come right back."

The dog barked and hurried outside. Ajay stood in the doorway, watching her until she rushed back in. Lizzy laughed as Pumpkin shook her fur coat, snow flying into the space around her.

"I swear she's smiling," Lizzy said.

Ajay laughed. "She does smile. You get used to it. She's a happy dog, and she loves being outside. The elements don't seem to faze her one bit."

"Happy means she's well cared for. You must be doing something right."

Ajay shrugged his broad shoulders, but he didn't bother to respond, seeming slightly embarrassed by the compliment. Lizzy felt her entire face pull into a large smile as she watched him, sensing his cheeks had heated under his warm, tawny complexion. He had the kindest eyes, Lizzy thought, a golden shimmer glistening in the cool brown orbs. His chiseled features were the stuff of high-fashion models, and she got the impression a camera would love him from any angle. She suddenly wondered just how soft his skin was, because his complexion looked butter smooth.

Ajay shifted the conversation back to his original question. "Can I get you something to eat? You have to be starving by now."

Lizzy smiled and nodded. "I could eat a little something," she said.

"Would you like to try some oatmeal? Or maybe some soup? We also have oatmeal and soup. Or if you prefer, soup and oatmeal."

She laughed. "Sounds like we're eating soup and oatmeal."

"Or oatmeal and soup." Ajay laughed with her. "Those are two items that are well stocked up here. They have four flavors of oatmeal—plain, cinnamon, apple spice and raisin. Then there's chicken noodle soup, tomato, broccoli cheese, cream of mushroom, chicken and stars or vegetable. Pumpkin ate the last can of corned beef hash."

Lizzy feigned a frown. "I really would have liked that hash."

"Me, too," Ajay responded as he met the stare she was giving him with his own forlorn look.

The duo suddenly laughed heartily, the moment lifting the mood in the room. Pumpkin barked along with them.

Lizzy suddenly clutched her head and winced. "Don't make me laugh," she said. "I have a raging headache."

Ajay moved to her side and pressed a large hand to her forehead. "You're warm," he said. "Do you feel nauseous or anything?"

"No, not really. I just have a headache. And I'm hungry. In fact, I think chicken noodle soup would make me feel better," Lizzy said. She gave him the slightest smile.

Ajay headed toward the kitchen area. "One microwaved can of chicken noodle soup coming right up! And if you eat it all up, I have a surprise for you after."

"I don't like surprises," Lizzy said.

He tossed her a look over his shoulder. "Everyone likes surprises."

"I'm not everyone," she countered.

Staring at her for a moment longer, Ajay finally nodded, then turned his attention back to the can of soup in his hands.

Lizzy grinned, reaching out to pet Pumpkin, who'd settled down against her side.

"So," Lizzy said, anxious to continue their conversation, "do you like the snow as much as Pumpkin does?"

Ajay tossed her a look over his shoulder as he stood in front of the microwave oven. "Not really. I prefer tropical heat. Put me on an island, and I'd be a happy man."

"So you moved to Owl Creek, Idaho? Did you know that we're not remotely tropical?" The barest hint of sarcasm was wrapped around her words.

Ajay chuckled. "I had to go where employment took me. I was working in Boise when I got this job offer. It wasn't one I could turn down. The snow was an added bonus."

"Do you like search and rescue?"

"I love it. I spent time in the military after I graduated high school. That led me to law enforcement and the rest is history."

Lizzy nodded, then took a sip of the hot soup he'd passed to her.

"What do you do?" Ajay questioned.

"I'm a starving artist working as a graphic designer. Are you familiar with Bark Design Company?"

Ajay shrugged his broad shoulders. "Sorry."

"No worries. I've only been in business for two years now.

My latest venture into the corporate arena. In all honesty, I'd love to be in my own tropical paradise painting landscapes. But I have a talent for graphic design, and it pays well."

"I'd love to see your work one day," Ajay said.

Lizzy lifted her gaze to study his expression. His interest felt genuine, not as if he were saying something just to be saying it.

He smiled, his lips lifting slowly.

She smiled back. "One day," she finally said. "One day."

A warm wave of quiet filled the space between them. Pumpkin stared at one and then the other. There was the slightest rumble of noise deep in her chest before she rolled over onto her side and closed her eyes.

"Tell me about your family," Lizzy said. "Unless that's too personal. I wouldn't want you to break any rules, but I figured since we're stuck here together…" Her voice trailed.

Ajay shifted in his seat. "There's not much to tell," he said. "I'm an only child. A military brat born in Germany. My father was a career soldier, and we lived on six different military bases while I was growing up. My mother was a stay-at-home mom. Now Dad's retired, tending to his gardens, and Mom is the librarian at the local elementary school where they live."

"An only child!" Lizzy exclaimed. "I bet that sucked growing up."

Ajay laughed. "Not at all. You don't miss what you never had. My mother kept me busy with sports and extracurricular activities. Since I never had a problem making friends, I had a great social life. My really good friends were as close as family. I was also very comfortable being alone with myself. I didn't have to share. All in all, I think I turned out okay."

"I guess growing up with three brothers, I never appreciated what being an only child might be like. It sounds like it had its advantages."

"There are only four of you?"

"More if you take into account our Jerry Springer history."

Ajay's brow lifted. "Now I'm definitely intrigued."

"Malcolm never told you about our family?"

Ajay shook his head. "The subject never came up, to be honest. I knew he had siblings, but I try to stay out of other people's Jerry Springer business."

"Well, keep up," Lizzy said as she leaned back against a mound of pillows. "This story's a doozy! It all started with our parents. Our mother, Jessie, has a twin sister, Aunt Jenny, who we call our Mama Jen. Even though the two are twins, they were never close and didn't much like each other."

Ajay winced as Lizzy nodded her head to emphasize her comment.

"In high school," she continued, "the two sisters both dated the star football captain, Robert Colton. After graduation, Robert chose Aunt Jenny, and the two married. This pulled the two sisters even further apart. But Uncle Robert had an older brother. And not to be outdone by her sister, Jessie married Robert's brother, Buck. Buck Colton is my father."

Ajay shook his head. "I think popcorn might be necessary here. This sounds like some serious tea. Some really good tea!"

Lizzy giggled. "Let me finish! Now, my Uncle Robert and Aunt Jenny had six kids, so I not only grew up with my brothers, but a half dozen cousins, too. My brother Greg was the first child my parents had. He was that *oops!* baby. Then came Malcolm and after him, Max. Max worked for the FBI until recently. And of course you know Malcolm. I am the youngest and the only girl. I was their other oops baby."

"That's funny," Ajay said. "Oops!"

"To be honest, I'm not sure any of us were planned."

"Your story's not that bad. It's kind of tame, actually. I was expecting a true scandal the way you started your story."

"I'm not finished. Get another handful of that pretend popcorn," Lizzy said. She shifted in her seat. "My parents divorced when I was a toddler, and my mother left us."

"I'm so sorry," Ajay said. He leaned forward, clasping both hands in front of him. "That must have been hard for you all."

Lizzy shrugged dismissively. "It really got hard when we found out about the affair between my mother and my uncle."

Ajay's eyes widened. "Your mother, Jessie, and your Uncle Robert?"

She nodded. "Not only did they have an affair, but they had pretended to be married, buying a home a few hours outside Boise. They even had two children together. My half-brother Nathan and my half-sister Sarah. And no one knew until just recently. Surprise!" she gushed, giving him dance hands.

Ajay's eyes bounced from side to side as he put all the pieces to the Colton family tree in place. "Wow!" he exclaimed. "That also makes Nathan and Sarah your cousins, too."

"Siblings, cousins, whatever. I just know we shared the same incubator. And they share the same sperm donor with my Aunt Jenny's kids."

Ajay shook his head. "Are you all close?"

"We're all working on it," Lizzy said softly. "I imagine future family holidays will be quite interesting."

"Save a seat for me," Ajay teased. "I don't want to miss the fireworks."

"We managed to all get through Uncle Robert's funeral, and after that the truth started to come out. He suffered a stroke a few months ago. At least, that's what we've all been told."

"You don't believe it?"

"I really don't have any reason not to, but I know some of his children have had a lot of questions. Then toss in a whole other family wanting to lay claim to their share of his estate, and I'm sure everything looks fishy."

"I'm sorry to hear that," Ajay said. "Losing a parent must be difficult enough without the added drama."

"Do you have a good relationship with your parents?" Lizzy questioned.

"I do," Ajay said with a nod of his head. "My father is one of my best friends, and my mother, well… She still spoils me when she can. I love them both dearly. How about you?"

"My dad is the best. I don't know what I would do without him. My mother, on the other hand, is a whole other story." She scowled. Her eyes moved to the window, and Lizzy seemed to drift off into thought.

Ajay could feel a shift in her energy. He hesitated to ask more about her mother after everything she'd shared. "So what's the big surprise you have for me?" she questioned, holding out the empty soup bowl. The sudden change of subject meant he didn't have an opportunity to push further.

Ajay jumped from his seat. He reached for her dirty dish and took it with him back to the kitchen counter. A moment passed as he shifted items in one of the cabinets. Stepping back toward her, he held his hands behind his back.

"Should I be scared?" Lizzy said, eyeing him nervously.

"Only if you have an irrational fear of… Twinkies!" His grin was canyon wide as he held out the cellophane-wrapped treat. His eyes met hers and held. "We actually have dessert to go with all that soup and oatmeal!"

Twinkies! Lizzy laughed heartily. Maybe things were beginning to look up after all, she thought.

"I hated cheese as a child," Ajay said. "I thought it was the worst thing in the world. Now, I can't get enough of the stuff!"

"It was cottage cheese for me. I hated it then, and I despise it now." Lizzy frowned. "Please, tell me you don't eat cottage cheese."

"It's not my favorite, but I can get it down if I have to. It just requires something sweet to go with it. Like pineapple. Or strawberries."

"Yuck," Lizzy responded with a scowl.

Ajay laughed. "So what's your favorite dessert?"

"The first cake I taught myself how to make, and it came out well, was a pineapple upside-down cake. I've perfected my recipe, and it's my all-time favorite dessert to make and eat. And my daddy loves it!"

"What about your brothers?"

"They don't count. I can make a pan of boxed brownies, and that makes them happy."

"Brownies are good!"

"What about you? What's your favorite sweet?" Lizzy asked.

"I would give everything away for a perfect banana pudding with lots of those vanilla wafer cookies."

"I don't know if I've ever made banana pudding."

"It has to be the cooked pudding, not the one where you mix whipped cream and pudding mix together. Homemade pudding with bananas and vanilla cookies. I could eat that all day, every day!"

"I'll have to give that a try."

"Now don't go messing up good bananas. If it's not good, I will tell you."

"Who said I was making it for you?"

Ajay whooped, the laughter deep in his chest. "Touché!" he said when he'd collected himself. "Touché!"

His smile was wide as he stared at her. Lizzy was beautiful. Her girl-next-door glow was captivating, and her cheeks had brightened with the rise of heat in the room. Her strawberry blond hair fell in natural waves around her face and down her back. Her facial features were perfection, stunning blue eyes and the most luscious mouth. He found himself wondering about the person allowed to kiss her lips with regularity. Who were they and how had such luck befallen them?

He wanted to ask but knew to do so was unprofessional and also none of his business. A low sigh blew past his full lips.

"So, what else do you like to do to entertain yourself?" he asked. "We've ascertained you're a good cook. What else are you good at?"

"I'm very good with my hands," Lizzy said, the barest hint of innuendo in her tone.

Ajay laughed. "I'm thinking you might need to explain that," he said.

She smiled, arching her eyebrows suggestively. Then she laughed. "I like to be crafty," she said. "I like to make beautiful things from useless scraps. I'm the queen of handmade gifts."

"I would throw useless scraps in the trash. I guess I'm not that good with my hands," he replied.

Lizzy laughed. "That's a shame," she said with an eye roll.

"Let me rephrase that," Ajay said. "I'm good with my hands, but I'm not crafty. Is that better?"

"That's for you to determine, not me!"

"But you have me feeling some kind of way."

"Don't put that on me!"

"Like I didn't see that eye roll and that look you gave me. I know how to take a hint."

Lizzy giggled. "You're a little sensitive, aren't you?"

Ajay pressed his hand over his heart. "I'm extremely sensitive and I make no apologies for it."

"I like sensitive men," Lizzy said, a sly smile pulling at her thin lips.

Ajay grinned, feeling his own lips pulling wide across his face.

Chapter 4

Lizzy Colton talked in her sleep. Ajay had been watching her for over an hour, and she had been tossing and turning and talking in her sleep the entire time. After one too many bad jokes about Twinkies and the sweet cream inside, they had chatted for a few minutes longer, the conversation mostly idle chatter about nothing of any importance. Sleep had come soon after.

There was still much about the woman Ajay wanted to know. Lizzy Colton was very much an anomaly in his little world, and he was enjoying her presence. Unlike the last woman he'd dated, she didn't take herself too seriously. She was funny and instinctively looked for the best in a bad situation. She also exuded confidence, and he had always found that kind of surety in a woman very sexy. He found himself enjoying the little idiosyncrasies that made her so intriguing.

He discovered she practiced tapping therapy or what was called EFT, emotional freedom technique. It was supposed to be a powerful stress reliever. She'd spent an hour teaching him the meridian points on his body, the acupressure points he tapped with his fingers while focusing on what was causing his stress.

He was hesitant at first, disbelieving, and she found his reticence amusing. It turned out he had only needed to be open-minded and adventurous. When he finally allowed himself to explore the possibilities, he was pleasantly surprised. She was an adept instructor, patient and skillful. There was a rhythm to what he learned, a structured dance of sorts that put him into a state of full relaxation. Then they'd both drifted off to sleep.

Now, watching her, he wished there was something he could do to ease her discomfort and help her find a semblance of peace. Because her beloved tapping didn't seem to have helped the anxiety she was clearly feeling.

Everything she'd gone through looked like it was beginning to haunt her dreams, despite her efforts to pretend like she wasn't bothered when she was awake. But Ajay knew that bottling up that kind of trauma wouldn't serve her well.

"Why are you staring at me?" Lizzy suddenly asked, her blue eyes open wide, her expression questioning.

Looking up, Ajay was taken aback. So lost in his own thoughts, he hadn't expected to get caught like his hand was in a cookie jar. "Was I staring?" he asked, feigning ignorance.

The look that crossed her face spoke volumes. Not only had he been staring, but every thought in his head could probably be read like a summer novel across his face. She must already know that he stared because he was concerned. Worried that she wouldn't be well despite his best efforts. He could keep her safe for the moment, but there was nothing he could do about the personal demons she refused to acknowledge. She was on her own in that battle.

"Okay, be like that," Lizzy said. She shifted against the mattress, sitting herself upright.

"Like what?"

"Like that."

Ajay smiled, but he didn't bother to reply. He changed the subject. "I keep thinking about your kidnapping. Do you know any reason why someone would want to take you?"

Lizzy shook her head. She blew out a soft sigh. "I really have no idea."

"Do you think it was random? That you just happened to be in the wrong place at the right time?"

"The story of my life," Lizzy muttered, seemingly pondering his question. "But no, something about it doesn't feel random. It felt like there had been some previous planning. I almost want to say he purposely meant to grab me. Showing up where I did just gave him the opportunity."

"And you're certain you never saw this man before?"

"Not that I really saw him, with the mask and all. But no. I have no idea who he is. I'd recognize his eyes, though. I'd recognize those eyes anywhere."

"Do you have any idea why he'd want to kidnap you, Lizzy? Is there anyone who has a grudge against you or who you've had beef with lately?"

She shook her head, and he could almost see her mind going through a list of everyone she knew. "No one," she said finally. "It just doesn't make sense to me."

"When you chased down the car, there was no one there, is that right?"

There was a hint of attitude in her response, as though Lizzy was beginning to feel like she was being interrogated. "I wouldn't say I chased it down. It was parked, and I went over to inspect it. I was hoping to find Justin and Jane inside, but it was empty. I started walking around the area, and that's when someone came up behind me and hit me on the head. Everything after that is really foggy. That's all I know!"

"One last question, if you don't mind. Do you remember what the car looked like?"

She nodded. "Yeah. It was an older model Nissan. A Maxima, I think." She repeated herself, needing to affirm that she was certain of what she saw. "Yeah. A black Nissan Maxima."

Ajay paused, replaying everything in his head that Lizzy had told him about being captured. He fell into thought as she pulled the blankets tighter around her torso and drifted back to sleep.

Ajay sat watching her toss and turn, her slumber restless and disturbed. He watched, almost afraid to pull his eyes away from her as if something might happen. Because clearly they were missing something, and he couldn't begin to know what that was, or if she was really safe.

When Lizzy next awoke, she was running a high fever and her chest rattled with congestion. She could barely open her eyes, and Ajay's concern rose exponentially.

It had been snowing for an entire day and didn't look like it planned to end any time soon. It had been hours since he was last able to get a signal on the radio, and he could only hope that someone would be headed in their direction sooner than later.

Pulling on his jacket and boots, he and Pumpkin headed outdoors. He carried a stack of towels that he dropped into the freshly fallen snow, rolling the towels about until they were wet and icy. Back inside, he wrapped one of the cotton cloths around Lizzy's neck and pressed another to her forehead. He knew he needed to lower her body temperature by any means necessary.

She shivered from the sudden chill as perspiration beaded across her brow. She moaned, the guttural sound pulling at Ajay's heartstrings.

"It's going to be okay," he said, his voice a loud whisper. "I'm not going to let anything happen to you, Lizzy."

Pumpkin dropped her head into Ajay's lap. Her puppy-dog stare shifted from Ajay to Lizzy, and she licked the side of Lizzy's face before burrowing her muzzle into her neck.

"She needs to rest, Pumpkin," Ajay said. "Leave her be." He stroked the dog's thick coat and nudged her down to the floor at his feet.

Hours passed as he sat at Lizzy's side. He felt helpless, only able to watch and wait. And the waiting was beginning to take its toll. Knowing he needed to keep his composure, to keep Lizzy from fearing the worst, he remained steadfast, determined that they would soon be home, safe and sound.

Ajay gently caressed the length of her fingers, her palm like smooth satin against his own. She had drifted back to sleep again, but her breathing was still ragged. She struggled for air, and that cough had become barking. Intuition told him things were only going to go downhill if help didn't arrive soon. Time wasn't being a good friend.

Lowering his head, Ajay closed his eyes. He pressed his forehead to the back of her hand, wanting to will whatever strength he had to her. Then he whispered a silent prayer skyward, wishing for complete and total healing. He still held her hand tightly, struggling against his desire to pull her into his arms.

The snow had finally stopped falling, but Ajay still wasn't able to get a radio signal in or out. Lizzy's fever had barely broken, but he'd been able to rouse her long enough to entice her with three tablespoons of soup and a few sips of hot tea and lemon. She'd fallen right back to sleep and seemed to be resting as well as she could under the circumstances.

With the fire burning in the fireplace and the snow-painted canvas outside, Ajay couldn't help but think that under different circumstances the cabin was probably a very romantic place for the right two people.

He found himself pondering the idea of himself and Lizzy Colton and blamed the fantasies on their current situation.

With nothing but time on their hands, they'd spent some of the hours in the cabin getting to know each other before Lizzy's fever spiked. He'd had dozens of questions for Lizzy, and she'd had just as many for him. He wanted to think they'd become fast friends as they'd traded stories about their childhoods and families.

With more in common than not, they'd discovered similar interests in food, music and movies. He had watched *Titanic* as many times as she had, if not more. They both loved Italian food, and she'd promised him a lasagna dinner when this was over and they were back to civilization. Learning they both kept Amythyst Kiah, Shy Carter and Ghost Hounds on rotation in their playlists had sealed the deal on a lifelong friendship both looked forward to exploring.

Lizzy's temperature spiked twice more, and twice more Ajay wrapped her in cold towels. Without her smile and laughter, it felt like an eternity had passed before the first sign of rescue sounded in the midmorning air.

Pumpkin heard the engines first, barking excitedly as she rushed to the door. Jumping from where he sat, Ajay grabbed his coat and hurried outside. Holding both arms high above his head, he waved his hands from side to side for their attention.

The line of newly purchased search-and-rescue vehicles was truly something to behold. The Owl Creek town council had approved the budget for them the previous year, and Ajay knew this was one of the first storms to put them into full use. There were five in total, SnowTrax vehicles that could easily get off the road and maneuver into tight spots without getting stuck. They put traditional ATVs, snowmobiles and trucks to shame, maneuvering around and through obstacles the other vehicles couldn't. Snow depth was inconsequential

as they literally floated above the snow. Each had been con-
figured for a driver, an EMT and a gurney if needed. And
they'd all been painted vibrant red with the Owl Creek town
logo adorning the side.

Malcolm Colton jumped from the first vehicle followed by
Max and Della. Emergency medical personnel pushed past
them as Ajay pointed them in Lizzy's direction.

"She's suffered a head injury and minor frostbite," Ajay
said. "Her fever's only been down for an hour or so, but she's
having difficulty breathing. I'm afraid it might be pneumonia."

"We've got it from here, Lieutenant," the EMT said, acknowledging the insignia on Ajay's jacket.

Malcolm extended a hand in his direction. "Thank you!
We've been worried, but I knew she was safe once you found
her. I appreciate you getting that last message to us."

"Lizzy's a fighter," Ajay said.

He watched as the two brothers hurried inside to see their
little sister. Seeing them together, there was no missing the
family resemblance. It was the eyes for Ajay—all telling,
sometimes brooding, most times full of light and energy.

Della moved to Ajay's side. She hugged him briefly before shifting into business mode. "Did Lizzy say what happened?" she asked.

Ajay nodded. "She was kidnapped. A man grabbed her
and was holding her hostage. She was able to escape when he
left her unattended, but she got turned around in the woods.
She fell and hit her head. When I found her, she was passed
out and suffering from hypothermia."

"Kidnapped? Did she recognize him?"

"No. He wore a mask. But he kept her in one of the abandoned cabins not too far from here. If we can find it, forensics might be able to discover something useful."

They both paused as the EMTs carried Lizzy from the cabin, moving swiftly to the rescue vehicle.

"There's a helicopter coming to take her to the hospital in Conners," Max said as he too rushed past. "We just need to get her to the clearing on the other side."

"I can help," Ajay said, starting after them.

Malcolm slapped him on the back as he moved past. "You've done more than enough. Thank you again for everything you did. We've got it from here. You go get some rest."

"You need to let the EMTs check you out," Della said as she and Ajay both stepped aside.

Ajay shook his head. "I'm fine. I just need a ride back to my car."

"Then you're going to need a shovel, too," Della said smugly. "Your car is buried under a few feet of snow right now. I'll arrange for a tow. You really just need to go get yourself some sleep. I'll drive you home." She headed toward one of the rescue vehicles, then paused, throwing him a look over her shoulder. "Good save, Lieutenant Wright. You did good out here. My future in-laws won't forget that."

In the distance, Ajay could hear the chopper blades turning in the air. He stared in that direction until he saw the Life Flight rise above the tree line and head in the direction of the hospital.

Pumpkin suddenly appeared at his side, pushing her head against the palm of his hand. She whimpered softly.

"It's all good," Ajay said as he tousled the dog's fur. "Lizzy's going to be just fine." His voice dropped to a low whisper. "She has to be, Pumpkin. She just has to be okay."

Chapter 5

There was an abundance of commotion that suddenly intruded on Lizzy's rest. Familiar voices were calling her name. Voices she recognized but still couldn't identify. One of her brothers, or maybe it was all three of them. Her father and a woman who was not her mother. A stranger, whose tone was nasal and high-pitched. Someone else whose voice was soft and smooth like the brush of cotton against her skin.

Her body felt heavy and disjointed. There were people poking and prodding at her, shifting her this way and that. She wanted to tell them to stop, to leave her be, but she couldn't find the words in the murky fog that clouded her head.

She opened her eyes and was blinded by the bright lights. She closed them again, wishing away all the noise. She kept listening for one voice, and no matter how hard she tried, she couldn't hear the sweet baritone that had become a singular source of comfort for her up at the cabin. She wanted to hear the bourbon-inspired growl of Ajay Wright's seductive laugh, the rich, sweet timbre like warm caramel and sweet butter against her ears. The last time he spoke to her he was holding her hand, assuring her things would be well. She had believed him, and now all she wanted was to have him back at her side.

Their time together had been emotionally intimate in a

way she would never have expected. During one of their conversations, the opportunity for a first kiss had presented itself, but Ajay had pulled himself from her, respectful of her injuries. Instead, he had tucked a second blanket around her, asking if she wanted to share the last Twinkie that had been in the box. Both had pretended like the moment never happened, and for a while Lizzy had wondered if she'd imagined it. Maybe what she wanted had nothing at all to do with what he had wanted. Maybe he hadn't given any consideration to kissing her and it had all been in her own head.

Lizzy had been drawn to the prospect of taking things further, but she had to admit, that yet again, it was the wrong place and the wrong time and, for all she knew, maybe even the wrong man. Because Lizzy's luck with men was a thing for the record books. The *boys* who always wanted her number were self-absorbed, self-centered and selfish. The few *men* she'd actually dated had been likable at the start, but things often crashed and burned before she could blink.

There was only one man who'd lasted for any length of time, and Lizzy had no desire to remember that disastrous relationship.

Lizzy heard her name, someone talking about her. Or maybe it was everyone talking about her. She wasn't sure of anything except she was missing Ajay and wished someone would tell her why he wasn't there.

"She'll sleep," a voice was saying.

"Should we be worried?" another voice questioned.

The words "…fever…antibiotics…time…rest…" floated through the air.

There was more chatter and whispered responses, none of it making any sense to Lizzy. She tried to speak, Ajay's name on the tip of her tongue. She attempted to call for him, but the words sounded foreign to her own ears.

"It's okay, Lizzy. Just rest, sweet girl." Lizzy recognized her father's voice. Only her father called her sweet girl.

It hurt to breathe, Lizzy thought, but oxygen in her nostrils made it easier. *It's okay*, she repeated over and over again in her head. *It's okay.*

Something beeped, the sound startling. She tried again to call for Ajay, and then she felt a hand gently caressing her forearm. She wanted to smile, to open her eyes one more time to see if he was there. But sleep was calling her loudly, pulling her back beneath a blanket of quiet and calm.

Everything was going to be okay, she thought as she gave into the slumber. Ajay had promised, and she knew with almost infinite certainty that Ajay Wright always kept his word.

He didn't dare tell anyone that he was missing Lizzy Colton, Ajay thought to himself. Heaven forbid he say it out loud, even if only for Pumpkin's ears. He had only been back in his home for a week, and he was missing her as if they'd been separated for an eternity. He blew out a soft sigh as he scavenged for a meal in his very empty refrigerator. It had been so long since he'd last shopped that the pantry of oatmeal and soup up in that cabin sounded pretty appetizing right then.

He scrambled himself an egg, the last one left from a container of twelve. There was no bread, nor anything that resembled bacon, to be found. That egg and a pack of peanut butter crackers became the meal, and when he'd consumed the last bite, he sat at the kitchen table feeling lost and, for the first time, alone.

He couldn't help but wonder if Lizzy was doing well. He had called the hospital the day before to check on her, and Malcolm had been happy to tell him she was finally out of the woods. She was expected to make a full recovery and was already giving her big brothers a hard time. Malcolm hadn't said whether or not she had asked about him, Ajay thought.

Ajay wanted to call to check on her again but knew that it would probably be frowned upon. He wasn't family, no one knew him as her friend, and his position on the search-and-rescue team dictated he file his final report and move on. Officially, he could be written up for calling a woman he'd rescued. Most especially if he wanted to invite her for coffee and maybe dinner, no matter what the circumstances. Personal relationships with clients were frowned upon. Doubly so since he was also in a leadership position, and he needed to be the example other officers followed. Besides, he thought, Lizzy might not be interested in seeing him again.

Pumpkin suddenly barked, running from the room and back again.

"You don't know," Ajay muttered at the dog. "For all you know, she might have a boyfriend."

"Ruff! Ruff!"

Ajay rolled his eyes skyward. He hated it when it felt like his four-legged friend was reading his mind. He hated it more when it felt like the animal was giving him advice.

He dropped down onto the sofa, flipping channels on the television remote. As promised, Della had arranged for his car to be in his driveway, the tow truck arriving the day after she had dropped him home. He had needed to sleep, but he hadn't rested well. There was a nagging feeling in the pit of his stomach that he couldn't shake.

He didn't feel comfortable with the idea that Lizzy's kidnapper still roamed the streets of Owl Creek, and no one knew who it was or why they'd taken her. How was her abduction linked to the missing Kraft children? *Was* there any connection at all? Had they intended to leverage her capture against the Colton family for a ransom? Had she been the next intended victim of a serial killer hunting innocent women for sport?

He still had more questions than answers and that left him feeling vulnerable. Because if Lizzy ever needed protection, it would be now. At least until they were able to solve her case. And if Lizzy needed protection, then he desperately needed to be where she was. He needed to trust that she was safe. Not knowing what was going on with her didn't leave him with any confidence.

"I need to go check on Lizzy," he said out loud. He jumped to his feet and reached for his keys and jacket. He was headed to the hospital. He paused briefly to reflect on the ramifications of his decision, deciding to hell with protocol as he rushed out the door.

As Ajay made his exit, Pumpkin barked again, her tail wagging in agreement.

Lizzy was so done with the hospital food they'd been serving her. She pushed whatever was on the plate in front of her from one side to the other. It looked like mashed potatoes and tasted like mush. She'd also had her fill of nurses taking her temperature and logging her blood pressure every other minute.

She was ready for a semblance of normalcy, if such a thing could ever exist again. She was grateful that her family had finally stopped hovering over her. Her brothers had returned to their jobs, and her father had finally been convinced to return to his ranch. There had been no sign of her mother, the matriarch not bothering to call or visit.

Lizzy was three years old when Jessie Colton walked out on her husband, leaving him and her children behind. Lizzy had no memory of ever calling her mommy or mother or mom. Jessie had never returned, not bothering to stay in contact with her offspring. The boys had missed her, having memories from when she'd been there to make them breakfast and lunch and take them to school. Whatever gap she'd left in their small worlds had been filled abundantly by their father, who hadn't taken the responsibility lightly. He had been, and continued to be, one hell of a father.

Jessie had missed every important moment in Lizzy's life, and Lizzy had learned to accept not having her around. It was all she had ever known.

Mama Jen had been there in Jessie's stead, showing Lizzy how to apply makeup, giving her the birds-and-bees talk, taking her shopping for her prom gown and being the voice of wisdom when her father and brothers lacked understanding of female things. Mama Jen had been a lifeline Lizzy never knew she needed until she was there.

Mama Jen hadn't left the hospital since Lizzy arrived a week ago, supporting her father and brothers and making sure all of Lizzy's needs were attended to. She was a nurse by profession and fell into the role easily. So not hearing from Jessie Colton hadn't bothered Lizzy at all.

But she had hoped to hear from Ajay Wright, and his not calling had her squarely in her feelings. It had pushed her knee-deep into a bad mood, and she was past ready to go home and sulk without being disturbed.

She reached for the phone to call Vivian. Her friend would understand, Lizzy thought. And if she didn't, she could at least be trusted to share her ideas without holding her tongue. As she scrolled through her contacts, she was suddenly distracted by a commotion in the hallway.

Looking out the room door, Lizzy was startled by a man standing by the nurse's desk. His back was turned, and he was leaning over the counter chatting with one of the nurses.

No one else was there to see what he was doing, but everything about his demeanor felt too familiar.

Lizzy shifted against the pillows, a knot tightening in the middle of her stomach. She leaned forward for a closer look.

His clothing was neat, black pants and a matching shirt with a black overcoat. It was the hiking boots, well-worn and dingy, that grabbed her attention. Boots she'd seen before.

And then he turned, his dark eyes locking with hers. He wore a mask, his face obscured, but those eyes were all too familiar.

Lizzy was suddenly dizzy, the room seeming to spin around her. The air felt thin, and she gasped loudly, fighting to catch her breath. Dropping the telephone, she clenched her fists, digging her nails into the palms of her hands.

The man lifted himself upright, staring in her direction. His gaze narrowed with hostility. He took one and then two steps toward her.

The ear-piercing shriek that echoed down the hospital hallway was deafening. It rattled the walls like a rumble of thunder. Lizzy screamed a second time, abruptly halting the man's steps. As her room suddenly overflowed with hospital staff, the man turned and disappeared in the opposite direction, Lizzy still screaming again and again.

Owl Creek's Express Medical Clinic was a staple in the community, and its location near the center of town made for easy access. It was also a central point of care and support services for residents, their mission devoted to patient-centered care and education. Its reputation was stellar for its size, but more complicated cases had to travel forty-five minutes to Conners and the big hospital there.

Ajay had prepared himself for the ride, making it from his front door to the hospital's parking lot in record time. As he pulled his SUV into an empty parking space, he was instantly on edge. Several Conners police cars were parked in front of the brick building. Uniformed officers were stationed at the exits directing traffic and eyeing each vehicle suspiciously. Someone or something had put them on high alert.

His gaze shifted around the parking lot, noting those who were as curious as he was and others who had no interest at all in what might be going on. Jumping from the Jeep, he locked the door and hurried toward the hospital entrance.

Inside, the number of uniformed officers standing around made it look like the entire police department from Conners and maybe even Owl Creek, too, had been called into work. Whatever was going on was serious, and Ajay found himself racing to find Lizzy to ensure she was safe. He flashed his badge at the hospital's reception desk and then the nursing station on the third floor.

As he neared Lizzy's room, the number of officers seemed to increase. Detectives he knew and occasionally worked with were interviewing nursing staff and taking statements from a number of visitors to the hospital.

Della stood at the door to Lizzy's room. He could hear her inside, crying hysterically, and it took every ounce of fortitude he possessed not to push his way inside to get to her.

"What's going on?" he snapped, greeting his friend brusquely.

Della's gaze widened. "What are you doing here?" she questioned.

"I wanted to check on Lizzy." He suddenly felt anxious and slightly embarrassed. "Did something happen?"

Della eyed him with a narrowed gaze and a wry smile. "Interesting," she muttered.

"Don't start, Della. I just wanted to make sure she's doing okay."

Della grabbed his arm and pulled him aside. "Lizzy thinks she saw her kidnapper outside her door. They haven't been able to calm her down since."

"Did you pull the security tapes?"

"And the building was locked down as we checked everyone coming and going," Della answered with a nod of her head.

"He didn't hurt her, did he? Did he touch her?" Ajay's mind was racing, his eyes darting from corner to corner.

"No. Lizzy screamed bloody murder before he could make it to the door of her room. Apparently, the man she saw was chatting up one of the nurses, trying to get a date. The doctors think she may have been hallucinating from all the medication they've been giving her. Max agrees. Now she refuses to let them give her anything to help her calm down. The family doesn't know what to do. They're even considering sedating her completely and transferring her up to the psych ward for an evaluation."

Ajay shifted his weight from one leg to the other. He desperately needed to lay eyes on Lizzy. He shook his head. "She'll be fine," he said as he turned toward the room and the two uniformed officers standing guard. "I need to go in to see her."

"I don't know if that's a good idea," Della said softly.

"Just be my friend," Ajay replied as he tossed her a look over his shoulder. There wasn't anything anyone could do to stop him, he thought, but he didn't say it out loud.

Della nodded for the officers to let him pass, and they stepped aside as he moved into the room.

The Colton family all turned at the same time, eyeing him warily. Silence surrounded Lizzy's low sob as they all stopped talking, their focus shifting to where he stood.

"I don't mean to interrupt," Ajay said. His gaze left her

brothers and settled over her face, noting the stream of tears that trickled down her cheeks. "I just wanted to make sure Lizzy..." he started.

"Ajay!" Lizzy screamed his name, extending her arms in his direction.

He hurried to where she sat in the hospital bed. As he neared, Lizzy's expression changed from gleeful to angry. She threw a punch, hitting him squarely in the chest.

"Ouch! What the hell, Lizzy? That hurt!" He rubbed where he suspected a bruise would rise in varying shades of black and blue.

"You ghosted me!"

"I did not!"

"So where have you been?" Lizzy said, her voice raised. "You promised to take care of me."

Ajay paused, suddenly aware of all the eyes on him, her family watching their exchange closely. "I'm here now," he finally answered, taking a seat on the side of the bed.

Lizzy threw her arms around his neck as he gently wrapped her in his arms.

"He was here," she whispered loudly. "That freak came after me here in the hospital. He was right outside my room! I saw him, and no one believes me."

"I believe you," Ajay whispered back. "And I promise, we're going to find him."

Lizzy exhaled the softest sigh, still clinging to him tightly. Her sobs had finally subsided to a recital of hiccups, but at least she was no longer shaking or railing at her family.

"We're going to step outside. Do you mind staying with her?" Malcolm asked, his question directed at Ajay.

Lizzy still clung to his neck as he nodded, his eyes lifting to meet the stare his friend was giving him.

As they headed out the door, he and Lizzy could hear the questions the family had wanted to ask the two of them.

"Who is he?" her father questioned, his voice booming.

"Did you know about this?" Max asked.

Della shrugged in response. "I don't know anything."

"I'm sure it's not serious," Jenny said. "Lizzy would have said something before now."

"Hero worship," someone else—Ajay wasn't sure who—stated. "What else could it be?"

The door closed tightly behind the last person, and with the room empty, Ajay pulled her arms from around his neck. Still holding tightly to her hands, he eased her back against the pillows.

"I'm not delusional," Lizzy snapped. "They all think I've lost my mind, but I know what I saw."

"I know," Ajay replied. "Now start from the beginning and tell me everything you remember."

As Lizzy spoke, Ajay noted the small crowd standing in the hallway. For a brief moment, he considered closing the blinds that covered the glass window to the space outside. The Colton family had gathered en masse, joining the medical personnel and the police detectives. No one seemed thrilled by the turn of events. He could only imagine what else was being said about her, and him. He took a deep breath, holding it in his lungs before blowing it out slowly.

"It was his shoes," Lilly was saying. "They were old and busted and seemed out of place with what else he was wearing. At first, I thought it was weird, then I remembered all the snow outside, so maybe he just didn't have proper winter boots. But then he turned around, and I knew it was him. Even though he was wearing a mask, I recognized those evil beady black eyes of his. I just started screaming, and he ran."

"What kind of mask was he wearing?"

"Hospital issue. One of those blue paper masks."

Ajay's head bobbed up and down as he took mental notes of everything she was telling him. He understood everyone's concern, but he believed her. He knew her family did as well but were trying to keep her calm considering her situation. He was certain Lizzy had seen the man who'd held her hostage, and he was willing to bet that if he'd come to the hospital, the man was now stalking her.

The door suddenly opened, the noise from the hall billowing into the room. Ajay didn't know the stranger who stood in the entrance with an oversize bouquet of fresh flowers. He stood as tall as Ajay, with an unkempt head of light brown hair. His eyes were bright blue, and his resemblance to the Colton family couldn't be denied. Ajay suspected they were related, but he still stood protectively, putting his body between Lizzy and the other man.

"May I help you?" Ajay asked, his deep voice a tad harsh and a lot possessive.

There was a moment of hesitation before the other man responded. "I'm Nate Colton," he said. "I'm Lizzy's...brother. Her half...brother," he suddenly stuttered, tripping over the words to explain who he was and why he was there. He gestured with the flowers as if the sight of them explained his intentions.

Lizzy sat up straighter in the bed, the slightest smile pulling at her lips. "Nate! What a surprise!" she said. She swiped the back of her hand across her eyes.

Nate smiled back.

Ajay extended his hand. "Ajay Wright. I'm a friend of your sister's."

"Nice to meet you," Nate said. "I understand you found her and kept her safe. Thank you."

"Ajay is a lieutenant with the Owl Creek Police Department. Search and rescue is his specialty. And Nate is a detective with the Boise Police Department. You two have a lot in common." Lizzy looked from one to the other, the two men standing like stone in the middle of the room. "You're both cops!"

"It's nice to meet you," Ajay said.

"Same," Nate muttered.

Ajay turned toward Lizzy. "I'll leave you and your family alone. I'll be right outside if you need me."

"I'll scream," Lizzy said, her smile widening.

Ajay chuckled as he made his exit and closed the door behind him.

Nate gave Lizzy a sheepish grin. "I came to check on you and to say hello before I headed back to Boise. You were completely out of it the last time I was here." He laid the flowers on the overbed table that rested in front of her.

Lizzy was sure her expression registered her surprise. "You were here before?"

"I came to help with the search when they said you were missing."

She shook her head ever so slightly. Family and friends had come and gone for days, and not knowing that Nate had visited left her feeling sad. "Thank you. I didn't know. That was sweet of you. And these flowers are beautiful."

Nate smiled, his entire face lifting with light. "I'm learning that's what family does for each other." His gaze shifted to the brothers standing outside the room. For a moment, he seemed to drift off into thought.

Lizzy smiled again, guessing what was on his mind. "It's going to get easier," she said. "For all of us."

Nate nodded. "I hope so. At the moment, it's still a lot to take in."

"How's Sarah?" Lizzy asked.

"She's good. She asked about you. She wanted to come visit you herself but wasn't sure you would want to see her."

"It's strange suddenly having a sister. I imagine it's a lot for her right now."

"Don't I know it!" Nate said with a low laugh. "We suddenly have four new sisters and six new brothers. I'm going to have to review my Christmas budget this year."

Lizzy laughed with him. "No worries. We do Secret Santa. You'll only have to buy one present."

Nate looked confused. "Secret Santa?"

"We throw everyone's name into a hat. You pick one name, and that's the only adult you have to buy a present for. It makes things super easy. And it's fun. There's always a gag gift or two tossed in with the real presents."

"You all are really close, aren't you?" A wave of sadness washed over Nate's face.

"We try. I've always had my brothers, and Mama Jen kept us connected to her kids. Chase, Fletcher, Wade, Hannah, Ruby and Frannie were more like siblings than cousins. They were always around, even when I wished they weren't." She smiled. "Kidding."

Nate shook his head. "Jessie really did us a disservice," he said, a hint of anger in his tone.

"At least you have a relationship with our mother."

"I don't have anything to do with her, especially now with this cult mess she's gotten herself into."

"Greg mentioned it briefly, but then the festival happened and all the drama with his babies. He said she's joined some church?"

"It's called the Ever After Church, but there's nothing at all Christian about it. It's some sort of shady operation, and only our mother would try to play like their leader is directly related to the next coming of Christ. In actuality he's a wolf in sheep's clothing, but she refuses to see it. It's always about power and money with her, and she thinks he has both. Her adoration for the man borders on obsessive. I'm sure it'll only last until the next schmuck captures her attention."

Lizzy shook her head. She could hear the frustration in Nate's voice, his anger rising steadily. She changed the subject for both their sakes. "Let's not talk about Jessie anymore. I can feel my blood pressure rising just thinking about her."

Nate smiled. "You don't have to ask me twice!"

"What's going on with you and my sister?" Malcolm asked. He and his brother Greg stood shoulder to shoulder staring at Ajay. "That's my sister, for Pete's sake!" he exclaimed. "My baby sister."

Ajay tried to put a friendly expression on his face, and he laughed. "Lizzy and I are just friends."

"You both looked a little too cozy to be just friends," Greg interjected. "Are you sure nothing happened between you two up in that cabin?"

Ajay wished he could explain what it was between him and Lizzy, but he didn't have a single word for what he, or she, was feeling. They were definitely friends. He wouldn't argue that with anyone, but there was more to their connection that he couldn't yet define. He just knew she needed him, and he would battle hell and high water to keep her safe.

Now her family was eyeing him as if he'd been the one to take her captive and hold her against her will. They wanted an explanation, and he didn't have one to give.

He said, "Well, I could give you the dirty details, but if I did, Lizzy would probably kill me!" He tried to use humor to diffuse the moment, nervous energy fueling the chuckle that passed over his tongue.

Greg took a step in Ajay's direction, his hand balled into a tight fist. "I will break your face," he snapped.

Ajay held up his hands as if surrendering. "That was a joke!" He shifted his eyes toward Malcolm. "Call your brother off me," he said.

"He has a weak punch," Malcolm said. "It's more like a bug bite. If I hit you, I'll make sure it puts you on your ass."

"I swear, I didn't do anything with your sister but keep her safe. I was a perfect gentleman the entire time. Just ask her if you don't believe me."

They settled into a brief moment of silence, the men seeming to stand off against each other.

"He's good," Malcolm finally said. "I'll vouch for him."

"You vouched for that Brian guy, and we all remember how that turned out," Max said. He and Della had eased into the conversation, moving to stand beside Ajay.

Malcolm quipped, "Brian was Greg's friend, not mine."

"That's why I didn't vouch for him," Greg replied. "Besides, Lizzy chewed him up and spit him out. His feelings are still bruised."

"I taught her that," Malcolm said. "Don't think my sister's going to be easy to handle. She's not."

Ajay changed the subject. "Della, were you able to find anything on the security tapes?"

"Nothing that can help," she answered. "There was a man at the nurse's station. We didn't capture a good look at his face, but it was just like she described. We can't say for certain though that he was after Lizzy. In fact, it looks like he was more interested in the nurse than in her."

"So, you've talked to him?"

Max shook his head. "No, he was gone by the time we arrived, but we did interview all the hospital staff. I've had an entire FBI team on this since you found her, and they keep coming up empty."

Ajay gave him a nod. "Hopefully, FBI involvement will help."

"Especially since I don't technically work for them anymore," Max said. "My *retirement* from the agency didn't last long, but we're talking about my sister here, and I don't trust anyone else to take lead on this. I had to pull some strings and call in a few favors, but I'll keep the FBI involved as long as I'm able."

Appreciation crossed Ajay's face. He and Max exchanged a fist bump before Ajay responded. "So, it's possible it was her kidnapper?"

Lizzy's brother shrugged. "We can't rule him out, but we do have to take into consideration that Lizzy has been heavily medicated. She might not have been in her right mind."

"She has been out of it," Greg added.

"She seemed perfectly lucid to me," Ajay noted.

"Because she's refused to take any more of her medication," Malcolm said. "In fact, she's threatening to check herself out of the hospital and go home."

"Would that be a bad thing?" Ajay questioned. "She'd be able to recuperate, and you could all keep an eye on her at the same time."

The family exchanged a wave of glances, looking from one to the other.

Ajay continued, "And if someone is stalking her, putting her where she'd be hard to get to might make it easier for us to catch him. He might make a mistake and show his hand."

"I don't know if that's a good idea," Greg said. "That might be like putting her out there to be bait."

"Ajay makes a good point, though," said Malcolm. "We

can keep her safe while she continues to heal and keep our eye out for anyone wanting to do her harm."

"Has anyone thought to ask Lizzy what she wants to do?" Della questioned.

The men all turned to look at her at the same time.

Her brown eyes danced across their faces as she flipped her light brown hair over her shoulder. Her gaze stopped on Max, and her brow lifted questioningly.

"We should probably ask Lizzy what she wants to do," Max said, his expression sheepish.

"That might be a good idea," Malcolm agreed.

They all turned to stare at Ajay. His eyes widened, and he suddenly felt like he was under a spotlight about to be dissected. He crossed his arms over his chest. "What?"

"Let us know what she says," Malcom said, tossing him a wink.

"We'll be downstairs in the cafeteria," Greg interjected. "Dad and Mama Jen went down a few minutes ago to grab some coffee. We'll go update them."

Della pressed her hand against Ajay's arm. "She trusts you, Ajay. And I really need to be able to have a conversation with her where she isn't calling her brothers names or cursing us all for being incompetent. The last few times I tried to question her, she went off on a rant that made that last blizzard look tame. She's very spirited when she wants to be."

Max laughed. "Aren't you being nice, honey!" he said. "I like that. Lizzy is *spirited*." He leaned to kiss Della's cheek.

Malcolm gave Ajay a look, rolling his eyes skyward. "Lizzy's a raving hellion when she's angry, and right now she's mad as spit," he said. "It looks like you're the only one she's *not* irritated with. So you're it."

"While you do that," Greg concluded, "we'll double-check with her doctors and get their thoughts about her leaving."

Ajay rubbed the tender spot on his chest. For reasons he couldn't explain, he wasn't quite sure any of them had any idea what the hell they were doing when it came to Lizzy Colton, most especially him. Taking a deep breath, he watched as her family all walked away, huddled together in conversation. Turning, he moved back toward Lizzy's room, hesitating just briefly before heading inside.

Chapter 6

"I'm not staying here a minute longer," Lizzy snapped. "I don't care what my brothers say. I know what I saw, and I'm not going to sit here waiting around for that man to come after me again." Her voice had risen an octave, and she folded her arms across her chest.

"I agree," Ajay said, his tone even.

"You agree?" Lizzy sounded surprised.

"I think home is the best place for you to be. You can recuperate at your family's ranch."

"I have my own home," she responded. "A very nice home. Thank you very much."

"You probably need to be where there's family to help you until you're stronger. Besides, I don't want to worry about you being alone. I also don't think your father and brothers want to be worried about you, either."

"Fine," Lizzy said grumpily. "I'll stay at the ranch, but there's one condition."

"And what's that?" Ajay questioned.

"I'll only stay if you agree to stay there with me. Just for a few days. I'll feel better if I know you're there to protect me."

Ajay hesitated. He hadn't anticipated her request, and staying with her at her father's house hadn't been on the top of his list of things to do. He tossed a glance in the patriarch's direction.

Buck Colton had arrived an hour earlier, catching the tail end of Lizzy's most recent rant. He was a tall muscular man, his complexion weathered from the sun and hard work. Lizzy had inherited her father's bright smile, and there was no missing his devotion to his children.

"It's settled then," Buck said, easing to Lizzy's side to kiss her forehead. "Lizzy will come home when the hospital releases my sweet girl, and Lieutenant Wright is welcome to stay at the ranch for as long as he's needed."

"I appreciate your hospitality, sir, but I'm certain I'll need to clear it with the police chief."

"No problem," Buck said. "Chief Stanton and I are old friends. He owes me a favor or two. And if need be, I'll even clear it with the mayor."

Ajay smiled. "You're friends with Mayor Carlson?"

"He taught my boys how to ski before he retired and became a public servant."

"Small world," Ajay muttered.

Lizzy laughed. "Smaller town!"

Her father winked. "Getting the proper permissions, son, won't be a problem. I'll take care of everything. You just keep an eye on my baby girl."

Ajay nodded. "Yes, sir, Mr. Colton."

A few short hours later, the senior Colton had arranged for Lizzy to be transferred to the family home with in-home nursing services to provide her care. Arrangements had also been made with Ajay's superiors for him to provide the Colton family with security.

Lizzy wasn't one hundred percent happy with the arrangements. She had wanted to go back to her own things, in her own space. But knowing Ajay would be where she was left her feeling a little better about the whole situation.

Vivian answered her phone on the second ring.

"It's about time," Vivian gushed. "I've been worried sick about you. Malcolm's been keeping me updated, but still…"

"I'm fine," Lizzy replied. "In fact, I'm headed home now."

"I'll meet you there," her friend said.

Lizzy shook her head into the receiver. "I need a favor. I need you to meet my friend Ajay at my house. He'll be headed in that direction in a few minutes. I need you to pack some clothes for me. I'll be staying at the ranch for a few weeks."

"Is everything okay?" Concern seeped through Vivian's question.

Lizzy smiled as if Vivian could see her. "Everything's fine now. I'm getting out of this hospital, but they're making me stay at the ranch."

"Then things aren't fine. What's going on?"

"I'll explain when I see you, but do you think you can meet Ajay? Please? You have the spare key to my house, and you know where all my things are kept. I trust you'll get everything I need without me having to make a list."

"Who is this Ajay person? Do I know him? The name sounds familiar."

"Lieutenant Ajay Wright. He's police. He's also the man who rescued me, and Vivian, he's gorgeous!"

"Is he the police officer that your brother is friends with? The cute one who looks like…"

The door to Lizzy's room suddenly opened, and Ajay peeked inside. He gave her a bright smile, his whole face seeming to lift with joy at the sight of her.

"I've got to go," Lizzy said, interrupting her friend's comment. "But come to the ranch later so I can catch you up. I promise to tell you everything!"

"You better," Vivian quipped.

"I'll text you his cell phone number," Lizzy said, "and give him yours so you two can touch base with each other."

"That's fine," Vivian replied. "Quick question before you hang up."

"What?"

"Doesn't he have a girlfriend?"

"Do you have a girlfriend?" Lizzy suddenly asked. "I don't remember you saying anything when we were at the cabin."

Ajay gave her a narrowed stare, his eyes drawing into thin slits. "Why do I feel like you were just talking about me?"

"Because I was. I was telling my best friend what a good guy you were."

Ajay's cheeks turned a brilliant shade of fire-engine red. He shook his head.

"So are you?"

"Am I what?"

"In a relationship? Do you have a girlfriend?"

"No," he answered, "but I don't think we should be talking about each other's personal lives. I'm on the clock, and I take my assignments seriously."

"That's good to know. I'd hate to have security that wasn't serious about protecting me."

Ajay chuckled. "The ambulance transport is here to take you home. I'll follow behind them."

"I need you to do me a favor and stop by my house. My friend Vivian is going to meet you there. I need clothes, and she knows exactly what to pack for me."

His brow lifted. "Now I'm running errands, too?"

Lizzy's eyes widened. "It's not like that. You and Vivian are the two people I trust most with my personal possessions. I don't even trust my brothers like that."

"I guess I should be flattered. But I don't think your family is going to be happy about that."

"My family knows how particular I am about my things. And who I do and do not trust, and why."

Lizzy didn't miss the odd expression that passed over Ajay's face. She sensed that he felt uncomfortable, and she was suddenly worried that she had made things between them awkward. That was the very last thing she had wanted for the two of them. Contrition furrowed her brow. If she could have kicked herself, she would have.

Lizzy had never been a wallflower, needing a man to take care of her. Despite growing up in a home where her big brothers babied her and her overprotective father coddled her every wish, she wasn't spoiled. She wasn't the fragile, weak female some thought her to be. With Ajay, she just wanted to be noticed and wanted, but she was behaving like a lovelorn teen desperate for a boyfriend.

But Ajay wasn't her boyfriend, and they weren't in a relationship, despite how she was behaving and how she was treating him.

"I'm sorry," she said, her voice dropping. "I should have asked how you felt about…well…everything." She took a deep breath, losing the words to explain herself.

"It's okay," he said, his smile returning. "There's just a lot happening. We need to sit and talk and maybe figure some things out. But until then, I'm fine with meeting your friend. I'll make sure someone follows the ambulance. Max and Della, maybe."

"I'm not usually so pushy," she said. "It's just…well…" She shrugged.

Ajay gently tapped her hand. "I need to go by the station first, then I'll meet your friend. After that I need to run by my own place to pack a bag and pick up Pumpkin."

"Thank you," she said. For the briefest moment, Lizzy wanted to press her lips to his, to seal their deal and move things forward. And then she remembered she was an assignment, with rules that he needed to follow. Kissing her wasn't part of the job description, no matter how hard she might have tried.

As he walked out of the room, Ajay tossed her one last smile.

The Owl Creek Police Department was quiet for the time of day. Quieter than he had expected. Ajay found the silence a little unnerving as he entered the building and moved past the reception desk to his office. He lifted a hand in greeting as he passed one familiar face and then another, but he didn't bother to stop for any lengthy conversation.

Inside, he shuffled through the mail that had been dropped on his desk, separating the junk from what might have been important. There were five messages reminding him that Pumpkin was due for her annual physical and that he, too, needed to schedule a date for his firearms recertification. Once he had cleared what was important, he shut off the lights and closed the door.

Heading down the hall toward the corner office, he greeted the officer sitting at a desk outside the police chief's door. She was a new hire and Ajay had only met her one time. He paused, trying to remember her name as he greeted her.

"Officer Bailey, good morning," he said finally.

"Lieutenant Wright," she responded. "It's good to see you again. And please, call me Bridget."

"Only if you promise to call me Ajay."

"How are you doing, Ajay?" she asked.

Bridget Bailey was a petite young woman with large brown eyes and a pixie haircut that made her appear younger than she was. Ajay remembered that she had graduated at the top of her class at the academy and was considered a feather in the department's cap, adding to an already impressive roster.

"I'm well," he responded. "Does the chief have a moment to speak with me, by chance?"

A booming voice called out from inside the office, their commanding officer never missing anything that was happening in his building.

"Get in here, Wright!" Police Chief Stanton bellowed.

The young woman gave Ajay a bright smile. "I think he can see you now," she said.

Ajay laughed. "Thank you," he said as he rounded her desk and moved through the office door. He closed it after himself, his gaze meeting the chief's evenly.

"Chief Stanton, good morning."

"What's good about it? I hadn't been here for an hour before I start getting calls about you wanting to be reassigned to a private assignment. People seem to forget I run this department."

"Yes, sir," Ajay said. The chief gestured for him to take a seat and he moved to one of the upholstered chairs in front of the desk and sat down.

"So, what's going on?" Stanton asked. "Buck Colton called me. Something about his daughter needing you to be her personal bodyguard?"

Ajay took a deep breath. "Miss Colton was my last rescue and she's having a difficult time. Her family thinks that since we bonded while we were trapped during the storm that she would do better if I were to stay with the family until her kidnapper is apprehended. I also think my being there will allow me to investigate the case and hopefully catch whoever is preying on her."

The captain nodded his head slowly. "So, you think you can do a better job than my best detectives can do?"

"Chief Stanton, I think I'd be in a unique position to gather evidence your best detectives will have a harder time discovering."

A pregnant pause billowed slowly between the two men. The police chief sighed, and his tone softened ever so slightly. "Ajay, you're one of our best search-and-rescue officers. We're good now, but if I need to call you back in, I will."

"Yes, sir."

"And this assignment is temporary, so don't you get comfortable. Buck Colton is a good friend and one of the police department's biggest advocates. Our citizens need to know we're here to support them and they can always depend on us. So don't do anything to embarrass us."

"Yes, sir."

"You'll be the point person on this case and have the full support of our detective unit. Use them. As well, the FBI will also be working this investigation, but you already know that, don't you?"

Ajay grinned. "Yes, sir. I do."

Stanton grunted. "Clear this case, Lieutenant. I want it solved yesterday!"

"If I can ask for one more favor, Chief?"

Stanton's brow lifted, his gaze narrowed. He waited, not bothering to respond.

"I'd like to request that Della Winstead be allowed to work this case with me. She and I work well together, and I respect her insight. Of course, it would only be temporary, sir. Just until we can catch our perpetrator."

Stanton sighed deeply. "I swear! I think folks forget who's in charge around here."

"No, sir! Not at all."

There was another moment's pause as the police chief considered Ajay's request. Finally, he shook his head as he moved back to the pleather chair behind his oversize desk. "You better be glad I like you, Wright. Now go impress me and take Winstead with you."

Ajay smiled. "Thank you, Chief! You won't regret it."

"I better not, son. Or there'll be hell to pay around here. You're dismissed."

Backing his way out of the office, Ajay gave his commanding officer a slight nod of his head as he made his exit and closed the door.

"How'd that work out for you?" Bridget asked.

"I have my work cut out for me," Ajay responded.

"Don't mess up," the young officer said. She gestured toward the closed door with her head. "He won't be happy if you do."

Ajay sighed. "Yeah! That's what I'm afraid of."

The phone rang a half dozen times before Della answered his call. When she did pick up, she was giggling on the other end, sounding slightly out of breath.

"Hello?"

"Are you okay?" Ajay asked. "Is this a bad time?"

Della giggled again. "I was just having a conversation with Max. What's up?"

Ajay didn't mince words, getting right to the point of his call. "I just spoke with the captain about this case. Apparently, Buck Colton called in a favor, and now I'll be taking lead on the investigation into Lizzy's kidnapping."

"Good for you!" Della gushed. "Not looking to make any friends with the detective's division, though, are you? You know how sensitive those guys are."

"I'm hoping they'll see this as a good thing. That it'll take some of the load off their plates."

"Aren't you the optimist!"

"I know you'll be able to help me sell it."

"Me?"

"The captain approved you working the case with me. He also stressed that it's temporary, and that you and I will still be on call for search and rescue if we're needed."

"Me?"

"What better way to sharpen those investigative skills of yours than on a case that's important to you? Besides, I trust you and I know you'll have my back if I get in over my head. I need you, and since Max has pulled in his FBI team, it's a win-win for all of us."

"Max is only doing this because it's his sister. He'd rather be making furniture."

"Then he, too, is motivated to solve this case quickly so he can get back to what he's truly passionate about."

"Don't get me fired, Ajay! I really do like my job."

"Thank you, Della," Ajay said, a wide smile pulling across his face. "I'm headed over to Lizzy's house to meet her friend Vivian. I'll call you when I'm leaving."

"Be safe out there, please. I hate worrying about you. It makes Max jealous."

Ajay laughed. "As it should!" he teased. "As it should."

The drive to Lizzy's didn't take as long as Ajay anticipated. The twenty-five-hundred-square-foot property was located between the Colton family ranch and where the north end of Owl Creek met downtown. It was a quintessential 1900s Craftsman bungalow that had been completely renovated. Its captivating, historic charm was warm and inviting with undeniable curb appeal. Lizzy could easily stroll or bike through the city or return to the family homestead in the blink of an eye. It was impressive from the outside, and Ajay imagined it was equally impressive on the inside.

Admiring the architecture, he was standing outside his vehicle with his arms crossed when a silver sedan pulled be hind him in the driveway. The woman who stepped out of the car was nothing like the woman Lizzy had described to him. This woman appeared timid and not as outgoing as her bestie. She wore a smartly tailored ocher-colored suit with a blouse the exact same color. The monochromatic look complemented her dark brown, shoulder-length hair and Mediterranean complexion.

"Are you Lieutenant Wright?" she asked.

He extended his hand to shake hers. "Please, call me Ajay."

"Ajay it is," she said softly. "I'm Vivian. Vivian Maylor. It's nice to meet you."

"The pleasure is all mine. Lizzy has told me a lot about you."

"That's interesting. She hasn't told me anything about you…yet."

"There's really nothing to tell," he said with a wide smile. Ajay wasn't quite sure what to make of the look Vivian gave him before she turned and headed toward her best friend's home. Ajay followed her.

Vivian suddenly came to an abrupt halt. She looked back at him over her shoulder. "The door," she said. "It's open. Lizzy would never leave her house unlocked or the door wide open."

Ajay grabbed her arm and gently pulled her back. "Call 911 and give them the address," he ordered. "And stay out here until the police give you permission to enter."

He reached for the pistol clipped to his waist and took off the safety. He gave Vivian one last look as she pulled her cell phone from her purse, then he moved through the door.

The interior of the home boasted an abundance of architectural molding, built-ins and stained-glass windows that adorned each room. Banks of grid-lined French glass reflected natural light onto original hardwood floors. The floorplan was a series of impressive yet cozy living spaces designed with generous scale and tall ceilings. Lizzy had married an eclectic mix of Bohemian and French country styles, integrating jewel tones with classic neutrals and bold floral prints. And someone had completely trashed her home, soiling fabrics, destroying furniture and leaving the place in complete disarray.

He moved past the dining room, through the living room and skirted from the kitchen to the screened-in patio and backyard. He had cleared the downstairs and was heading up to the bedrooms when a uniformed police officer came through the front door.

Ajay flashed his badge and kept his weapon pointing where he was headed. He had no intention of rounding a corner and being surprised. An officer he didn't recognize followed on his heels up the stairs. Minutes later, the Owl Creek police officer shouted down to the others, "All clear!"

Ajay recognized a familiar voice shouting orders from the floor below. He stood in the middle of Lizzy's bedroom staring at the wall above the king-size bed. When Della hurried up the steps and joined him, there was no hiding the distress on his face even if he had wanted to. Ajay shot her a quick look as she turned to stare where he was focused.

Time felt as if it had come to a standstill. Nothing moved, the air in the room blistered with the stench of something dangerous and ugly that Ajay couldn't touch or run from or keep far from Lizzy.

"This isn't good," Della finally said, her voice a loud whisper.

"We have to find this guy, Della," Ajay whispered back. "We have to find him now!"

The two friends took a step closer the wall. Someone had marred the soft blue paint with what looked like blood. It had dripped and dried, its consistency dark and viscous. Printed in bold, block letters were the words, *We're coming for you.*

Chapter 7

Ajay had called three times to check on Lizzy. He knew he needed to head toward her father's house, but he was anxious to hear what the forensics team found in her home. If anything at all.

When he had called the first time, she was sleeping soundly, finally settled into her bed. By the time he placed the second call, Vivian was there, and Max was explaining to Lizzy all that had happened and what little they knew. With the third call, she was still sobbing, shaken by the violation of her private space and the threat they'd found there.

They had ruled out the intrusion being a random act of vandalism. Lizzy had purposely been targeted, and Ajay still didn't know why. He didn't know who to blame or how to stop the threat. He disliked how that left him feeling. He hated the anxiety that dropped across his shoulders. He had no control, and that left him feeling vulnerable and weak. His thoughts were suddenly interrupted by one of the technicians who was collecting samples.

"This guy has a fetish for undergarments."

"Excuse me?" Dread and confusion felt like a gut punch to Ajay's abdomen. He could only imagine what he looked like, feeling as if the color had drained from his face. "What kind of fetish?"

The tech pointed to a pile of silk panties on top of the chest of drawers. Ajay had spied them earlier, but the graffiti on the wall had grabbed his attention and held it. Lizzy's undergarments had been pulled from the enclosure and laid neatly across the surface in order of color. Someone had clearly spent far too much time with them, and the technician seemed to take great pleasure in sharing that information.

"From what I can ascertain, he's spent the last few days using them for his own pleasure. He's ejaculated into each one, and he's clearly had multiple happy endings, unless there was more than one person. We'll run the DNA when we get them back to the lab to confirm how many offenders there were. With any luck, we'll get a hit in the database." The old man smirked as if he were amused. "And if she had any in her dirty clothes basket, they're gone. All her panties and bras are gone from her laundry. Except for what was left here on her dresser."

Ajay shook his head, still staring at the pile of soiled little underthings Lizzy had kept tucked away in a top drawer. He didn't know how to even begin to explain that violation to her.

The technician made another crude comment, laughing as if something were funny. It was the last straw, breaking whatever calm Ajay may have had left. He snapped, laying his frustration squarely in the other man's lap as he snatched the guy by his collar.

"I'm sorry! Sometimes you have to joke about it," the guy said, blood rushing to his cheeks. He lifted his hands to protect himself from the punch he thought was coming.

Della was standing at the bedroom door, clearly not amused after witnessing the exchange. Disgust painted her expression like bad makeup as she relieved the other man from his duties.

Ajay let him go, and he hurried out of the room and down the stairs, muttering under his breath about suing the department.

"Sorry," Ajay said. "I wasn't going to hit him. I just wanted to scare him. He really got under my skin."

"I know. That's why you need to head out," she said. "The team and I have got this."

Ajay gave her the faintest smile. "The team… You work fast."

"I called in favors this time. You told me to sell it and I did. Now, I'll call you if we get a hit on anything."

Ajay nodded. "I still need to run home and get Pumpkin. I'm headed to Colton Ranch right after that."

"Max said Lizzy didn't take the news well. The doctor wanted to give her something to calm her down, but she's adamant about not taking any more medication. It's probably going to be a long night."

As he eased past his friend, Della tapped him on the shoulder, a wave of compassion sweeping between them. With the last bit of energy Ajay could muster, he blew out a heavy sigh and hurried down the stairs to the front door.

The Colton family were gathered in the home's family room, everyone circling around Lizzy and trying to calm her. She had stopped crying, and now she was simply angry, fueled by fear and frustration.

When Ajay entered the family's home, Pumpkin by his side, he knew there wasn't anything he could say that could make things better.

"That was my home!" she hissed between clenched teeth.

"We'll buy you a new home," her father responded.

"I don't want a new home. I loved that house. Now it's tainted!"

"Lizzy, let the nurse give you something," an older woman was saying. "Something to help you sleep. Darling, you need to rest."

"She's right," Ajay interjected. "You need to rest."

"Ajay!" As Lizzy called his name, Pumpkin pushed her way through the crowd and jumped onto the sofa beside the woman. The slightest smile pulled at Lizzy's thin lips. "Pumpkin! I missed you!" Lizzy hugged the dog to her, gently stroking her fur coat.

Pumpkin settled into Lizzy's side, her position protective. It was clear to Ajay that she had no intention of being moved.

"Pumpkin! Where are your manners?" Ajay said. "Get down off that couch."

Lizzy laughed. "She's fine. Don't scold her."

The older woman moved swiftly to Ajay's side to shake his hand. She had those familiar blue eyes and short, dark blond hair streaked with strands of gray. Her presence was warming, and he instinctively knew she was Lizzy's favorite Mama Jen.

"Welcome to the ranch," Jenny Colton said. "We're glad to have you here."

"Thank you," Ajay said. "And I apologize for my friend there. She can be very possessive about people she becomes attached to."

"We love our animals around here, isn't that right?" Jenny said, giving Buck a nod.

"We certainly do. And that beauty is quite a specimen. I hear she was instrumental in helping you find our Lizzy."

"Yes." Ajay nodded. "I don't know that I could have done it without her."

"Then she's welcome here at Colton Ranch, too."

"Let me get you both something to eat," Jenny said, heading in the direction of the kitchen.

"Please, don't go through any trouble," Ajay replied. "I really couldn't eat a thing right now."

"One of the boys will show you to the guest room," Buck said. "You make yourself at home during your stay. We want you to be comfortable."

"Not too comfortable," Malcolm said with a dry laugh.

Lizzy gave Ajay a nod of her head as she continued to stroke Pumpkin's coat.

When he returned, Pumpkin was still in the same position, and Lizzy was arguing with Max.

"If scaring me was what this creep hoped to do, he's done a good job," she snapped. "I'm scared. He broke into my home. He touched my things. I'm officially scared to death!"

"We're not going to let anything happen to you," Max said.

"Like nothing was going to happen when I was at the hospital? The police are making a lot of promises they have a hard time trying to keep," she quipped. "And the FBI aren't much better!"

"It wasn't an FBI case," Max snapped back. "They didn't have jurisdiction, but as a favor to me, they're trying to help."

"They should be trying harder!" Lizzy yelled, her voice vibrating around the room. "What if I had been home? Or worse, if I hadn't gotten away or been saved by Ajay in the snow? Would it have been an FBI case then?"

"You can really be irrational sometimes," Max countered.

Lizzy pulled her knees to her chest, her arms tightening around Pumpkin's neck. She buried her face into the dog's neck, her tears falling for the umpteenth time.

Pumpkin whimpered softly.

"I think maybe we should squash this conversation until later. Everyone's tired, and Lizzy should probably go lie down," Ajay said, trying to keep his tone calming.

There was the briefest of pauses, then Lizzy jumped from

where she'd been resting. Pumpkin jumped with her, staying close to her side as she moved toward a bedroom at the end of the hall.

The family stared after her, no one saying anything as she stormed out of the room.

"I'll go make sure she's okay," Ajay said. He turned to follow her.

Like birds being shooed away, her family suddenly took flight. Everyone moved in opposite directions, heading for their own homes and beds. There was a lot of muttering and an occasional curse uttered into the late-night air. Their vexation was palpable, each consumed with worry and concern but wanting to be pillars of strength for their baby sister.

"Good night," Jenny called after Ajay.

"Let us know if you need anything," Buck concluded.

And just like that, the Colton Ranch was as quiet as a library, not a single sound to be heard.

Lizzy had thrown herself face down across the bed. She lay crossways, a pillow tucked beneath her head, her arms wrapped tightly around the pillow. She wasn't crying, instead staring into space still fuming with rage.

Ajay stood watching her, knowing there was little he could say to ease the hurt and anger she was feeling. Pumpkin lay at the foot of the bed, giving him a side-eye like he didn't belong in the space. A clock on the desk ticked loudly, and Ajay found himself counting time away in his head.

He didn't know just how long he stood watching, but when Lizzy sighed heavily, rolling over onto her side, it shook him from the daze he'd fallen into.

"Do you want to talk?" Ajay asked.

"No," Lizzy snapped. "I just want this to be over."

"I know."

She took a deep breath and held it before blowing it slowly past her thin lips. "I'm having a hard time finding balance. I think it's all going to be okay, and then *boom*, something else hits."

Ajay moved to the side of the bed and sat down beside her. Lizzy rolled herself closer to the center of the mattress to give him more room. Without missing a beat, Ajay lifted his legs, shifted his torso and gave himself permission to relax into the moment. He eased his body against hers, his arm falling over her waist. Ajay felt her entire body relax against him. He pressed his face into her hair, the scent of her jasmine shampoo wafting up his nostrils.

Neither spoke another word, allowing themselves to savor the intimacy of the moment. Lizzy clasped her hand atop his, their fingers entwining one with the other. Her touch was warm and gentle, and Ajay knew he would miss it whenever she let his hand go.

The room's windows were open for the fresh air, and a chilly breeze blew into the space. A full moon sat high in the deep black sky, light reflecting over the layers of snow on the ground.

An aura of peace filled the air, washing over them both like a gentle kiss pressed against an eager cheek. Ajay pulled a heavy comforter over them, the two snuggling closer beneath the warmth. Sleep came easily. Ajay had no clue who dozed off first, but in no time at all, the two of them were both sleeping soundly.

It had been ages, if ever, since Ajay had heard the crow of a rooster in the early morning hours. But the familiar cock-a-doodle-doo snatched him out of the sweetest dream.

It took him a moment to collect himself, his surroundings unfamiliar. And then he remembered where he was, Lizzy still resting in his arms.

Exhaustion had finally beaten them both. He vaguely remembered the nurse rousing them some time in the middle of the night, and Lizzy had allowed her to add a sedative to her medications. He imagined she would continue to sleep, her body reclaiming the rest that it was owed.

He, however, couldn't afford that luxury. He needed to assess the landscape in daylight and learn everything he could about the Colton family and Lizzy. It was the only way he imagined he could beat her stalker and keep her from harm.

Easing himself from around her, he lifted his body from the bed. Extending his arms above his shoulders, he stretched, leaning as far back as the tightness in his lower back would allow. He gave Lizzy one last glance. She looked peaceful with her hair splayed across the pillow around her face. Her cheeks were tinted a rosy shade of pink from the heat in the room. He wished he could climb back into the bed beside her, but there was too much he still needed to do. He turned and headed toward the door.

Pumpkin jumped up from where she'd been sleeping at the foot of the bed to follow behind him. "So, you *do* remember me," he whispered to the dog. "I can't believe you threw me over like that."

Pumpkin nudged his side and made him laugh.

Everything about Colton Ranch reminded Ajay of how wonderful a home could be. Just north of Owl Creek, it was some eight hundred acres of working cattle ranch with plenty of fertile space to grow a variety of crops.

Lizzy's father, Buck, had built his fortune on two brands: Colton Produce, which monetized the agricultural side, and Colton Beef. He'd been an astute businessman, building value in the land to pass down to his children. Greg and Malcolm both worked on the property, choosing to follow in their father's footsteps.

The family home was a renovated red wooden barn with a two-story living and dining area, multiple bedrooms, quaint sitting areas and angles that gave the home a rustic appearance. Buck's gardens in the backyard lent character to the landscape. It was an impressive property.

From what Lizzy had told him, her mother, Jessie, had always hated the idea of living in a barn, despite the high-end designer renovations that made it a home. Buck had added an Olympic-size swimming pool for the kids and a guesthouse, where Greg currently resided with his new wife, Briony, and their two adopted children. Not far from the home was a working barn, horse paddock and shared house where the ranch hands stayed if they chose to live on site or just needed a place to lay their heads.

Ajay ran down the length of driveway that had been cleared of snow and ice. Pumpkin ran with him, leaping into the high mounds of snow as she played and exercised her legs. He laughed at her antics, understanding that feeling of freedom she seemed to be reveling in. It was a good workout for them both.

By the end of the hour, Ajay had raced along the property's perimeter, crossing a short length of field that led him past a small pond. He stopped at the barn to catch his breath and admire the horses inside. He was about to head back to the main house when Malcolm waved for his attention, heading toward him on an ATV.

"Good morning," Ajay said.

Malcolm greeted him warmly. "How'd you sleep?"

"Like a log. It felt good to get some rest."

"Max followed Della to Lizzy's house. They wanted to check it out one last time before the police release it back to her."

"I don't want her seeing it like that," Ajay said. "This situation has her shook, and I think if she sees the damage the intruder did, it might break her. Can you arrange for someone to put the place back in order and give it a good cleaning before she returns home?"

"Yeah." Malcolm nodded. "I'll make sure it gets handled."

"I appreciate it. I don't want Lizzy more traumatized than she already is."

"You've got it bad for my little sister, don't you?" Malcolm's brow lifted.

Ajay's eyes darted back and forth, and he pondered his response. "I care about your sister," he finally replied.

He wasn't ready to admit that his heart was riding a roller coaster of emotions when it came to Lizzy. Despite all the warm and fuzzy feelings he was having for her, he was conflicted. This was uncharted territory for him. All his previous relationships had been casual encounters. There had been no one he went to bed thinking about and woke up missing. Lizzy had him out here like a grade schooler with his first crush. She occupied his thoughts every single minute of his day from the time he opened his eyes till he closed them again at night.

Yeah, he thought, he had it bad.

"Is that what we're calling it now?" Malcolm said with a smirk. "You care? Dude! Just admit you have the hots for her!"

"Does it show?" Ajay asked.

"Stevie Wonder could see it."

Ajay sighed. "I'm not going to lie to you. I like your sister. I like her a lot. But I also know that this is not an ideal situation for either of us. I don't want her idolizing me because of what I've done and then thinking those feelings are something they really aren't."

Malcolm turned serious. "And what about your feelings? How do you know you're just not going through some savior complex?"

"I've been doing this job for too long and have never thought about the women I've rescued the way I think about Lizzy. Your sister is an incredible woman, and when this is over, I hope we can continue to get to know each other."

"Damn!" Malcolm said, feigning revulsion. "You know that's so not cool for a girl's brother to hear, right?"

Ajay laughed. "Sorry, guy!"

Malcolm nodded. He hesitated, mulling over the conversation before responding. "You have my blessing," he finally concluded. "But I'm not sure Max is ready to give you a green light."

"I get that. What about your father? Has he expressed any concerns?"

"Dad just wants Lizzy to be happy. Don't think he hasn't noticed the change in her disposition with you around. We've all noted the transformation."

"Then we're good. I'm sure I can win Max over once he gets to know me better. Besides, Lizzy and I are still discovering what we like about each other. For all I know, she might decide that I'm not the one, and Max can say he told you so."

Malcolm winced. "Please, don't mess up," he said with a snort. "I hate when Max is right!"

Ajay laughed. "I'll do my best!"

"Do you want a ride back to the house?"

"Thanks, but I need to finish my run. I'm still getting the lay of the land. Just in case."

"I'll meet you at the house then," Malcolm said, jumping back on his four-wheeler. "Mama Jen just got here, and she said she's making pancakes!"

* * *

"So what's going on with you and that young man?" Jenny sat in the sunroom beside Lizzy. The two women were enjoying the early morning sunshine and their first cup of coffee for the day.

Lizzy took a sip of the hot brew from the mug she held, hesitating. She could feel something like joy pulling at the muscles in her face, widening the smile in her eyes.

"I don't know," she finally answered. "I really like him, Mama Jen. He seems like a great guy, and I can see myself in a relationship with him. But I can't imagine him wanting a woman who is so needy! And since we met, I've been like a need magnet. Just one blunder after another. What guy wants to be bothered with that?"

Jenny chuckled. "Obviously, he doesn't feel that way. I can tell by how he looks at you that he clearly cares a great deal about you. And his concern feels very genuine."

"Exactly!" Lizzy tossed up her hands. "He's concerned. It's like I'm a project he's suddenly responsible for, and when this is over, I'll just be a finished assignment."

"You don't give yourself enough credit, Lizzy. You're a strong capable young woman. Lieutenant Wright can see that, and I think he respects and admires that about you."

Lizzy shrugged her shoulders. "Maybe."

"No maybes. That man is very interested in you, and you are interested in him. Don't waste years of your life being unhappy when love is right beside you trying to get your attention."

"Did you do that? Waste years of your life?"

Jenny sighed. "When I married Robert, he was like a shiny new penny. After a while, that shine started to dull and tarnish. I kept trying to polish him up and shine him back up. I ignored all the dings and dents and scuff marks.

Before I knew it, there were just too many blemishes for him to ever be new and pretty again."

"What about you and my dad? You both seem very cozy with each other."

"Your father and I have a lot of history together. He's a good man and an even better friend."

Lizzy smiled. "Just a friend?"

"Worry about you, Lizzy. This family has enough relationship drama to contend with. Your father and I have no interest in adding to it."

Lizzy persisted, "So you have thought about it?"

Giggling, Jenny lobbed an accent pillow at Lizzy's head. The two women enjoyed a good laugh.

"This is pretty," Lizzy exclaimed a moment later. "I don't remember it." She held the embroidered pillow out in front of her. Its watercolor-inspired design was a nice complement to the decor.

Since she'd been fifteen, her father had always allowed her free rein when it came to their home. Lizzy's love of art came from her first interior design endeavors. Buck had supported all the changes she wanted to make, cheering her on during each of her decorating stages. Art school had helped her tone down some of her choices, and now the space was a beautiful mesh of bright colors against white walls and cabinets. It still retained its rustic flair and exuded comfort in every room.

Jenny answered, "Your dad and I found two of them at the flea market back in the summer. Shortly after Fletcher returned home, if I remember correctly. I thought they'd be a nice addition to this room. I'm so glad you like them. Your taste is much better than mine."

Lizzy hugged the pillow to her chest and tried to keep the glee out of her expression. She wasn't sure how she felt about her father being with any woman, but she definitely didn't hate the idea of him and Mama Jen being together.

As if she could read Lizzy's mind, Jenny tossed her a quick glance, and the two burst out laughing for the second time.

Ajay was confident that no one could get onto the property and close to the Colton home without being seen. Strangers would set off all kinds of alarms, and everyone had been given implicit instructions to ensure no one passed through the front gates without being thoroughly vetted. He had all the confidence in the world that Lizzy was safe as long as she kept close to her family home.

After a quick shower, Ajay joined the Colton family for breakfast. Jenny had prepared pancakes just as Malcolm had promised she would—light, fluffy, silver-dollar-size flapjacks dripping with maple syrup. There were also strips of crisp bacon, fresh scrambled eggs and one of the best cups of coffee Ajay could remember ever having.

The noise level in the house had risen substantially since he and Pumpkin had gone for their run. Laughter was abundant, and the conversations were loud.

Lizzy and Malcolm sat at the dining table teasing their father about his new obsession with lilies. Apparently, lilies occupied over half the garden, bulbs planted during the fall to be ready for the spring. Buck had carefully charted their placement, variety and growing needs, preparing himself for the impending growing season. His family found his obsession amusing, and Ajay was impressed with his determination.

"Have you given any thought to adding a greenhouse to the property?" Ajay asked.

"Don't give him any ideas," Lizzy said with an earnest laugh.

"That's actually something to think about," Buck said.

"And Colton Florals is born!" Malcolm teased.

"I kind of like that," Buck said. "We might be on to something!"

Jenny shook her head. "I don't think starting a new business was what retirement was supposed to look like." She giggled.

Buck winked at her and laughed. "Maybe not. But that's why I'm always open to suggestions."

Lizzy looked from her father to her aunt and back. She shot her brother a look, then turned her gaze on Ajay. He didn't miss the amusement that danced in her eyes as the two seniors fell into their own conversation. She smiled, bright white teeth blessing the moment. Ajay couldn't help but smile back.

"I need to run," Malcolm said, rising from his seat. He wiped his mouth with a paper napkin. "We need to chase down a few stray cattle that knocked down the fence on the back field. My search-and-rescue skills come in handy during times like this."

"I'd offer to help you out," Ajay said, "but my search-and-rescue skills wouldn't be handy at all."

They all laughed, everyone shifting in their chairs.

"Please, be careful out there," Jenny said as Malcolm waved goodbye and disappeared out the door. She rose from her seat, moving to clear away the dirty dishes from their breakfast.

Ajay stood to help. "Breakfast was amazing," he said. "Allow me to do the dishes."

"I can help," Lizzy said. She reached for her father's empty plate.

Ajay's gaze narrowed. "Shouldn't you be resting?" he asked, his concern rising.

"I load a mean dishwasher," Lizzy answered. "I don't think putting a few plates in the tray is going to tax my strength. Besides, the doctor says I need to start moving more. Physical therapy for my weakened muscles."

Ajay didn't look convinced.

"You two have at it," Jenny said, sitting back down. "Buck and I will enjoy one last cup of coffee."

"You do that," Lizzy said, tossing the two a look over her shoulder. She purposely bumped into Ajay as she moved through the sliding barn-style doors to the kitchen.

He eyed her curiously, noting the piercing stare in her eyes. "What?" he asked, his voice dropping to a whisper.

"Do you get the impression that those two might be enjoying a little more than coffee?"

Ajay laughed as Lizzy peered past him, watching the other couple closely. He reached for the dirty plates she carried in her hands. Easing past her, he leaned to whisper in her ear. "I'm more excited about finishing that puzzle you and I started." He winked at her. "I do good puzzle," he said teasingly.

"Lieutenant Wright!" Lizzy grinned, her smile pulling full and bright across her face. "I don't know how you do it, but that actually sounded like you were being fresh," she said as she pretended to clutch a strand of pearls at her chest.

Laughter rang sweetly between them.

Lizzy disappeared into her father's office. Ajay watched from the doorway, not wanting to interrupt.

She sat with a sketch pad in her lap, singularly focused on the work she'd tasked herself with. When she sat back in the leather executive's chair, her arms folded across her chest, Ajay called her name. He moved into the room to her side.

"Is this a good time?" he questioned. "I don't want to interrupt if you're working."

Lizzy shook her head. "No, I'm not working. Not my day job, at least. I just can't get that creep off my mind, so I figured I'd put my artistic skills to work for me. Della said you don't have a sketch artist on the payroll, so I've given myself the job."

She reached for a stack of paper from the corner of the desk. She passed it to him, pulling her legs beneath her butt in her seat. "This is the man who was holding me hostage. And this was the same man who showed up at the hospital outside of my room."

Ajay stared at the images she passed into his hands. He shuffled through them, clearly impressed. "How did you..." he started.

"I'm really good at what I do," Lizzy said. She sat back in the chair, her expression smug. Satisfaction seeped like water from her eyes.

An actual photograph couldn't have captured the details of the man's face better. She'd done mock-ups of him in his two masks as well as one without. Clearly, Ajay thought, it took a particular skill level and a good eye for detail to generate the images she'd created with a heavy lead pencil.

"I'll get this to Della and the detectives investigating your case. It should definitely help."

Lizzy pulled both hands through her hair, twisting it into a messy topknot. "I'm tired," she said, "and I imagine you're bored and ready to go home."

"In time," Ajay replied. "Right now, we worry about you. Not about me."

She nodded. "In that case, right now, I need a nap. Care to join me?" Her smirk was teasing as she lifted her brow seductively.

Ajay laughed. He waved the sheet of paper at her. "I still have work to do, Ms. Colton."

"You are absolutely no fun, Lieutenant Wright. No fun at all!" Lizzy giggled.

Chapter 8

Ajay had settled into a comfortable routine in the brief time he'd been staying with Lizzy in her family's home. During the day, he and Lizzy were able to spend a good amount of time together. Their conversations ran the gamut from the nonsensical to the sagacious. They debated the benefits of dryer lint, discussed the world financial crisis and pondered everything else of interest in between.

Sometimes her family would join them, and sometimes they didn't. They flirted with each other unabashedly. They laughed a lot and even shared a tear or two. Every waking moment together served to bring them closer as they spent time learning each other's idiosyncrasies. What they'd proclaimed a friendship had been firmly solidified, and time had served to further cement their mutual respect and admiration for each other.

"Dinner was exceptional tonight," Ajay said as he moved into Lizzy's bedroom. He dropped down to the tufted ottoman that rested at the foot of her queen-size bed.

"I told you I could cook."

"I didn't believe you. I said I could cook, too, but that didn't make it true."

"So, you lied? You can't cook?"

"That's not what I said."

"That's what it sounded like."

"Well, I can cook. I make a mean scrambled egg with cheese. There are levels to cooking. My level of expertise may not be your level. That doesn't mean I can't do it."

"You can't cook!" Lizzy exclaimed. "And my vegetable lasagna just outdid whatever egg thing you think you can cook!"

Ajay pressed his hand to his heart. "Ouch! That hurt!"

Lizzy laughed. "Not as much as discovering you are a kitchen fraud."

Pumpkin barked.

Ajay shook his head. "I can't believe you're taking her side," he said as he scratched the dog's head. "Where's your loyalty?"

Pumpkin jumped onto the bed and lay herself down beside Lizzy. She tilted her head to stare at Ajay.

Lizzy laughed again. "You tell him, girl!"

"Della and I are going to have to have a conversation about your training," he quipped, his eyes rolling skyward.

Pumpkin barked, then laid her head against Lizzy's leg and closed her eyes.

After an hour of watching the evening news together, Lizzy shifted her legs off the bedside to kick off her leather cowboy boots.

"Do you need help?" Ajay asked.

"If you don't mind," Lizzy responded, "I could use a little assistance."

"I don't mind at all," he answered. He reached for her foot, grabbing at the heel of her boot. Lizzy pulled her leg up toward her chest. The joint gesture helped the boot to slide off and Ajay dropped it to the floor as he reached for the other foot. When both had been discarded to the floor, he was still holding on to her heel, his eyes wide.

"Don't look at my toes!" Lizzy exclaimed as she tried to pull the appendage from his hands. "I need a pedicure!"

"You really do," Ajay said, his head bobbing in agreement.

"I don't recall asking for your opinion," Lizzy snapped, a wide smile on her face.

"I can take you tomorrow," Ajay said. He was still holding her heel, despite her efforts to disengage his grip.

"I'm not ready to go out," she said. "Besides, no one will see my feet."

"I've seen your feet!" he exclaimed.

Lizzy giggled. "I cannot believe you! There are extenuating circumstances. Give a girl a break."

"I think I need to give a girl a pedicure," he said, rising from where he sat and heading into her bathroom.

Lizzy's gaze was wide-eyed, shock and awe washing over her expression. She listened as he seemed to be rummaging in her bathroom cabinet. "What are you looking for?" she asked him.

Ajay poked his head out the bathroom door. "Do you have one of those footbath things? Or a small washtub?"

She nodded her head. "Look in the linen closet. On the top shelf."

Ajay winked his eye at her, then disappeared back into the bathroom. Minutes later he returned with a foot tub of warm water, a towel, a tube of moisturizer and the brightest pink nail polish she owned.

"You're kidding, right?" Lizzy questioned.

"Not at all. You have a need, and I can help. Why wouldn't I?"

Lizzy hesitated. She didn't really have an answer to give, so she said nothing. She watched as Ajay placed the tub at the end of the ottoman and gestured for her to take a seat. She slid from the bed to the cushioned top, easing her feet into the warm bath of water that he'd scented with her lavender bodywash.

Ajay poked her big toe with his finger, amusement dancing across his face.

"Do you know what you're doing?" Lizzy asked.

"Nope! It's my first time, but I'm pretty sure I'll figure it out. How hard can it be?"

Lizzy lifted both her feet out of the water. "Now I'm scared," she said with a laugh.

Ajay pushed her toes back beneath the suds. "You act like I run into woman with crusty feet on a regular basis."

Lizzy gasped. "My feet are not crusty! They are not that bad!"

Ajay shot her a look. "Okay," he said. "If you say so."

"Take that back, Ajay Wright!"

Ajay drew his fingers down the inside of her calf, his hands dropping into the water as he continued to caress her skin. "Nope!"

Lizzy moved as if to stomp her foot and splashed him with water. "I mean it," she said. "Take that back!"

Ajay laughed. "I will not. My feet look better than yours."

"I swear! I liked you much better before you started hanging out with my brothers. They're starting to rub off on you."

"Honesty is not a character flaw, Lizzy."

"Being mean is."

"Would you rather I send you out into the world with jacked-up feet or tell you the truth?"

Lizzy didn't respond, pretending to pout. She crossed her arms and turned her head from him. She enjoyed bantering with him, but his touch was beginning to take on a life of its own, her entire body responding to the gentle caresses. She feared her voice would crack or she would say something she couldn't take back if she spoke.

"That's what I thought," Ajay said smugly.

"Enjoy your little moment," Lizzy muttered. "I will get even. Just watch your back."

Ajay chuckled. "Duly noted."

Lizzy closed her eyes and settled into the sensations sweeping from her female center. Heat burned in every direction as she focused on his touch, his hands gently kneading the muscles in each toe, across the bottom of her foot and over the top. He twisted the appendage from side to side, gently stretching each ankle. As he massaged each sinewy muscle and caressed every nerve ending, Lizzy could feel herself falling deep into the warm sensations sweeping through her entire body. It was quickly becoming the best pedicure she'd ever had, and she could tell from his expression that he knew it.

"You are so wrong, Ajay!" she sputtered.

"What did I do?" he questioned.

"You know exactly what you're doing and it's not fair."

Ajay laughed heartily. He continued to caress and tease her flesh and she let him. Minutes passed before she suddenly snatched both feet from the bath, lifting them high in the air.

"I think they're good," she muttered.

"Are you sure?" Ajay said as he reached for the towel to pat her toes dry. "I still need to moisturize them and update your polish."

"No, that's good. I can finish them later."

"I don't mind. I want to make sure you're satisfied."

"Clearly, this has to be the devil's work. You've got me heated and now I can't even think straight."

Ajay sat upright. Amusement seeped from his eyes as he stared at her.

Lizzy pointed her index finger at him. "Don't you dare try to deny it. You've got me ready to rip my clothes off and you did it on purpose, knowing that you would have to turn me down."

"I did no such thing," Ajay professed.

The two sat staring at each other, neither speaking. Lizzy finally broke through the quiet that had filled the room.

"I really like you, Ajay. I like you more than I should and definitely more than I like any of my other male friends. I don't want to embarrass myself if the flirting and teasing is just that and not something more. So, I really need you to be honest with me about what you're feeling. Please don't leave me feeling foolish."

Ajay paused before answering. He lifted himself from where he'd been kneeling to sit on the ottoman beside her. He reached for her hand, entwining her fingers between his own.

"I like you, too," Ajay finally responded. "And you know that whatever is happening between us is definitely more than two friends casually flirting and teasing each other. It's a lot more, but it can't get in the way of me keeping you safe and finding your kidnapper. No matter what the two of us are feeling."

Lizzy blew a soft sigh. She closed her eyes and sat in the silence for a good few minutes. When she opened them, Ajay was staring at her, his eyes misted ever so slightly. Shifting her body to face him, she pulled her hand from his and pressed her palm to the side of his face. There was no need for words. His eyes danced across her face, his gaze reflecting every emotion he was feeling. She felt her heart skip a beat, and then two, the entire universe feeling as if it was syncing the two of them together.

Leaning forward, Lizzy pressed her closed lips to his, the kiss lingering ever so sweetly. Rising, she moved toward the bathroom, pausing for a quick minute before closing the door after herself. Minutes later, when she returned, Ajay was gone, and Pumpkin snored softly against her pillow.

* * *

Every evening, they would talk until they were completely talked out, their eyelids heavy. Ajay would send Lizzy off to her room as he double-checked the doors and windows. Most nights, Pumpkin would follow Lizzy, tossing Ajay to the curb.

With regularity, his internal clock pulled him from a deep sleep at 2:00 a.m. every night. Rising, Ajay would ease down the hall to first check on Lizzy. Most times, Pumpkin would be in her room or her bed, the two sleeping soundly. Ajay would check doors and windows a second time before returning to his own room to fall back to sleep alone.

On two occasions, her father had been sitting in the family room, sipping bourbon from a cut-crystal whiskey glass. The last time the two had talked, Buck had peppered him with questions to learn more about him.

"My daughter is quite smitten with you, Ajay." Buck's stare had been searing, pulling hard at Ajay's heartstrings.

Buck continued. "I understand these are unusual circumstances for both of you, but I wouldn't want either of you to misinterpret your feelings. Lust is a far cry from love."

Ajay had nodded. "Yes, sir. I agree."

"My sweet girl doesn't fall easily for any man, but when she does, she falls hard. I won't sit back and watch her heart be broken."

"I would never do anything to purposely hurt Lizzy. She means the world to me."

Lizzy's father eyed him sternly. "Jenny says you two are falling in love and don't even realize it."

Ajay felt his cheeks heat with color. He wasn't sure how to answer that, so he didn't say anything, allowing Buck to continue the conversation.

"Personally, I think you both realize it and are trying hard to deny it. As a father, I can appreciate you taking things slowly. Caution will serve you both well. It will also keep me from putting my foot up your backside if you get it wrong and make my baby girl cry." Buck lifted his glass and took a long sip of his bourbon. As he swallowed, the conversation shifted like a spring breeze, the two suddenly talking about football and their favorite teams.

Ajay had great appreciation for those nights, even learning a thing or two about himself that Buck had been all too willing to point out. And his corny dad jokes were actually funny despite Ajay's best efforts to not laugh.

This night was different. As he double-checked the doors, he immediately sensed that something was amiss. It was a feeling deep in his gut, a flutter of apprehension that moved him to retrieve his service weapon from the nightstand drawer before starting his rounds.

Outside Lizzy's room, he heard Pumpkin growl, the guttural noise low and threatening. He opened the door, and the dog stood ready to pounce on any intruder.

Ajay gestured her back toward Lizzy, who was sitting upright in the bed. He knew it was on the tip of her tongue to hit him with a barrage of questions about what was going on, but she bit back the words, seeming to trust he would do whatever was needed. As Pumpkin jumped back on the bed, she wrapped her arms around the animal's neck and nuzzled her face against the dog.

Ajay moved swiftly through the home, checking each room as quickly and as quietly as he was able. Traversing the hallway toward the family room, Ajay realized someone had left one of the sliding glass doors to the screened porch wide open. The family room was cold, the icy breezes from outside intruding on the space.

When he was certain no one was there who wasn't supposed to be, he moved outside, not bothering to grab his boots or a jacket. The icy remnants of the last snow against his bare feet shocked him wide awake, leaving him no reason to think that this was an accident.

The night sky was dark. The temperature had dropped, and it felt like another storm might be brewing. He turned on all the outside lights and slowly circled the perimeter of the family's home.

Outside the screened porch, Ajay noted two sets of footprints, both from heavy boots with thick treads. He lifted his eyes to follow where they led, the darkness eventually stalling his view. Then a flicker of light in the distance grabbed his attention.

Someone had come through the gates and was headed back down the driveway toward the main road. Ajay suddenly had no doubt that same someone had been in the house. So close that any of them could have been targeted.

He turned to go back inside. When he looked up, Lizzy was watching him from the doorway. Their eyes connected and locked. Tears puddled beneath her eyelids, her lashes fluttering to keep them at bay. There was nothing he needed to explain.

"I called Max and Della," Lizzy said softly. "The police are on their way."

No one had seen or heard a thing. The intruders had come and gone under the cloak of darkness. Nothing had been taken, everything left neatly where it belonged, except for a note that had been slipped beneath Lizzy's bedroom door. She gave it to Ajay, who took it gingerly by its corner and passed it to the Owl Creek forensics team. The two sat watching as it was dusted for fingerprints, the officer noting that both had handled it.

The single-ruled note paper was nondescript, torn haphazardly from a composition notebook. Blue ink was scrawled as crudely as the tear in the paper, but the scribbled words left nothing to interpretation. *We're coming for you.*

"Pumpkin woke me up," Lizzy said, her voice calmer than he would have expected. "She jumped from the bed, and I heard her growl. Somehow, I knew it wasn't you, and then this note was pushed under the door. Whoever was there didn't stay longer than a minute or two before I heard them move away. Not long after you opened the door."

Ajay nodded. "Did they even try to enter your bedroom?"

She shook her head. "No. Not at all. I think they just wanted me to know they were there."

He felt like he had failed her. "I should have been there," he muttered.

"You were there. And you did the best you could," Lizzy whispered. "This is not your fault, Ajay." She reached for his hand, gently caressing his fingers.

Ajay slid his hand from hers, suddenly feeling self-conscious. He didn't think her family was at all concerned by her public display of affection, but he didn't feel worthy of her touch. He was taking the intrusion harder than she was, and Lizzy's calm aura had him feeling off-kilter.

"I'm installing a security system first thing in the morning," Buck said. The patriarch had spent the better part of the last hour calling every member of the family to rule out it being one of them paying a late-night visit. Despite his best efforts, they all knew the task was futile. No one in the family would have come and gone at such a late hour, sneaking around like thieves in the night. Nor would they have left Lizzy this threatening calling card.

"Who all has a key to the house?" Ajay asked. "I didn't see any forced entry."

Lizzy's eyes narrowed. "It would probably be easier to

list who doesn't have a key. When my father said this would be the family home, he didn't mean it figuratively. All of us have keys, even my cousins. Everyone has always had a place to stay without needing to ask. And you can come and go as you please. There's always a stocked pantry, full fridge and an empty bed."

"Family's important to me," Buck said.

"It's important to all of us," Lizzy responded.

"Which is why we will do whatever we need to do to protect this family," Buck concluded. "Besides, all these doors still have the original locks. I never even thought to change them after your mother left. I guess now is as good a time as any."

Lizzy shook her head, tossing Ajay a look. "Even my mother probably still has keys," she said flippantly.

Buck scoffed, waving a dismissive hand in Lizzy's direction. "I'm sure Jessie tossed her keys the day she walked out. She never liked this place. Said I had her living in a barn like the farm animals."

Ajay watched as Lizzy pulled her knees to her chest and wrapped her arms around her legs. She hugged herself tightly. He had no doubt that her father's comment hit a nerve. Lizzy was proud of their family home, believing their barn had been everything they'd needed, and more. As if reading her mind, he knew that she would never understand how anyone could have found their home, or them, lacking. Most especially her mother.

His attention shifted back to their current situation. Ajay's frustration was on a low simmer. He was finding it difficult to accept that whoever was stalking Lizzy had been so close. Being there and still not catching the man, or men, had him feeling inadequate. It wasn't an emotion he was accustomed to or one he was willing to accept.

He'd been so caught up in the joy he felt spending time with Lizzy that he'd forgotten his mission. He was there to protect her, and he knew the first line of defense was always a good offense. He needed to change his tactics, and hers, if they were going to catch this guy.

"We need to get some sleep," Ajay said. "We're going to have a long day tomorrow."

Lizzy looked confused. "I don't understand."

"You're going back to your life, and I'm going back to mine."

"I don't understand. What does that mean?"

"It means we're done hiding, and we're definitely not running. We're going to take back control."

"Does that mean you're leaving?"

"It means if I stay, it's because I want to be here. And the same goes for you. If you're ready to head back to your place, I'll support that and do what's necessary to ensure your safety. If you don't want that yet, that's fine, too."

"I don't think I'm ready yet," she muttered. "I feel safe here. I don't know if I'll feel safe back at home."

Ajay nodded. "And that's okay. We can both stay right here at the ranch until you feel comfortable."

Lizzy hesitated, seeming to process everything that had happened and all that had been said. Ajay knew she still didn't have a clue what he intended for the two of them, but she did know she could trust him. In fact, she could trust him with her life, and her heart.

Retreating back to her bedroom, Lizzy dropped onto the carpeted floor. She had thought herself safe in her own family's home, but she wasn't. There was still a threat out there, and it had been close enough to reach out and touch her. She had grown comfortable, thinking she was safe here at home with the family that loved her best. But that was a lie. She wasn't safe anywhere.

But why? She still couldn't figure out who was doing this or why this was happening to her. She wanted to scream and yell and wake up from the nightmare of it all, but this wasn't a dream, and she couldn't deny the reality of her situation.

She hugged herself tightly, curling her body around a pillow as she lay in the fetal position. She didn't want her family to know her fears. She refused to let them see that this thing had her scared beyond words. She needed them to think she was healing and would be well. And, she was desperate to keep Ajay from thinking she was weak or fragile. Even if it was only an illusion, she needed him to believe that she was strong and capable in trying situations. *Smoke and mirrors*, she thought. *Smoke and mirrors!*

The knock at the door was unexpected, and she jumped. She stared but didn't respond. Lizzy's heart began to race, and her palms were suddenly clammy. She could feel the onset of a panic attack, and she began deep breathing and tapping to quell the emotion.

Minutes passed before the second knock. This time, Ajay pushed the door open slowly, peeking inside. "I just wanted to check on you," Ajay said softly.

At the sight of him, tears began to roll out of her eyes and down her cheeks. So much for trying to be strong, she thought. She swiped at her face with the back of her hand, not wanting Ajay to see her be emotional. Lizzy shook her head, words caught deep in her chest. Whatever needed to be said rained from her eyes.

Ajay dropped down to the floor beside her. He pressed his hand against her knee, gently caressing the cool flesh.

Desperate to hold back her sobs, Lizzy was good until he touched her, and then the floodgates opened. As she cried,

Ajay wrapped his arms around her torso. He didn't speak, simply allowing his presence to be a comfort to her.

As the first hint of a new day's sun began to peek over the horizon outside, he was still there with his arms around her, her tears damp against the front of his shirt.

After the commotion of police and investigators in the house, sleep had been difficult for everyone. After tucking Lizzy into her bed, Ajay was still roaming the house looking for clues. He hadn't shared his thoughts with anyone, not even Della. But there was just something about the intrusion that concerned him.

How well did the interloper know the family? Whoever it was had found Lizzy's bedroom easily, having no problems discerning her door from all the others. Why did he feel like this wasn't the first time the intruder had been in their home, by invitation or otherwise? Was the man stalking Lizzy foe disguised as a friend? Ajay was determined to find the answers.

He moved from the family room to the kitchen. Jenny sat at the kitchen table, a cup of coffee in her hand. She gave him the sweetest smile and beckoned him toward the seat beside her.

"I didn't mean to interrupt," Ajay said, his voice a loud whisper. "I wasn't expecting to find you here."

"It was so late after the police left that I just slept in the other guest bedroom. I figured if Lizzy or Buck needed me, that it would be easier if I stayed close. I heard you scurrying around and figured I'd get up to make us all some coffee. Can I pour you a cup? Or would you prefer juice? I made some green juice last night before I headed to bed. It's good!"

"Thank you," Ajay replied. "The juice would be perfect."

"Juice it is." Jenny rose from her seat to the refrigerator.

She lifted a large container from a shelf and brought it to the counter. Grabbing a glass from an upper cabinet, she filled it with the neon green beverage and returned the pitcher to the fridge. "It's kale, cucumber, ginger and green apple."

Ajay nodded his appreciation as he took the glass from her hand and took a sip. "It's very good," he said, genuinely enjoying the flavors against his tongue.

"And good for you! I haven't been able to convince Buck and the boys of that just yet. Slowly but surely, though."

Jenny sat back comfortably in her seat and watched him for a few moments. Ajay quickly sensed that something was on her mind, and the matriarch didn't hesitate to speak her thoughts. "Lizzy is fragile right now. She's trying to pretend that she's okay, but she's not."

"I know. This can't be easy on her. Or any of you for that matter."

"Lizzy is leaning on you for support, and I'm not sure that's a good idea."

Ajay felt himself bristle, his nerves tensing. He took a deep breath as Jenny continued.

"What are your intentions with our Lizzy? When this is over, do you plan to disappear from her life? Because that may be even more traumatic than what's happening to her now."

"I want to think that Lizzy and I have become good friends through all of this. So me disappearing isn't an option. I'm hopeful that we can explore our relationship more when we're not always worried about what might happen next. I've enjoyed getting to know her and hope we can continue that momentum. I really care for Lizzy."

Jenny nodded and paused before letting her next words drop, hitting the floor with a thunderous thud. "Lizzy has fallen in love with you. But I think you know that already. Because I think you've fallen in love with her, too. All of us really want her to be happy, and we're probably more excited than the two of you are. But I don't want her to get her heart broken."

Ajay paused, reflecting on her comment. When he looked up, the older woman was staring at him intently, studying his reaction. He nodded. "I promise you," he said, lifting his hand to his heart. He made the same promise to her that he'd made to Buck days earlier. "I won't do anything that will ever break Lizzy's heart."

Lizzy lay in her bed staring up at the ceiling. She'd been awake for hours, trying to process all that had happened and everything she was feeling. She was even more frightened after this last incident.

But she was equally determined not to let Ajay see her break a second time under the stress of not knowing who wanted to hurt her. From being abducted to having strangers in her personal space at her home and the family ranch, it was all chilling. It was taking every ounce of courage she possessed to stay sane.

After leaving the hospital, Lizzy had figured if she stayed close to home and shut out the rest of the world, everything would be okay. She knew that if she broke, there might not be enough that anyone could do to fix the pieces and make her whole again. She exhaled softly as she adjusted the pillow beneath her head.

Pumpkin had gone for a morning run with Ajay, and Lizzy was feeling discombobulated without her canine companion. Ajay's last words replayed over and over in her head.

You're going back to your life, and I'm going back to mine.

She wasn't sure she wanted to go back to her previous life. That life didn't include Ajay. She wasn't ready to see him disappear from her day-to-day existence. She had grown fond of having him around to laugh with, to tease, to sit quietly with and just be nearby. She didn't want to miss him.

Neither of them had broached the subject of what would happen to them after her stalker was found and danger no longer existed. There had been no deep discussion about relationships or feelings. Even after she'd professed her adoration, they'd gone back to business as usual.

But there was something that brewed between them like morning coffee. It was heated and necessary and perfect. It had left an impression and a longing that couldn't be denied if they were honest with each other. And Lizzy wanted more, a second and third cup that could soothe the weariness in her spirit and lift her up on a high the likes of which she had never experienced before. She would have called it love, but labeling it and having it disappear on her would be heartbreaking.

Some things were best left alone, she thought, and maybe a relationship between her and Ajay was one of those things.

When her cell phone rang, she rolled her eyes skyward. Without looking, she knew it was Vivian. Vivian seemed to have her number on repeat, dialing her every hour on the hour, but Lizzy was ignoring her bestie. Not because she didn't want to talk to her friend, but because she didn't want to hear a lecture on what she was doing wrong and needed to be doing right. Lizzy already knew and had no need for any reminders.

Vivian would *tough love* her until every thought of her and Ajay was nothing but a memory, and Lizzy wanted more than memories for as long as she could hold on. That was why she wasn't going to answer Vivian's calls or return them until she was ready. She promised herself a conversation with her friend when she was ready to let Ajay go.

You're going back to your life and I'm going back to mine.

What Lizzy trusted was that she and Vivian knew each other well enough that Vivian wouldn't take her disregard personally. Vivian would give her time and space, and when Lizzy was ready, the two women would pick up where they left off as if nothing tragic had happened. They would laugh and gossip, and Vivian would remind her that Ajay's kindness had been a condition of his employment. He hadn't been a summer fling to love and leave. He'd just been in the right place at the wrong time.

Her phone suddenly chimed, an incoming text message calling for her attention. Her first thought was to ignore it, too, but when it beeped a second time, she forced herself to glance at the screen. The message was from Ajay.

Get up and get dressed.

She texted him back. NO!

Get dressed Lizzy. We have to go.

Where?

Lizzy waited for a response, but none came. She asked a second time.

WHERE!

Don't worry about where. I'm leaving in 30 mins. Be ready or you can go as you are. But you are going.

Lizzy giggled. She had no doubt that he would probably sling her over his shoulder in her pajamas and slippers if he needed to. She also liked that he didn't take her crap when she was shoveling it with both hands. He was no-nonsense, straight as an arrow and everything she could have ever needed.

Rising from the bed, she headed toward the adjoining bathroom. She needed a quick shower if she were going to be ready in time. She would return Vivian's call when she and Ajay went back to their respective lives. Why give her bestie a reason to be a killjoy when she was actually having fun?

"I don't mean to be a killjoy," Della said, "but we're coming up empty."

Ajay adjusted his cell phone against his ear. "Who is this guy?" he snapped. "And why do I feel like he's always one step ahead of us?"

Ajay knew the frustration in his tone had to be off-putting. He heard Della gasp as he spewed a litany of curse words over the phone line.

"Sorry," he said. He took a deep breath.

"Don't take this the wrong way," Della said. "But maybe you should recuse yourself from the case? It's starting to mess with your head, and if you and Lizzy are in a relationship, that's not going to help."

"So, you're policing my work now?"

"I'm being your friend. We have always been straight with each other. I'm not going to stop now. This case is starting to get to you and it's getting to you because of your feelings for Lizzy. Why can't you admit that?"

Ajay shifted the conversation, not wanting to answer questions about his emotional stability. He also wasn't willing to admit that Della might be right—he was too closely involved to successfully investigate the case and find Lizzy's stalker.

"Were there any prints on that sheet of paper?"

Della blew a soft sigh. "Nothing. It came up empty."

"Did any of the cameras in the area catch anything?"

"Nothing that we can use."

A lengthy silence swelled thick and full between them. It was Della who spoke first.

"I have an obligation at Crosswinds today. I'll be there if you need me."

Ajay nodded as if the woman could see him. "I'm getting Lizzy out of the house. I'm hoping it will draw out her stalker. I know she wants to visit Ruby and Sebastian's new baby, so we might do that."

"How about we put a police tail on you just to be safe?"

"That's fine. Just make sure they keep their distance. I don't want Lizzy worrying about one more thing."

"No problem."

"We'll probably run errands tomorrow. She has a physician's appointment first thing in the morning."

"It's not anything serious, is it?"

"Just a follow-up, I think. Jenny will be going with her, too. I'm just playing chauffeur."

"Well, come see me if you drop by Crosswinds. I'll be down in the kennels."

There was a moment of hesitation before Ajay spoke. "Thanks, Della," he said softly. "I did get your message. Loud and clear."

"Whatever you decide, you know I'll support you," Della said.

"I do," Ajay answered. "And I appreciate you for being there for me."

Chapter 9

Ajay hadn't completely thought through their next steps, but he figured he had a better chance of catching the criminal if Lizzy were out in the open, taunting him to take his best shot. He'd spent most of the morning on the phone trying to get answers. The captain had reamed him for not letting the detective team help him and Della do their jobs, claiming Ajay's insistence on working single-handedly on the case hindered the search. Even he and Della had exchanged words, his friend claiming he was too close to the case to be of any real help.

He didn't have the words to explain how furious he was about someone getting that close to Lizzy on his watch. Maybe he had done everything he could do, but it still wasn't enough as far as he was concerned. It wasn't enough because the kidnapper was still out there. Still lurking in the shadows. And clearly hunting the woman he was falling in love with.

The air in his lungs blew out in a heavy gust of warm air. He could never say aloud what had been going through his mind about Lizzy. There was no one he could tell about the growing feelings he was having for her, not even his dog. They still didn't know each other that well, but Lizzy had grabbed a large chunk of his heart and was holding tightly to it. She'd gotten under his skin, and it felt as if he'd been plagued by a virus of magnanimous proportions. It had him feeling happy and foolish and completely out of his element. He was so enchanted with her, he was willing to fight tooth and nail for the opportunity to discover everything he could about her. He was willing to step out on the front lines and go up against anyone or anything determined to do her harm.

Her Aunt Jenny had called it love, claiming they had both fallen hard for each other. She could very well be right, but Ajay would keep that tidbit of information close to his chest until he was ready to have that conversation with Lizzy.

Lizzy relaxed into the passenger seat of Ajay's ride, allowing her body to melt against the warmth of the leather seats. Pumpkin sat upright in the back seat, her head hanging out the open window. A country singer was serenading them from the radio. The sun was shining, and the air was crisp. They couldn't have asked for a more perfect day.

"Where are we going?" she questioned.

Ajay tossed her a look. "Hunting."

Lizzy's gaze narrowed. "I think that's going to require further explanation."

"We're going to find the man trying to terrorize you. When we find him, I'm going to make sure he never gets an opportunity to cross paths with you again. Even if I have to hurt him to keep him away from you." Ajay's tone was stern and straight to the point.

"I don't know if this is a good idea," Lizzy said. She shifted her body and turned to face him. "I have to be honest with you, I don't know if I'm ready. My anxiety is sky-high right now."

"You can't keep hiding. You are sitting around waiting for something to happen, and that will make you stir crazy. You need to get out, visit with your family, hang out with your friends. When's the last time you spoke with Vivian?"

Lizzy cringed, suddenly feeling like a real jerk for ignoring her bestie's calls. Vivian had stopped leaving messages, but she continued to call her like clockwork.

"I owe her a call," Lizzy said, contrition wrapped around her words. "I haven't been a good friend lately."

"Good friends are hard to come by," Ajay said.

"What if I'm putting her in danger? If anything happened because of our association, I would be devastated."

"I won't say it's not a risk. I honestly don't know. But I do know it's highly unlikely that, whoever this guy is, he's going to harm anyone else. He's had ample opportunity, and he hasn't taken it. My sense is this is more about making you his possession, either for profit or his own perverse gain."

"Well, that makes me feel better," Lizzy said facetiously. The snark in her tone was thick.

"Everything's going to be fine," Ajay said as he gave her a wide smile. "I promise."

She blew out a sigh of relief, wanting to believe because Ajay seemed both determined and certain. She turned her attention back to the road.

From the back seat, Pumpkin eased her snout over Lizzy's shoulder, nudging her. Lizzy smiled, that little gesture of comfort taming the angst in her heart.

When Ajay turned onto Cross Road, the private drive into the Crosswinds Training Center and the Cross family home, he wasn't sure who got more excited—Lizzy or Pumpkin. He turned left past the medical building toward the kennels and training areas. The single-family home was in walking distance of the kennels, and he turned into the parking area between the two.

Both woman and dog were bouncing up and down in their seats. Lizzy squealed as if she'd won the biggest prize at the state fair, and Pumpkin whined as if she'd been given a treat for her good behavior.

Crosswinds was Owl Creek's pride and joy. The facility was owned by former marine Sebastian Cross. Sebastian was well-known in the community for his expert training and handling of search-and-rescue dogs. He also supported veterans with PTSD, providing them with service dogs to help with their healing.

Sebastian's new love, Ruby, was a Colton, Jenny's eldest daughter and Lizzy's first cousin. She owned Colton Veterinary Hospital, and her vet services surpassed all others in the area. Both Sebastian and Ruby were thriving, living their best lives. Friends and business associates, they worked well together, focused on building their respective businesses.

When Sebastian became a target, his land considered prime real estate, no one had expected that Ruby would get caught in the cross hairs of a fanatic claiming to do God's bidding. Fighting side by side for what they believed in had given the couple a new look on what life could be like for them. Now they were celebrating the birth of their first child, a baby boy named Sawyer Colton Cross.

Lizzy hadn't seen her cousin for a little while, only hearing bits and pieces of the drama from other family members. Mama Jen had told her of the new baby's birth, but Lizzy's current situation had kept her from visiting.

There weren't enough words for Lizzy to express to Ajay how happy she was. He had made her entire world turn on its axis. She was beyond ecstatic.

"I'm going to take Pumpkin over to the kennels so she can nuzzle some of the puppies if they have any. Ruby and Sebastian are at the house. I'll catch up with you in a few minutes," Ajay said.

"Thank you," Lizzy said as she threw her arms around

Ajay's neck. She pressed her mouth to his, kissing him with an intensity that bordered on ravenous.

He couldn't help but kiss her back, his lips dancing in perfect sync with hers. He tasted like mint, she thought, wintergreen, fresh and airy. When his tongue darted past her lips to tangle with her tongue, Lizzy felt like she might have dropped to her knees had she been standing.

They both pulled away at the same time. Ajay's eyes were wide, and he looked as if he wasn't certain what was expected of him next. Lizzy's palm was pressed against his chest, and she could feel his heart racing. He was visibly fighting to catch his breath.

Lizzy pressed her mouth to his for a second time, giving him a quick peck on the lips, then she jumped from the car and sprinted down toward her cousin's home.

Ajay shook his head. Clearly, he and Lizzy were headed down a path of no return. Neither was going to be able to come back from the growing tsunami of emotions swirling between them. He bit his bottom lip as he exited the vehicle, Pumpkin on his heels.

Inside the kennels, Della sat at the front desk, her dog, Charlie, resting beside her. Charlie barked in greeting, moving to Ajay's side for a scratch behind his ears. Pumpkin pressed her nose to her friend's, the two engaging in typical scratch-and-sniff doggie behavior as they greeted each other. Ajay motioned for Pumpkin to take a seat, and she lay down on the floor, curling her body against Charlie's.

"This is a surprise! I wasn't expecting to see you out and about." Della stood to give him a hug.

"I thought it would be good to get Lizzy out of that house, and she hasn't seen the new baby."

"Babies always make you feel good, and that one is a cutie!"

"How's it going?" Ajay questioned.

"Work is work. Still no news on Lizzy's stalker. It's really starting to mess with everyone's heads. It's been a minute since I've seen the team so frustrated by a case."

"Glad I'm not the only one."

"You need to let this go, Ajay."

He rolled his eyes skyward. "Didn't I just hear this lecture from you?"

"You need to hear it again. Go back to search and rescue and do what you do best. The captain has put his best detectives on the case to help you. I know how important this is to you, but you don't need to let it consume your entire life. They'll catch him."

"I think whoever it is, they're known to the family. It's someone they're friendly with and maybe even someone they trust."

"Why do you say that?"

"No forced entry into the home, which suggests they had a key, and the intruders knew exactly where Lizzy's bedroom was. They didn't waste time looking for it."

Della nodded. "I'll pass that information on. In the meantime, though, want to tell me how things are with you and Lizzy?"

Ajay's brow lifted, the question putting him on edge. "What do you mean, how things are with me and Lizzy? Things are fine."

"I saw you two swapping saliva. Things looked more than fine."

"How the hell…?" Curiosity turned to embarrassment.

Della laughed as she gestured to the security cameras. One was pointed toward the parking lot, his vehicle front and center. "Sebastian had these put in when the trouble was going on a few months back. Just to be safe." She tapped her hand over her heart. "They've been good for my voyeuristic spirit!" Her raucous laugh was teasing.

Ajay shook his head slowly. "Let's keep this between us, please. I still don't know what's happening with me and Lizzy."

"Looked cut-and-dried to me. I mean, that was some kiss!"

"She kissed me," he said sheepishly.

"It didn't look like you were putting up much of a fight, my friend."

Ajay laughed. "I got caught up. It won't happen again."

"That's your lie," Della said with a shrug. "Tell it any way you want to tell it."

The two laughed cheerfully together.

Chapter 10

Lizzy and Ruby were clinging tightly to each other when Sebastian entered the small family room. He stood patiently, allowing the two women a moment that both clearly needed. Ruby kissed Lizzy's cheek. Even though she had her biological sisters, Lizzy had always been special to her. She'd been the baby girl of all the babies, and Ruby had been especially protective of her since she'd been the only girl in a house filled with yucky boys.

"I've been worried sick about you," Ruby said as she grabbed Lizzy by the hand.

"I'm fine. But you had a baby!"

Ruby grinned. "I did." She pointed toward Sebastian, who was cradling their infant son against his broad chest.

Lizzy squealed, her excitement brimming out of every pore. "Can I hold him?" she asked, her arms extended.

The noise startled the dog reclined in front of the fireplace. Oscar, Sebastian's golden retriever, sat up and looked around.

"It's okay, boy," Sebastian said as he took a step forward. His smile was bright as Lizzy reached for the baby, lifting their bundle of joy from his arms.

Lizzy moved to the sofa and sat down. The small person in her arms had chubby cheeks and suckled his tongue. His blue eyes opened and closed and opened again as he looked up at her. Lizzy declared him the most beautiful baby she had ever seen.

"He's absolutely precious," Lizzy gushed.

"He's a sweet baby," Ruby said as she unfolded a white spit cloth and laid it against Lizzy's shoulder. "I think we'll keep him!"

"I just want to know how you carried him for nine months and he comes out looking just like his father. I don't see an ounce of Colton in him."

Sebastian laughed. "He did get my good looks, didn't he?"

"I swear I think it's karma for something I did in a former life," Ruby said.

The doorbell suddenly chimed.

"Were you expecting someone else?" Sebastian asked, his eyes shifting toward Ruby.

She shook her head again. "No."

"It's probably my bodyguard," Lizzy said, nonchalantly, her gaze still locked on the baby.

The married couple exchanged a look. Sebastian moved to the front door and pulled it open. Laughter exploded as he greeted Ajay warmly, showing him into their home.

"Ajay!" Ruby exclaimed. "We heard you were pulling watchdog duty."

Ajay laughed. "Is that what they call it?"

"Whatever it is you're doing, I'm just happy to know my baby cousin is in good hands."

Ajay stared where Lizzy was sitting. There was a glow on her face that he hadn't seen before. Her joy was palpable, filling every corner of the room. She looked good with a baby in her arms and before he could catch them, those words seemed to jump out of his mouth on their own accord.

Lizzy gave him a smile. "Why, thank you, Lieutenant

Wright. That's very sweet of you to say. I hope to have my own babies someday."

Ajay could feel his face warm as he blushed profusely. Sebastian and Ruby grinned at them both.

"So, what's up with you two?" Ruby asked. "Mama says you're staying at the ranch, Ajay?"

"Just until they can get a lead on whoever has been threatening Lizzy."

"I told you I had a bodyguard," Lizzy said teasingly.

"For a small community like Owl Creek, we've had a lot going on these past few months. And not a lot of it has been good," Sebastian said. "Della and Max were telling us about what's been happening with you, Lizzy, and it's almost as wild as what Ruby went through."

Ruby nodded. "It was bad enough when we thought you were lost. But then to find out that someone had actually taken you was really frightening."

Lizzy shifted her gaze from Ruby's face to Ajay's. "Something similar happened to Ruby not too long ago."

"Turned out to be some lunatic from that new church that's pitched their tent here in town," Sebastian said. "They're called the Ever After Church. He was one of their ranking members and claimed he was ordered by God to lay claim to the property here. Setting his sights on Ruby to get to me was his first and last mistake."

"If you ever need to talk," Ruby said, turning toward Lizzy, "you just call me. I know how it feels to have someone coming after you like that. I've never been so scared."

"And you were pregnant," Lizzy added. "I can't even imagine keeping it together under those circumstances."

Ruby reached for Sebastian's hand. "I don't know what might have happened if Sebastian hadn't been going through it with me. He was my rock!"

"I guess boys do come in handy!" Lizzy snuggled the baby against her shoulder.

Ruby laughed. "Only if they're not related to you! Brothers are still butts!"

Both men shook their heads and rolled their eyes, but seemed to be amused. Ajay finally took a seat beside Lizzy, cooing at the little boy who was the spitting image of his friend. Laughter filled the room, ringing warmly through the air.

"Have you two eaten?" Sebastian asked. "I was going to toss something onto the grill for lunch. There's more than enough to share."

"We don't want to wear out our welcome," Lizzy muttered.

Ajay added, "I should probably get Lizzy back to the ranch."

"And Mom brought us a cake," Ruby interjected. "Chocolate mousse cake! If I remember, that was one of your favorites, Lizzy!"

"Besides," Sebastian added, "you're going to need a crowbar to pry my son out of her arms and that might take a while."

Ajay chuckled. There was a moment of hesitation as he and Lizzy had a silent conversation. She attempted to plead with him with her eyes.

"We'd love to stay," he finally said. "And if you have a crowbar I can borrow, it would be appreciated."

Sebastian laughed. "Steaks and a side of crowbar coming right up!"

Lizzy hadn't stopped talking since they'd left Crosswinds. After spending time with Ruby and Sebastian, they stopped down at the kennels to collect Pumpkin and bid goodbye to Della. Once they were in the car, Lizzy was a bundle of joy and happiness. Her exuberance was infectious, and before Ajay knew it, he was almost as giddy as she was.

Almost.

Despite their moment of relaxation and fellowship with the other couple, Ajay was still on high alert. Still looking over his shoulder, and hers, for anything out of place. He understood Lizzy wasn't safe until they captured whoever was after her. And Lizzy's safety had to be foremost in his thoughts.

Lizzy asking him a question pulled him from his musings. "How many kids do you want?"

Ajay blinked, his lashes fluttering. "Kids?"

She laughed. "Kids! Those really small people who cry a lot. Have you ever thought about having kids of your own?"

"Not really," Ajay answered honestly. "I've always been singularly focused on my career. I hadn't considered what my future might look like with a family. I figured there was plenty of time for that."

"I want at least six kids," Lizzy said definitively.

"Six?" Ajay was incredulous. He shot Lizzy a quick glance, then shifted his eyes back to the road.

"I've always imagined I'd have a big family. When I was younger, I was determined to only have one child. But then I thought how lonely that must be, and well, coming from a big family, why not *have* a big family?"

Ajay chuckled. "As an only child, I can attest to the fact that not having a big family isn't a big deal. I could probably see myself with two kids. Maybe even three. But six? I can't wrap my mind around six."

Lizzy laughed. "I think we could handle six kids easily. Four boys and two girls. I want the boys to come first and then the girls. Big brothers can be pretty cool."

"While we're at it, why not put in an order for twins?" Ajay said facetiously.

"Twin girls! Yes!"

He shook his head. "I can't with you!" he said, laughing heartily.

"We should probably get to work on that. Don't you think?"

"I think we need to end this conversation before you say something that gets me in trouble."

"What kind of trouble?"

"The kind of trouble that makes babies," he replied.

She grinned. "Would that be a bad thing? Practice would be half the fun!"

Ajay changed the subject. "Tell me about Brian. From what I heard, that was a devastating crash and burn for him."

Her brow lifted, surprise washing over her expression. "Who told you about Brian?"

"One of your brothers might have mentioned him. He was a friend of Greg's, and from what I hear, you chewed the guy up and spit him out."

Lizzy rolled her eyes skyward. "He was my last boyfriend. He was a real douchebag!"

"Ouch!"

"I thought he was the one. I'd already planned to name our first child Brian Junior. Then I discovered he already had a son named Brian Junior. Two in fact. And a daughter named Brianna. But he never bothered to tell me. His wife did."

"Three kids *and* a wife?"

"Three kids, a wife and a mistress."

"Greg didn't know he was married before he introduced you?"

"No one knew. Not even the mistress who named his second son Brian, too."

"What a douche!"

"Exactly!" Lizzy exclaimed, tossing her hands up in the air.

"What did you do when you found out?"

"You really don't want to know."

"No, I really do," Ajay said, stealing another glance in her direction.

"I negotiated a meetup with the other two women and their kids and invited him to a surprise party. And we met in the conference room at his job."

Ajay laughed. "Please tell me how you managed to pull that off at the man's job."

"I'd been hired to do some marketing work for his firm. I had a presentation to give. He just happened to be the star on my program."

"What happened then?"

"Before or after his wife slapped him with divorce papers?"

"I don't need to know anymore. You are ruthless, Lizzy Colton!"

"I'm not a woman to be played with. If I give you my heart, then I'm trusting you to protect it. Hurt me, and I will cripple you. And that's after I sic my brothers on you."

"And here I thought you were this nice, kind, sweet..."

She cut him off. "I'm all those things. But I'm also vicious, and I can be mean if you cross me. So don't ever cross me."

Ajay smiled. "No worries. I imagine I'll be too busy with four sons and twin daughters."

Lizzy giggled like a teenager. "Seriously, though. This thing with us..." She paused, seeming to search for the words to explain what was on her heart.

"This *thing* is scary," Ajay said. "And I don't want either of us to make a mistake. We've been thrown together under unusual circumstances. I think we really need to take things slow. Very slow."

"So no more kissing?" Amusement danced across Lizzy's face. "Because I really liked kissing you."

"I think we should table the kissing for a minute."

"No."

"Excuse me?"

"No." Lizzy folded her arms across her chest. "I like kissing. And I really liked kissing you. So, no! I'm not tabling kissing, and you can't make me. Well, you could, and of course I'd respect your decision, but still…"

Laughter billowed through the interior of the vehicle. Ajay shook his head from side to side. "Why are you making this so hard?"

Lizzy paused, seeming to choose her words carefully. She took a deep breath before finally responding. "Because I really meant it when I said I liked you, Ajay. And I think you feel the same way about me." Her tone had changed, humor shifting to something more serious. "And although I heard what you had to say about not letting what's between us get in the way of your responsibility, I don't want us to miss out on what might be the best thing that's happened to us because we're too busy trying to be proper and listen to what other people say we should be doing. I want us to follow our hearts for as long as it feels right."

Ajay turned his head to stare at her. The look she was giving him was filled with promise, the shimmer in her eyes drawing him in. He could feel himself falling headfirst into her stare, and all he could do was nod. He turned back to the traffic they'd gotten stuck in.

A knot tightened in Ajay's throat as he pondered their conversation. There wasn't anything else he could say, so he didn't say anything at all. Instead, he reached for her hand, pressing his palm against hers. He entwined her fingers between his own, lifting her hand to press a damp kiss against the back. He hoped Lizzy already knew he would have moved heaven and earth to kiss her again and again.

Ajay's gaze suddenly paused on his rearview mirror. The car coming up behind them was moving too fast for the icy roads. He had seen it swerve in and out of traffic earlier but hadn't given it much thought until now. Because now it seemed to be trying to catch up to him, bearing down with disregard for everyone else on the road. He slowed, ready to maneuver defensively out of the sedan's way if necessary. It passed one last car to fall in line directly behind them.

"What's wrong?" Lizzy asked, her brow furrowed with concern.

"Do you recognize the car following us? It's been on our tail since we left the training center."

Lizzy glanced at the side mirror, then turned in her seat to stare out the back. "No," she said with the shake of her head. "I've never seen it before."

The road had cleared, only a few vehicles headed in their direction. Ajay signaled, then pulled into the right lane to allow the other car to pass by them. Instead, that car pulled right, continuing to follow him.

Despite his best efforts, Ajay couldn't see inside the other vehicle. The windows were tinted, making visibility difficult at best. The car was so close to his rear end that if Ajay hit the brakes suddenly, they were sure to collide.

"Should we call someone?" Lizzy questioned as she dug into her purse for her cell phone.

Pumpkin, who had been sleeping peacefully on the back seat, sat up, seeming to sense the tension that had risen in her owner. She barked, a low yelp as if she knew something was going on.

"It might be nothing," Ajay said. "Just hold on."

He stepped on the gas, his truck accelerating swiftly. The car behind him picked up speed as well. Ajay was driving too fast for comfort, and the other driver seemed determined to keep up.

As they approached the intersection headed away from the center of town, the car pulled up beside them. As the driver lowered the window, Ajay readied his service weapon at his side.

The other car suddenly sounded its horn, and a teenage boy hung out the window to give Ajay his middle finger. The others inside all laughed as if he'd actually done something amusing. As the light turned green, the driver hit the gas and barreled through the intersection, making a right turn directly in front of Ajay. He narrowly missed hitting another car before jetting off.

Ajay reached for his police radio and engaged the microphone. "Dispatch, ten-thirteen. Officer needs assistant."

"This is Dispatch."

"We have a ten-fifty-five in progress. It's a late model Ford sedan, license plate three, nine, eight, Adam, Zebra, Lincoln. I repeat…three, nine, eight, Adam, Zebra, Lincoln. The driver and passengers appear to be in their teens." Ajay gave the dispatch officer their location and the direction the car was headed in.

"Ten-four, Lieutenant. Traffic officers are in pursuit."

"Thank you, Dispatch. Over and out."

Minutes later, Ajay reached the front gates of the Colton Ranch, noting the new security box that had been installed since they'd left. He pressed the call button, and Buck answered immediately.

"This thing is fancy!" the elder Colton exclaimed. "Let me buzz you in."

As the gates swung open, Lizzy finally breathed a sigh of relief. "All this excitement isn't good for my nerves," she said.

Ajay chuckled softly. At the home's front door, he reached out for her, wrapping his arms around her shoulders. Lizzy sighed as she melted against him, relaxing into his chest as if nothing had happened.

In the distance, the sun had made its descent, darkness quickly claiming its place. There was the barest sliver of a crescent moon, and the chilly air was eerily still. Their visit with Sebastian and Ruth had lasted longer than initially planned. A late lunch had become an early dinner, and dinner had ended in a round of board games with coffee and a second helping of dessert. Lizzy had held their baby, fed him a bottle, changed his diaper and ordered a bundle of baby gifts from an online app on her cell phone. Laughter had been abundant and greatly needed, and Lizzy and Ajay were able to relax in a way that felt nurturing. Both were now exhausted as the late-night hour was pulling at the last of their energy.

"Thank you for a great day," Lizzy said. "It felt good to get out. I had so much fun I'm not ready to end the day yet."

"You're welcome. But you really need to go get some rest. I can't have your people mad at me for keeping you up past your curfew!"

Lizzy giggled, her head shaking from side to side. "You worry about the darndest things!"

Ajay smiled. "One of us needs to," he replied. "I'm going to stay out here for a minute to decompress. I'll see you in the morning."

"Another adventure?"

He smiled. "Maybe. After your doctor's appointment."

Lizzy's eyes widened as she suddenly remembered the obligation. It was her follow-up appointment to get the doctor's all clear for her to return to a semblance of normalcy. "Shoot," she replied. "I forgot about that."

"I didn't. Someone needs to keep you on track."

"I hate going to the doctor," she said. "He has clammy hands!"

Ajay chuckled. "I'm sure everything will be fine. Good night, Lizzy." He leaned to press the gentlest kiss against her cheek.

"Good night, Ajay," she whispered.

Pumpkin barked, leading Lizzy into the home, and all Ajay could do was shake his head.

Chapter 11

Ajay rose early the next morning. He hadn't slept well and figured he would start the new day with work. After a cup of hot coffee courtesy of the Keurig coffee maker on the counter, he'd dressed, checked on Lizzy and his dog, and then headed toward town. Driving to the police station to check in and follow up on the progress, or lack of progress, in Lizzy's case had him irritated, and it was barely light out. He needed to work out to ease his stress, and he wasn't certain when that would happen.

Today's schedule was mapped out, starting with driving Lizzy and Mama Jen to her doctor's appointment. He had a meeting with the police captain after that. Pumpkin was due at the groomers for a bath, and who knew what might blow up before his day ended.

Thinking about Lizzy had him in a strange headspace. No woman before her had been able to push him to such an emotional crux the way she did. And there had been plenty of other women. Women who passed through like the birds that settled about in the warmer season and disappeared with the cold. Women who wanted nothing from him but a few good memories, and women who wanted more than he was able to give. And now he'd fallen in love with a woman who wanted a six-man football team to go with the husband, the house and the picket fence.

He loved Lizzy. As crazy as it sounded after such a short period of time, he was in love with Lizzy Colton. Saying so felt as natural as breathing, and if he could have shouted it out to the world, he would have. For now, though, he felt like he couldn't even tell Lizzy what was in his heart and in his head, and that burdened him more than everything else.

"Ajay, hey, dude! What's up?"

Ajay had been sitting at a back table in Hutch's Diner. After leaving the police station, he had just enough time to kill before needing to head back to the ranch to pick up Lizzy and Jenny for her doctor's appointment. The morning breakfast spot was a town favorite, serving the best coffee in Owl Creek. The business had been started by Hutch Maddox. After his death a few years back, Hutch's wife, Sharon, and their son Billy had taken over running the establishment. True to her husband's vision, Sharon had maintained that 1990s vibe, and the welcoming atmosphere had made the diner a staple in the Owl Creek community.

Ajay looked up to find Billy staring at him. The two men bumped fists in greeting. "How's it hanging, kid?" Ajay asked.

"A little to the left, a little to the right," the young man answered jokingly.

Ajay laughed with him.

"We haven't seen you in a while. Not getting your coffee at some other place, are you?"

"Never! Besides the coffee, I'm addicted to your mother's biscuits and gravy. No one does sausage gravy like your mom."

Billy held up a coffeepot. "Would you like a refill?"

"Thank you," Ajay said as he tilted his cup toward the young man. "How are things going with you, Billy?"

"No complaints. Work keeps me busy. Mom keeps me busier."

"Moms will do that. You're lucky to have yours."

"Everybody keeps telling me that," Billy said with a shrug.

"Everyone's telling you right."

Billy nodded, but his expression seemed to say otherwise. Ajay knew that against his mom's wishes he'd taken a gap year from college, unsure what he wanted for himself. But mom and son had always seemed content with the decision once it had been made.

"If you're still here after I make my rounds and get the orders out, I'd like to sit and talk for a minute," Billy said. "If that's all right?"

"Always," Ajay answered.

Billy turned and headed in the opposite direction. Ajay watched as the young man circled the diner, filling empty cups with fresh coffee.

The room was beginning to fill, the morning crowd looking for breakfast before starting their day. His gaze was suddenly drawn to a man sitting on the other side of the room. He looked comfortable in his seat, as if he'd been there before. But he also looked out of place in his expensive wool suit and silk tie. He didn't give Ajay tourist vibes, and Ajay couldn't think of one business in town whose employees needed to bring a Wall Street flair to their positions. Not even the local bank employees dressed so conservatively.

Under different circumstances, Ajay would probably have not paid him an ounce of attention, but he was staring in Ajay's direction and that instantly put Ajay on the defensive.

When Ajay stared back, the man nodded his head, every strand of his dark blond hair staying in place. With the horn-rimmed glasses he was wearing, he almost reminded Ajay of Clark Kent. His shoulders were broad and his physique trim, but Ajay didn't get *superhero* from him.

Ajay nodded back, the gesture polite but dismissive.

Billy suddenly plopped down into the seat beside him. "I have to be quick. We're short one waitress this morning."

"Not a problem," Ajay responded. "What's going on?"

"I've been thinking about joining the police department. I just wanted to get your thoughts about that."

"Obviously I consider it a good profession. Are you still considering school?"

Billy nodded. "Boise State University has a really good criminal justice program. They also have one of the best forensic science programs. It would keep my options open. Or do you think I should just apply to the Idaho State Police Academy?"

"There are some specific requirements you have to meet to get into the academy. First, you have to be twenty-one years old."

"That's almost two years away."

"Sounds like college would be the best route. Plus, it'll afford you the opportunity to discover exactly where you'd like to see yourself in our criminal justice system. You may discover being a peace officer isn't for you."

"That's what my mother said."

"Smart woman, your mother."

Billy's smile spread across his face. "Thanks. I may have some more questions, so you need to come back more often."

Ajay laughed. "Deal!" He suddenly leaned forward in his seat. "Actually, I do have a question for you, Billy. Do you know the gentleman sitting in the booth there by the window? The one in the blue suit."

Billy shrugged. "He's one of those Ever After Church guys. He likes to come in and talk to people. The tourists mostly. Mom says he's a snake oil salesman. But I think he's growing on her, 'cause she agreed to go to one of his services this month."

Ajay and the man locked eyes again. This time, the man stood, carrying his cup of coffee in Ajay's direction.

"Thanks, Billy," Ajay muttered.

"Good morning, sir!" the man greeted him.

Ajay smiled. "Good morning to you."

"Do you mind if I join you? Good coffee is best shared with a new friend."

Ajay pointed toward the seat on the other side of the table. "Please, have a seat."

"Thank you," the man said as he adjusted his suit jacket before sitting down. He extended his hand. "My name is Acker. Pastor Markus Acker. My flock and I are new to this fine city, and I'm still getting to know my way around. This establishment has become one of my favorites for breakfast and for fellowship."

Ajay shook his hand. "It's a pleasure to meet you, Pastor Acker, and welcome to Owl Creek."

"I apologize for staring at you earlier, but I could tell that you were a deeply troubled soul. And troubled souls are my specialty." His smile was charismatic, and his voice was like butter, smooth and easy.

"I wasn't aware I had any issues for anyone to be concerned about," Ajay said calmly.

The pastor suddenly quoted, "Incline thine ear unto my cry; For my soul is full of troubles: and my life draweth nigh unto the grave. I am counted with them that go down into the pit; I am as a man that hath no strength…"

Ajay nodded. "Psalm 88, verse 3."

"You've studied your Bible. I am impressed."

"As a man of faith, I'm sure you know others of faith stand on the teachings of the Bible, too. Just as you do."

"Yes, yes, yes." Acker closed his eyes, his head waving slowly from side to side. When he opened them, Ajay was watching him closely. The pastor smiled his saccharine smile. "I would love to invite you to one of our services." Acker reached into the inner pocket of his jacket for a business card, passing it to Ajay. "Our programs are open to the community so bring your family. And your friends. All are welcome."

"Thank you," Ajay said.

Acker stood, lifting his empty coffee cup from the table. "I didn't catch your name, my brother."

Ajay smiled. "Ajay. Ajay Wright. *Lieutenant* Ajay Wright with the Owl Creek Police Department."

If Ajay hadn't been studying the man so intently, he would have missed the flutter above his left eye. The pastor visibly bristled but didn't seem to allow the information to throw him completely off guard. Instead, he took a deep breath and smiled. "Well, Lieutenant Wright, it's been a pleasure. I hope that we run into each other again soon."

"Very soon," Ajay replied in a friendly manner. "Very soon."

Acker walked back to his own table. He reached into his pocket and pulled cash from a worn leather wallet, tossed the money onto the table and headed out the door.

Ajay continued to watch him through the window. Acker had only been standing outside a few minutes when he was suddenly joined by another man. One of his *flock*, Ajay mused. But when the man turned to stare into the diner, he met Ajay's gaze.

Ajay's eyes widened as he recognized the man Lizzy had drawn. The man they suspected of stalking her.

Without thinking, Ajay jumped from his seat and bolted toward the door. Not paying attention to his surroundings, he collided with Billy's mother, Sharon, knocking a tray of food out of her hands and onto his clothes. He knocked the poor woman to the floor, practically falling on top of her himself. They both cursed, an oration of profanity filling the midmorning air.

"I'm so sorry," Ajay exclaimed. "Just charge me for the meal!"

"What's wrong, Ajay?" Sharon asked.

"It's an emergency," he shouted as he clumsily helped her up. He continued to apologize as he turned back toward the door.

By the time Ajay made it out the entrance and onto the sidewalk, both men were gone, neither anywhere to be seen. Ajay looked up one side of the street and down the other. Not even a vehicle passed him by.

He pulled his cell phone to his ear, shaking off what looked like scrambled eggs from the screen. Three rings later, Max answered.

"Is Lizzy okay?" Max asked, not bothering to say hello.

"Lizzy is fine. She's at the ranch. But I think I just saw her kidnapper. I'm down here at Hutch's Diner. He's with a man named Markus Acker."

"Markus Acker?" The shock in Max's voice was thick as clabber. "Are you certain?"

"Do you know who he is?"

There was a moment's hesitation before Lizzy's brother answered, "Markus Acker is the pastor of the church Jessie recently became affiliated with."

Lizzy stood naked in front of the full-length mirror in her bedroom. Her complexion was pale, but she no longer looked ghostly. The bruises had finally begun to fade, and the bruised ribs beginning to heal made breathing so much easier.

Were she to consider getting naked in front of a man in general, she would only be a little embarrassed. Getting naked in front of Ajay, however, was a different beast. She wanted him to see her at her very best. If the moment presented itself, makeup would have to be her very best friend. Having his attention long enough to get into bed meant pulling out all the stops to keep his attention.

She stared a moment longer, then wanted to give herself a swift kick. Ajay wouldn't care if she were perfect or not. Ajay would love her because she brought him joy and made him happy. She imagined he would look past any scars that marred her body. He would only care if he thought it important to her. And even then, she imagined he would tell her she was being silly. He would say she was beautiful, and he'd kiss each mark and touch every part of her, because in his eyes, she was perfect.

She imagined the warmth of his fingers as they trailed down the length of her arms and across her back. He'd tease one rock-candy-hard nipple and then the other, and where his fingers led, his tongue would follow.

Lizzy suddenly shook away the reverie, moisture beginning to puddle in places it had no business being. Thinking of Ajay had her heated, and she couldn't dwell on fantasy. But, if anything at all, Lizzy thought, a girl could certainly hope.

She slid into fresh panties and a bra, then dabbed her favorite perfume on all her pulse points. A hint of powder in those places where she might perspire and deodorant over freshly shaved skin helped boost her confidence. Black leggings, an oversize sweater and red Timberland boots completed her look. After pulling the length of her hair into a high ponytail, she polished her lips with a neutral gloss.

With one last glance in the mirror, Lizzy took a deep breath, then she went looking for Ajay.

"How the hell did you manage to lose him?" Max snapped.

Ajay cut a narrowed eye toward Lizzy's brother. The two

men were pacing in front of the diner, looking like both had just lost their best friend.

"You act like I purposely let him go," Ajay snapped back.

"Did you?"

"Both of you need to stop," Della said, her eyes darting from one to the other. "You know Ajay didn't do anything on purpose and you know Max is just in his feelings."

"We were that close," Ajay muttered.

Frustration played like music from a violin, a slow vibrato that was mesmerizing. Max nodded. "My guys are pulling all the security footage now. With any luck, we'll get a hit and a name."

"What do you know about Acker?" Ajay questioned.

"He's a grifter. The agency has had him and his church on their radar for some time now. They just haven't been able to get anything concrete on him to take him down."

"And his affiliation with your mother?"

Max shot him a look, clearly not happy with the question. "Let's just leave Jessie out of this for now."

"I can't do that. Lizzy needs to know that her mother may be involved in this."

Max snapped, "Lizzy needs to know no such thing."

"You can't keep this from her," Ajay said, his voice rising.

"You don't get to say what we can and cannot do with regards to my little sister. I get that you care about her. And I'm fine with you wanting to protect her, but you don't know anything about her relationship with our mother. You didn't wipe her tears away when she cried herself to sleep because that woman wasn't here. So, you are not about to add any more pain to a wound that is still raw."

"I'm not going to lie to her," Ajay hissed between clenched teeth.

The two men were now standing toe to toe, looking as if they were about to come to blows.

Inside the diner, customers had taken out their cell phones, cameras recording in hopes of capturing a viral moment they could post and exploit. Della stepped between the two, pressing her palms against Max's chest.

"You two aren't going to solve this butting heads like two bulls in a china shop. Just agree to disagree and circle back to it when you've both calmed down."

"I still think she needs to be told," Ajay quipped.

"I don't really give a damn what you think," Max barked.

Recognizing they were at an impasse, Ajay took a step back. He and Max were still shooting daggers at each other as they stared.

"We're not done with this conversation," Ajay said. He turned and began walking away.

"Where are you going?" Della questioned.

"Home to change. Then I need to go get Lizzy. I'm already late."

"I'll go get my sister and take her to her doctor's appointment." Max's expression was just a tad shy of a full-blown snarl.

Ajay tossed him one last glare over his shoulder. He turned slightly to stare at the man. "Fine. I'll meet you after to pick her up. And you have until the end of the week. If we don't come up with anything by then, Lizzy will need to be told."

"Look," Max started. "You don't get to say—"

Ajay interrupted. "I'm saying. I understand you don't want your sister to be hurt. I don't want her to be hurt, either. But keeping secrets from her isn't going to help. Lying to her will only hurt her more. The end of the week," he said, and then he turned and stormed away toward his car.

* * *

Lizzy was not happy with him. Ajay could hear her frustration over the phone when he called to say that he was running behind schedule and would have to meet her and Mama Jen after her appointment at the physician's office.

She had not wanted to hear that he needed to go home and change his clothes. Nor was she happy that Max had dropped everything he was doing to fill in for him, ensuring she was protected for however long she was away from home.

Her telling him not to bother coming at all to get her had been a defense mechanism. He knew because him telling her that was fine with him had been his.

He and Max making a quasi-agreement not to tell her about her mother didn't make him feel comfortable. Secrets had a way of coming back to bite you in the ass when you least expected. He had no intention of starting their relationship on half-truths and full-blown lies. After their semi-heated discussion, the two men had agreed to keep it between them until the end of the week. If the detectives didn't have any answers by then, Ajay would tell Lizzy everything they knew. It was a compromise of sorts, both agreeing that not hurting Lizzy or causing her any angst was first and foremost for both of them.

With Pumpkin at the groomer's, he had a moment to himself, and he needed to process all that was happening. He also needed to straighten up his home, the place looking like the aftermath of a frat party. He'd hurried out after pulling clothes from the closet and drawers, forgetting the dirty dishes he'd left in the kitchen sink and the carpet that desperately needed a date with the vacuum. He'd be highly embarrassed if visitors showed up unannounced. Realizing he needed some time, telling Lizzy he needed to be home for a minute had been necessary.

She responded exactly how he expected. Expressing her disappointment wasn't an option but keeping it out of her voice and off her face was nearly impossible.

"Whatever," she said, a hint of attitude in her tone. "It's fine."

But it wasn't fine because she was fuming. She wasn't interested in his explanation. She was just unhappy that she couldn't have her way. Then they both said some things neither could walk back.

"Lizzy, I'm not in the mood. With everything going on right now, you're being selfish. I'm only asking for a few hours to myself."

"I said fine, Ajay. Do whatever you want."

"Why are you giving me attitude?"

"Attitude?"

Lizzy's tone was sharp, and Ajay could just imagine the unhappy expression on her face.

"Yes, attitude! You're acting like a spoiled brat right now!"

"Go to hell, Ajay. You were the one who promised to be here if I needed you. I'm not breaking that promise. Clearly, you are useless to me if you can't keep your word!"

"Useless?"

"I don't need to be surrounded by weak men, so maybe it's better you don't show up."

"Now you're calling me weak?"

"I said what I said."

"That's fine, Lizzy. Now that I know where I stand, we're good. You have a great day!"

Ajay slammed the phone down, disconnecting the call. The conversation left him cold, his stomach tied in a tight knot.

The phone rang almost immediately, Lizzy calling him back. When he answered, she was still spewing venom, still wanting to hurt him to assuage her own pain. She had called him back to curse at him some more and he disconnected the call again, throwing the phone to the other side of the room.

Two days had passed since they'd spoken. Two days that had left him feeling riddled with guilt. He'd taken his anger out on her. He hadn't tried to be understanding of her feelings. He'd allowed his disagreement with her brother to get the best of him and she had borne the brunt of his anguish. Now, every effort he made to call her back and apologize was being ignored. Lizzy had no interest in speaking with him, and he wanted nothing more than to be back by her side, everything right between them.

He thought back to the kiss they shared, her lips plush against his own. She'd tasted sweet like honey, and it had taken everything in him to stop, his desire for more surging voraciously. He wanted to kiss Lizzy and hold her and feel her skin against his own. He wanted to take her and claim her and be everything she needed him to be.

That one kiss would never feel like enough, and for that reason alone, he needed to take a step back to assess what was happening between them.

He couldn't help but wonder if Lizzy even had a clue that she had such a hold over him.

"You can't hold the man hostage, Lizzy," Max said.

"No one was trying to hold him hostage. I just…" She paused, turning to stare out the window of her brother's car. Tears pressed hot against her eyelids, and she was determined not to let her brother see her cry.

From the back seat, Buck cleared his throat. "Max, leave your sister alone. Things have been hard enough for her without you boys giving her a difficult time."

Max shook his head. "I wasn't giving her a hard time. She's sitting here pouting because Ajay couldn't be here."

"No one's pouting!" Lizzy snapped, her ire rising with a vengeance.

"Everyone calm down," Mama Jen said. "You don't need to fuss at each other. We need to be celebrating the doctor clearing Lizzy to go back to a little normalcy. That will help once she's feeling safe and settled," she said. "We're just excited to see you feeling better, Lizzy."

Lizzy turned toward the back seat to meet the stare her aunt was giving her. She didn't miss how close the two elders were sitting beside each other. It made her smile.

"I'll be fine," she said. "I do feel better, and with the new security at the ranch I'm not worried about anything happening to me there. I know Ajay needs to go back to his own life." She took a deep breath. "I'm just going to miss Pumpkin," she said softly.

"We'll get you a puppy of your own," Max said. "I'll call Sebastian as soon as we get home."

"Let's just try to find one that's already house-trained," Buck said with a deep chuckle. "I'm too old to be running around with a pee pad trying to catch accidents all day long."

Max and Lizzy laughed.

Lizzy said, "You don't run around with a pee pad, Daddy. You teach the dog to go on a pee pad."

"Well, whatever. I'm too old."

"Buck Colton, I'll have you know that sixty-three is not old. Most especially if you consider the alternative." Mama Jen tapped him with newly manicured fingers. The duo giggled.

"I'm hungry," Max said, changing the subject.

"Head to the ranch. I'm sure your dad has got plenty of food. I can make us something good to eat."

"Are you sure, Mama Jen? We can always stop somewhere in town," Max said.

"I'm certain. No point in wasting good money for no reason."

Max turned his car toward Colton Ranch. He and Lizzy fell quiet as the couple in the back seat chatted with each other.

When Mama Jen suddenly giggled, Lizzy turned to look over her shoulder. Her father was whispering in the matriarch's ear, and Jenny was blushing profusely.

Lizzy smiled, then turned back to stare out the window. She was already missing Ajay, and she knew neither a new puppy, nor an old dog, was going to take that feeling away.

Chapter 12

It had been one week since Lizzy last saw Ajay. One week, twelve hours, thirty-two minutes and ten seconds. But who was counting, she thought. She lay in her bed, her body curled in a fetal position. She had barely left the room since she last spoke to him. She was sure that the last conversation had not left him with the best impression of her. Even she had thought she had sounded like a spoiled child.

It had been well over a week since their family home had been invaded and her personal residence had been broken into. She knew there had been no news about her abductor, nor had he done anything else to try to get to her. She wasn't certain if that was a good thing or the calm before the next brewing storm.

When Buck knocked on her bedroom door, easing it open to peer inside, she was actually surprised. She sat upright, turning to give her father a look.

"You have a visitor," he said.

Lizzy's heart shifted into another gear. She wanted to think that Ajay had finally come to see her. "A visitor?"

Buck gestured at the person in the hallway standing behind him. "I'll just let you two catch up," he said cheerily.

Vivian eased past the man, a wide grin across her face. "Thank you, Mr. Colton."

"Anytime, young lady. It's good to see you again," he said as he closed the door.

Vivian turned toward her, that smile disappearing so quickly that Lizzy thought she might have imagined it.

"Don't be mad," Lizzy said.

"Really, Lizzy? That's all you have to say. Don't be mad? I've been calling you every day, and you haven't shown me the courtesy of calling me back. Not even a message to tell me to drop dead. Nothing! Do you know how scared I've been?"

"I'm sorry?"

Vivian dropped onto the bed beside her. "You better be glad you're my best friend. I wouldn't take that from anyone else. What's going on with you?"

Lizzy leaned her head on Vivian's narrow shoulder. "I'm just having a hard time."

"This isn't good, Lizzy. What's worrying you most? The kidnapper? Ajay? Your family?"

"All of the above. I'm a hot mess, Vivian, and I don't know what to do. I'm scared one minute. Depressed the next. Sad. Angry. Sad again. I should be over this by now."

"You've been through a lot of trauma. No one says you have to get over it in a specific amount of time. Have you talked to your doctor? You might need anxiety meds."

"I have a prescription, and I've been taking them when it gets really bad."

"Have you thought about seeing a therapist?"

Lizzy shrugged. "Mama Jen made me go see someone once."

"It takes time, Lizzy. It would probably help if you could get back into your normal routine. Have they said when you can go back to your house?"

"It's still a crime scene, but I don't know if I plan to ever go back. He was in my things! For all I know, he could have been playing with my vibrator."

"Eww!"

"Exactly!"

"What about work? Do you have any assignments you need to finish?"

"I've been able to do everything here. But maybe I could go back to the office for a few hours each day."

"Well, that would be a start. But I think what you can probably use in this very moment is a drink. Let's go to The Cellar."

The Cellar was a wineshop downtown that hosted numerous events during the week. One of their more popular events was the wine tasting and food pairing where they partnered with area restaurants for a full dining experience.

Lizzy frowned. "I don't know…"

"Get dressed. I've already reserved a table. Besides, I need to get out so I can tell you about my love life and what's not happening in it."

Lizzy laughed. "I thought you had something new to share with me."

"You and I have a lot of catching up to do. I want to know about that man, too."

"What man?"

"You know what man I'm talking about."

"I don't want to talk about Ajay."

"Too bad. I do." Vivian stole a quick glance at the watch on her wrist. She wriggled her nose, a scowl crossing her face. "You need a shower. I'll find something in your closet for you to wear. Let's go!"

"Are you saying I stink?"

"I'm saying you don't smell fresh. Now let's do something about that."

Lizzy sighed as she lifted herself from the bed. She headed toward the bathroom, dragging her feet as if she were headed to the guillotine.

Vivian called after her, "I love you, Lizzy!"

Lizzy hesitated, turning around to stare at her bestie. "I love you, too, girl!" she said. "Even if you did say I smell bad!"

Both women were laughing, two glasses of wine each fueling their mood. It was live music night, and a local husband and wife duo, James and Elaine Mercy, performing as Mercy! Mercy!, were playing their guitars and singing. The indie folk music was upbeat and a nice mood lifter. The wine, a rich and spicy cabernet sauvignon, had been paired with a delectable beef bourguignon.

It was comfort food with a luxurious flair, and with each bite Lizzy was thankful that Vivian had dragged her out of the house. She was having a great time, and the two women had fallen in sync as if no time had passed since they'd last been together.

They'd been discussing Lizzy and Ajay for a good while. Lizzy recapped every moment she'd spent with the man. She told her friend about the kiss, about them sharing time together that had been intimate without taking their clothes off and how much she enjoyed how they laughed together. There was no detail she didn't want to share.

"Correct me if I'm wrong," Vivian said, "but it sounds like you've fallen in love with the handsome lieutenant."

"I'd prefer to say I'm in serious *like* with a boatload of *lust*."

"What you'd prefer and what your reality is are two different things. You're in love, and you might as well just say so."

"I got it bad," Lizzy gushed. "And I miss him so much!"

"You can call him, you know."

"I'm embarrassed. He called me, and I didn't answer or return any of his messages."

"You really need to stop doing that, Lizzy. There are people who genuinely care about you and want to know that you're okay, and I'm not talking about your brothers or your family. You can't keep ghosting people when you feel bad. Let us be there for you!"

Lizzy took another sip of her wine. She didn't bother to respond, not wanting to acknowledge that Vivian was right. Vivian was always right when Lizzy was getting it wrong. And her not being afraid to put Lizzy in her place was a testament to their friendship. She could trust her best friend to always give it to her straight, whether she liked it or not.

Vivian continued, "You can always attribute it to your head injury. I don't think telling the man you were just being thoughtless will win you any girlfriend points."

"So let's talk about your love life now," Lizzy said. "We know I screwed mine up."

Vivian laughed. "I'm sure if I had a love life, I'd be making mincemeat out of it, too!"

"We should teach a class on self-sabotage. We're so darn good at it."

"Maybe we should plan one of those ex-bestie parties?"

"Ex-bestie?" Lizzy raised a brow curiously.

"We invite all our friends. Then they invite their ex-boyfriends and best guy friends that they would vouch for. It's a meet-and-greet to see if we can make any love connections."

"Do you really want to date any of my exes?" Lizzy asked, amused. "Seriously?"

"Not any of yours, but one of our friends might have a good guy friend we might like. You could invite your brothers."

"Which brother?"

"Not for me, but one of them that's not dating some bimbo and would interest one of the other girls."

"My brothers have dated most of my friends. Which is why a few of them aren't friends anymore."

"Okay, so scratch that bright idea."

Their laughter rang through the room, dancing with a joy that wafted like a summer breeze through the air.

"Thank you," Lizzy said as she lifted her third glass of wine. It was Vietti Moscato d'Asti, a sweet wine with notes of peaches, candied ginger and honeysuckle. It paired nicely with the winter fruit tray and the glazed berry tart they were served for dessert. "I needed this more than I realized."

"You're welcome."

For another hour, the two women laughed, cried and had a great time. They talked about Vivian's business, the Colton family scandal, a romance novel the two had both read and a potential girls trip to Bermuda after the holidays.

"What do you plan to do for Thanksgiving?" Lizzy asked.

"Come to your house."

"And Christmas?"

"Your house. Unless I'm finally in a relationship. Then I'm going to meet the family."

Lizzy laughed. "Wouldn't it be funny if that was at my house, too?"

Vivian giggled. "That would so not be funny!"

Lizzy's phone chimed, a text message calling for her attention. She read it quickly, then downed the last swallow of wine in her glass. "All good things must come to an end," she said. "My ride is outside waiting for me."

"What ride? I had planned to take you back home." Vivian turned in her seat to stare toward the front door.

"I know. But I texted Max and asked him to come get me. I didn't want to put you out any more than I already have."

"You wouldn't have put me out."

"Dinner's on me," Lizzy said, gesturing toward the waitress with her credit card.

"This was supposed to be my treat."

"Next time. I want to get it this time."

"I'm not going to argue with you," Vivian said.

"Good," Lizzy said as she signed the receipt. "Max is waiting to walk you to your car, and we are going to follow you home to make sure you get there safe."

"That's so not necessary."

"It'll make me feel better," Lizzy said.

Rising from their seats, the two women embraced, wrapping each other in a warm hug.

"Call Ajay," Vivian whispered into her ear. "You deserve a happy ending, and I'm going to be really pissed if you mess this up for us."

Lizzy laughed. "Us?"

"Darn right, us! If I never find a man of my own, I'm going to have to live vicariously through you."

"Then we're both in trouble," Lizzy concluded.

"When are we not in trouble!" her friend said with a giggle. "Just call the man and don't forget to give me an update once you talk to him."

"Vivian said not to forget to call her when you do that thing," Max said as he slid back into the driver's seat of his car. "What's that thing?"

Lizzy gave her brother a quick look. He had just walked Vivian to her front door and ensured she was safe and secure inside. He shifted the vehicle into gear and pulled out onto the road.

They were midway between Conners and Owl Creek and had a good few minutes before arriving at the ranch. Lizzy hadn't said much as they had followed Vivian home. She'd been lost in her own thoughts, trying to figure out what her next steps needed to be. And she still didn't have a clue.

"I think I messed up," Lizzy said. She turned to look at her brother.

Max glanced back at her. "Does this have to do with Ajay?"

She nodded, biting back the rising emotion that threatened to bend her heart and spill her tears.

"What did you do?" Max questioned.

"I got mad when he said he needed to take some time to himself. I felt like he was abandoning me, so I decided to ghost him first."

Max nodded. "Do you like that guy, Lizzy? I mean *really* like him?"

There was a moment of silence as Lizzy pondered her brother's question. When she finally answered, tears were streaming down her face. "I think I'm in love with him, Max. I've fallen in love with him. I really wanted things to be good between us. But what man would want me and all the baggage I come with? And let's be honest. Our family puts a whole other spin on dysfunction. Then I thought, what if I turned out to be like Jessie? What if years from now I was a bad wife and horrible mother? I figured he might not have wanted to take the risk of tying himself to someone who's broken. I thought it would be better if I just pushed him away." She sobbed. "So, that's what I did. I pushed him away."

Max sat and let her cry. He didn't say anything as he drove on toward the ranch. He let her cry until she didn't have any tears left.

By then he had reached the front gates of their family home. He pulled the car through the entrance before stopping the vehicle. The two sat quietly as the darkness settled in around them. Finally, her sobs turned to a barrage of hiccups.

Max shook his head. "You are such a crybaby!"

"I am not!" Lizzy exclaimed.

"Are, too! Crybaby!" Max smiled.

"You have always thought you were the boss of somebody," Lizzy said as she swiped her eyes with the backs of her hands.

"Then don't be a crybaby! Do you want me to kick his ass for you? Because I will kick his ass. And so will Greg and Malcolm. No one messes with our little sister."

Lizzy laughed. "I know how to fight! You taught me. I could kick his ass myself if I wanted to. I want you to tell me how to fix this!"

Max took a deep breath. "You need to talk to him. You need to apologize for being a brat. Then you need to tell him how you feel and what you want. After that, you need to sit and listen to everything he has to say."

"What if he says he doesn't want me?"

"Then I'll kick his ass!"

Lizzy punched her brother in the shoulder. "I'm serious, Max."

"So am I."

Lizzy rolled her eyes skyward.

Max laughed. "One step at a time, Lizzy. Talk to him. You'll figure it out from there."

Ajay picked up his cell phone, eyeing it for a quick moment before dropping it back down to the tabletop.

He wanted to call Lizzy. But he didn't want to seem desperate. Clearly, she wasn't interested in hearing from him. She hadn't returned his calls or answered any of his messages. He hadn't thought it would bother him as much as it did, but if he were honest, his feelings were hurt. He pushed the phone aside and reached for the bottle of cold beer on the table.

"We tried to warn you," Malcolm said, laughing. He sipped on his own bottle of beer. "Our sister can be a handful."

Greg laughed with his brother. "Most men make the mistake of thinking Lizzy is fragile and weak and needs a man to take care of her. Lizzy might be a little spoiled because of us, but she definitely doesn't *need* a man. That's because of us, too. She can keep up with any guy and even outdo most of them. She's tough, and she can be mean as spit when she wants to be."

The trio sat at a table at Tap Out Brewery. Popular for the local brews they served and the party-like atmosphere on game nights, it was a great place to sit back and relax after a long day of responsibilities. When Malcolm had called Ajay to come and join them for a beer, he'd welcomed the opportunity to sit and relax with the guys.

Malcolm nodded in agreement. "She was so small when our mother left. We wanted to protect her, but we also wanted to make sure she could protect herself. She seems to be doing a good job of it so far."

"Except I would never hurt her. I thought she would have known that," Ajay said a little defensively.

The two brothers exchanged a look and laughed.

"Look," Malcolm said. "She's still a woman. And I haven't met a woman yet who doesn't pose a challenge from time to time. But if you care about Lizzy, then let her know. Fight for her."

Greg nodded. "Women like when you're willing to go to battle for them. At least that's what someone told me." He lifted his brow as he sipped the beverage in his glass. "And we've got your back if you need us."

"Max might not be, but we're good with you!" Malcolm said. "The two of them being the youngest means they were always super close, so he's even more protective of her than Buck is."

"What about Max?"

They all turned to see the man standing over them. Max reached for an empty chair and pulled it up to the table. "Why are you talking about me?" he asked as he sat down.

Malcolm laughed. "I was just telling Ajay that we have his back with Lizzy, but that you might not be a fan of his."

Max cut an eye in Ajay's direction. Ajay met his stare with a look of his own. The two men sized each other up.

"Exactly what are your intentions with our baby sister?" Max questioned.

"I honestly don't know," Ajay said. "I had hoped she and I would be able to take some time to really get to know each other without all the drama of what's happening now. But I think she's mad at me right now, so I'm not sure where that puts us."

"She's not mad. She's scared," Max said. "She's not used to feeling so vulnerable."

"Neither am I," Ajay muttered.

"What took you so long?" Greg asked Max. "We expected you over an hour ago."

"I had to pick up Lizzy," Max answered.

"Is she okay?" Ajay questioned. "Did something happen?" Concern may as well have seeped like water from his pores.

"She's fine. She's at the ranch."

Ajay blew out a sigh of relief.

Greg laughed. "You almost gave this guy a heart attack." He slapped Ajay on the back.

"Why are you messing with him like that?" Malcolm chuckled. "He's a good guy, and he's got it bad for Lizzy. You need to cut him some slack."

Max shrugged. "He's all right."

Ajay tossed him a look. "So we're good?"

"As long as you don't hurt my sister, we're fine."

"Lizzy was always his baby! Like Malcolm said, he's more overprotective than our father. I'm going to hate it when he has kids," Greg said.

"Like you wouldn't do the same for Jane and Justin," Max teased.

"Speaking of…" Greg said as he rose from the table, his cell phone in his hand. "I need to call Briony and make sure everyone's okay."

"How's Della doing?" Malcolm asked, looking at Max.

Max nodded. "She'll be better as soon as I get home."

"In that case, the last round is on me," Ajay said as he gestured toward the bar.

Loud cheers suddenly rang through the air. On the big screen televisions throughout the room, a college basketball game was going into overtime, and the two teams were battling hard. Malcolm headed to the bar to grab their tray of drinks from the bartender.

"Any advice you can give me about your sister?" Ajay asked Max.

"Yeah," Max answered. "Don't let her kick your ass. We will never let you live that down."

Ajay laughed.

When Malcolm returned with a tray of drinks, he grabbed one without sitting down. "I just ran into an old friend of mine. I'm going to chat him up for a minute. I'll be back," he said, tossing them a glance over his shoulder.

The two men returned to their conversation.

"Seriously," Max said as he leaned forward, folding his hands together on top of the table. "She's having a hard time, but she doesn't want anyone to know. She cares about you, and she's afraid she's blown her chance."

"I just need to talk to her," Ajay said, his frustration palpable.

"I told her that. I gave her the old communication is key speech, and I think she's still processing it all. Just give her some time."

"There seems to be plenty of that on my hands."

"You haven't been cleared back in the field yet? Since Lizzy fired you, I figured you'd already be reassigned back to search and rescue."

"I have. I'm just holding off for now." Ajay continued, "Have you heard anything about the case? Technically, I've been pulled. Della tries to keep me in the loop without risking her own access, but I haven't heard anything of value that would help us find this guy and get him off the street."

"You know I can't talk to you about this case. It's an ongoing investigation."

"Can't or won't?"

Max stared at him, hesitating briefly. "Fine, and only because I really do like you, and I think you might be good for my sister." He leaned in further, his voice dropping. "We got a hit on the DNA that was taken from Lizzy's home. It matched the DNA found in the cabin."

Ajay's eyes widened, and he leaned in closer. "Who is it?"

"His name is Tiberius Wagner. He's got a lengthy rap sheet. Assault and battery, attempted murder, rape, robbery, fraud. He's bad news all the way around."

"Why haven't you picked him up?"

"We're working on it."

"Do you know what his connection is with Markus Acker and the church?"

"From what we've been able to figure out, it looks like he's one of Acker's more devoted disciples. He's been following him around the country for years now. He's been Acker's bodyguard and his muscle in their more illicit dealings. He's bad news, but we don't know why he targeted Lizzy. That's where it gets particularly nasty."

"Why so?"

"We have evidence showing that Wagner and Jessie Colton have had business dealings together. Jessie and Acker are also in a romantic relationship. My mother is drawn to men with money and power, but she couldn't care less how they make that happen. Only that she benefits from the fruits of their labor."

Ajay didn't miss the snark in the man's tone at the mention of his mother. "Do you honestly think she might be involved with this?"

Max shrugged. "I don't want to think my mother would do something like that. It's possible she has no idea about his more illicit dealings. But I also felt that something was off with the second break-in. Like you pointed out, it's unusual for someone to gain entry like that unless they had a key. If it was Wagner, the only way he would have known where Lizzy's bedroom was located was if someone familiar with the home told him."

"But why..."

"I'll have to prove it obviously, but I think Lizzy was snatched so they could blackmail my father for money. That whole church is an unscrupulous bunch of villains and thieves."

Ajay shook his head as he pondered the news. This put a whole other spin on everything they might have believed.

"I'm trusting you to keep this to yourself," Max said. "One, we don't want him to know we're on to him. If he gets spooked, we run the risk of him leaving the state. And two, it's going to devastate Lizzy. She doesn't need that right now. It's better that she continues to think we're a bunch of incompetent fools not doing our job. She'll learn the truth soon enough, and then things really will be hell for her."

Ajay hesitated. "I don't know about that. Keeping secrets from your sister is certain to blow up in my face."

"I get it. But isn't Lizzy's well-being more important than you taking a hit if she gets mad? What I just told you is classified, and although I'm already out the door at the FBI, I'd like to make sure they don't ding my clean record. I need to know I can trust you."

"You have my word," Ajay said as he considered the ramifications of Lizzy discovering her birth mother might have purposely put her in harm's way. Learning her mom had ties to a known criminal was bad enough.

He sighed heavily and tossed back his mug of beer. Then he went to the bar to ask for one more beer with a shot of Jack Daniels.

Chapter 13

When she woke that morning, Lizzy was determined to fix what she had broken. She had practiced what she planned to say a hundred different ways. She still hadn't perfected her apology, but figured by the time she reached Ajay's home, she'd have gotten it right.

After a long shower and a breakfast of mixed fruit, granola and almond milk, she felt ready. She dressed in her favorite black jeans, a black turtleneck sweater and fuzzy Bearpaw boots, then slipped on a black leather jacket. With her hair pulled back into a ponytail, she felt cute.

Moving through the house, she called for her father but got no answer. When she reached the kitchen, she noticed Mama Jen headed out the door.

"Hey! I didn't know you were here," Lizzy said.

"Actually, I'm just leaving. I came by to drop off a casserole for dinner tonight."

"Do you know where my father is?"

"Down at the barn, I believe."

"I wanted to check with him to see if I could borrow his truck."

"He took the Range Rover, so I'm sure he won't mind. The keys are hanging on the hook in the mudroom. I'm headed down to the barn to say hello before I take off. Do you want me to tell him?"

"Please. Just let him know I won't be gone long."

Mama Jen gave her a thorough gaze, eyeing her from her head to her feet and back. "Are you sure you're okay to be going out by yourself?"

Lizzy nodded. "I'm fine. Everyone needs to stop worrying about me."

"Worrying is what we do. It comes with the job description when you have kids."

Lizzy smiled. "Good to know."

"Just be safe out there, please," the matriarch concluded before heading out the door.

"I will," Lizzy said. In the mudroom, she grabbed the keys and headed to her father's Ford F-150 pickup truck.

This would be the first time Lizzy drove anywhere by herself since she was abducted. Having other people chauffeur her around had begun to take its toll. There were errands she needed to run, shopping she would have liked to do, and she trusted she wouldn't have any problems getting around. Besides, it wasn't like she was going too far from home.

As she pulled the car out of its parking space, she felt her heart begin to race. She rolled down the window for a fresh breeze. Mama Jen's words echoed in her head, a vibration that began to feel like a jackhammer against concrete. *Be safe out there. Be safe out there. Be safe out there.*

But she wasn't safe, Lizzy suddenly thought. She couldn't be safe until they found the man who was haunting her, or he found her first. Truth be told, she might never be safe again.

She slammed on the brakes and shifted the truck into Park. The engine was still running as she jumped from the driver's seat, fighting to catch her breath. A full-blown panic attack had her feeling like her heart was about to burst. She couldn't breathe, and everything around her was spinning.

She suddenly felt an arm around her waist and a familiar voice in her ear. Her father's tone was soothing, and she tried to focus on what he was telling her. "Breathe, Lizzy. Breathe slowly. In and out. In and out. That's it."

"Should I call an ambulance?" Max questioned.

"No," Buck answered. "She's okay. It's just a little anxiety. Once she catches her breath, she'll be just fine. Isn't that right, my sweet girl? Everything is going to be all right."

Lizzy was bent forward at the waist, her hands clutching her knees. As her breathing began to slow, she no longer felt as if she might pass out and fall over. She felt a sense of calm returning, her body shifting back into sync. She took another deep breath and held it down in her lungs before blowing it out slowly.

Buck continued to soothe her. "That's my girl. Easy peasy. In and out. In and out."

Lizzy lifted herself upright, her gaze sweeping between the two men eyeing her with concern. She nodded. "Thank you," she said. "I'm okay."

"Where were you going?" Max asked.

She shook her head. "I just had some errands to run. I thought it would be okay."

"Why don't we go back to the house?" Buck said, his arms still wrapped around her shoulders. "I think you should lie down for a minute. I can send someone to get whatever it is you need."

She shook her head vehemently. "No... I... It's important... I..." she stammered, unable to find the right words.

Max took a step forward. "It's okay. I'll drop you off."

A wave of gratitude washed over Lizzy's spirit. She clasped her hands together as if in prayer, then dropped her face into her palms. Buck pulled her to him, and she dropped her head against his chest. Her father stood hugging her until

she stopped shaking, beginning to be embarrassed about causing a scene.

"I really am fine," she said. "I'll be okay."

"Are you certain?" Buck questioned.

Lizzy nodded. "Yes. I'm good."

"You make certain she gets where she wants to go safely,"
Buck said to Max.

Max gestured for her to get into the passenger seat of the
truck. He held the door open until she was settled, the seat
belt secured around her waist. Seconds later, they were pulling past the gates onto the main road.

"I'm never going to be normal again, am I?" she whispered.
"I just want to be better."

Max shrugged. "That all depends on how you define normal. Will you get past this? Yes, definitely. But you need to
remember that it's going to take some time. Stop trying to
rush your recovery. It'll happen in its own time."

"Well, I don't have your confidence," Lizzy said.

"What I have is experience, and no, you don't have that.
Now, where would you like me to take you?"

She stammered, "Well, I wanted… I need… It's only…"

Max laughed. "Got it. Did you call him first to tell him
you were coming? In case he had a date or something?"

Lizzy's heart skipped a beat as she suddenly considered
that Ajay could be on a date with someone. Or worse, someone was visiting with him in his home.

She tossed her brother a blank look. "I hadn't thought…"

"No worries," Max said. "I don't think Ajay is that kind
of guy!"

Ajay wasn't totally hungover from the night before, but
he did have a raging headache. He was off duty for the next
thirty-six hours, so he and Pumpkin planned to do abso-

lutely nothing for the entire day. He especially wasn't going to allow himself to think about Lizzy Colton.

He figured a date with a good book would help with that, and he palmed the latest copy of a historical fiction novel Della had recommended. The author was a woman writing about people of color during the Regency period. Entwined with mystery, her story had been sitting on his nightstand for weeks, waiting for him to find time to read. Now seemed as good as any other.

He reclined on the sofa, his legs atop a leather ottoman. Pumpkin had curled up against his side, determined not to be moved. She'd been moody since she last saw Lizzy. It amazed him how quickly and how intensely their connection had been cemented. Pumpkin had been moping around as if her heart had been broken, too.

He had just turned the page on the third chapter when Pumpkin jumped up to rush toward the front door. She barked excitedly, her greeting coming even before the doorbell rang. There weren't many people who got that kind of welcome from his four-legged friend, so the list of who might be on the other side of the entrance was slim.

He was not prepared, however, when he opened the door and found Lizzy standing there. Behind her, Max stood at the curb, leaning against a truck with his arms folded over his chest. When the two men locked gazes, Max gave him a nod, climbed back into the driver's seat and disappeared down the street.

Lizzy's eyes were wide, a hint of fresh tears dancing against her lashes. She looked nervous, twisting her hands together. "My ride would only bring me one way," she said softly. "I told him I didn't think you'd mind giving me a ride back home."

Ajay smiled, hoping that his excitement didn't show on

his face. "That shouldn't be a problem. Would you like to come in?"

"If I wouldn't be interrupting anything," she said, peering past his shoulder.

"Nothing at all. I was just hanging out with my favorite girl."

Lizzy's gaze narrowed, her smile fading slightly. "Oh."

"Come on in. I think she's missed you, too," he said, pointing at Pumpkin.

The yellow Lab stood patiently, her tail swishing like a windshield wiper against his hardwood floors. She jumped excitedly when Ajay signaled that she could move. Her energy was infectious, and even he had to laugh as she jumped excitedly around Lizzy.

Lizzy dropped to the floor, wrapping her arms around the dog's neck. She pressed her face into Pumpkin's fur. Her winter coat was thick and soft, and Ajay could see Lizzy relax against the animal's frame.

Quietly, he closed the front door and secured the lock, then stood and waited. Time felt as if it had come to a standstill, the moment surreal. He waited as she seemed to collect herself, and then she stood up, turning to face him.

Contrition rounded her shoulders and pinched her cheeks a brilliant shade of crimson. Her lengthy lashes batted down a rise of saline, and she held herself tightly. "I'm sorry," Lizzy said. "I acted childishly, and I apologize for my bad behavior."

Ajay stood like stone. There was a lengthy pause, silence rising between them like a morning mist.

"Oh," Lizzy added, "I promise it won't ever happen again." Her bright blue eyes danced across his face, as if searching for a sign that her apology had moved him to forgive her.

Ajay shook his head. Amused, he reached out and snaked his arm around Lizzy's waist. His fingers pressed hot against the small of her back. He pulled her against himself, the gesture sensual and possessive. He stared into her eyes, falling fast into her oceanic gaze.

Then he pressed his lips to hers, kissing her sweetly.

Lizzy knew beyond any doubt that this moment would solidify whatever it was that was between her and Ajay. She hadn't thought it possible to be so intrinsically connected to any one person as she felt to him at that moment. It was as if he'd grabbed hold of her heart with a vise grip and intended to hang on for as long as she would let him. Whether he knew it or not, Lizzy had no intention of him ever letting go.

"I'm sorry, too," Ajay whispered against her lips. "I should never have said what I said. I should never have spoken to you that way. And I promise you that it will never happen again."

"It better not," Lizzy quipped. She kissed him again.

"You're really not very good at apologizing, are you?" Ajay said.

Lizzy smiled brightly. "Not really. I had to practice that one."

Ajay chuckled as he entwined his fingers between hers and pulled her to the living room sofa. "Can I get you something?" he asked as they settled comfortably against each other.

"No, thank you. I'm good. I just needed to tell you how much I missed you."

He slid his hand into her hair, the strands tangling around his fingers. He drew her closer and kissed her one more time. She tasted like butter rum candy and ginger. "I'm glad you came. I was going crazy without you, Lizzy. I missed you more than you will ever know."

"I almost didn't make it," Lizzy said, telling him about her panic attack.

"Are they happening often?" Ajay asked.

She shook her head. "No, not really. I've had some anxiety, but this was different. This was bad. I was petrified to step off the ranch property by myself. The fear was unbearable."

"Why are you afraid?" Ajay questioned. "You're more than capable of protecting yourself."

"Tell that to my kidnapper. He got the jump on me, and the next thing I knew I was tied to the floor in some abandoned cabin. My abilities were clearly lacking. What if that happens again? I might not be so lucky."

"First, he got the jump on you. Hitting you from behind was not a fair fight. And you were not adequately prepared to defend yourself after that. Especially after you tried to get away and he beat you. We'll make sure that never happens again. The fact that you survived cracked ribs and a head injury says more about your abilities than you give yourself credit for."

"I still feel like I'm damaged goods," Lizzy said quietly. "I just can't shake the feeling that I'm putting everyone around me at risk. Especially you."

"Why especially me?" he queried, his brow furrowing.

"Because I insisted you stay with me. Because I always want to be around you. I've been a thorn in your side, and you've just been too nice to say anything."

"That's not true. If I hadn't wanted to be there, I would have told you no. I was there because I wanted to be. I wanted to protect you and make sure no one could hurt you. And then I was there because of how I'm feeling for you. I'm falling in love with you, Lizzy."

Lizzy looked him in the eyes as he proclaimed his truth, expressing the emotion that had been such a force for both of them to reckon with since they had met. He told her what was on his heart, and then he kissed her as if he were kissing her for the very first time.

"Ajay, you make me so happy!" Lizzy said, monumental joy wrapped around the words.

Everything about the moment felt like a fairy tale, and then Pumpkin whined, sitting at their feet as she stared up at them. She gave them the slightest bark, and it felt like love had completely encompassed the room.

Ajay settled down on the sofa beside Lizzy. He had made them both a cup of ginger tea and had plated a small charcuterie for them to snack on. The afternoon was passing so quickly that Lizzy had begun to think someone had played with the clocks to prank them.

"This is very nice," she said.

Ajay nodded. "It is and I hate to ruin the mood, but we need to talk."

The look Lizzy gave him made Ajay chuckle.

"You're not getting out of this, Lizzy. We have to clear the air before we can move forward."

She sighed, a heavy gust of air blowing past her lips. He had mentioned their argument earlier and now his insistence they rehash her bad behavior felt like it could well be the beginning of the end. Again. She felt as if they had reached a point of no return and their next decision would greatly impact what would come next for the two of them.

"Fine. What do you want to discuss?"

"We both said some pretty awful things to each other. I know I was in my feelings and just wanted us to stop arguing. But I need to know what you were thinking because some of what you said really hurt my feelings. I'm not going to lie about that. I felt like you'd sucker punched me when you called me weak. Especially since I was already feeling inadequate about not keeping your stalker from getting close to you.

"I said what I said just to be mean. I missed you and I didn't want to hear that you wanted to do something else. It was childish on my part and I'm really sorry for everything I said."

"And I apologize for anything I said that hurt you. It was just a bad time and your tantrum hit me the wrong way."

"My tantrums have always gotten me my way. They've always worked on my father and my brothers. It's a bad habit I know I need to break," Lizzy conceded.

"You need to understand that they aren't going to work on me. I will call you out just like I expect you to call me out if I'm not on my best behavior with you. We will never be able to make this work if we're not willing to have hard conversations. We can agree to disagree, but there should be no name-calling or cursing or being disrespectful to each other. I'm not going to tolerate that, and neither should you."

Lizzy reached for a cracker and a slice of cheese. As she bit them both, she found herself feeling liberated. It wasn't often she could express how she felt without fear of condemnation. She didn't like feeling vulnerable, but letting her guard down for Ajay felt right in a way she could never have expected.

As the weight of her anxiety and his lifted off their shoulders, Lizzy knew beyond any doubt that things going forward would be everything she could ever want with any man. She shifted her hips closer to his, allowing herself to wallow in the warmth of his body heat. Ajay reached for a grape and fed it to her, a comforting glow shimmering out of his eyes.

She looked around the living space. It was tastefully decorated, although it could have used a splash of color, Lizzy thought. He'd chosen gray tones with textured fabrics, woven rugs and leather furniture—overall, very bachelor pad-like. With his permission, she was excited to explore his personal sanctuary, to discover something about him that she hadn't yet learned. She rose from her seat to look around and be nosy.

White cabinetry, gray granite counters and white tiled

floors made the kitchen feel slightly antiseptic. Lizzy was already considering the changes she could make to warm up the space. Nothing decorated the walls, and it was clearly the home of a man who didn't spend much time there.

There were three bedrooms. The master featured its own tiled bathroom and an expansive walk-in closet that Ajay put to little use. That space was also a dichotomy of cool whites and various shades of gray. Ajay didn't blink an eye as she pulled open his drawers and closets to peek inside. Not even when she discovered the box of Magnum condoms tucked away in his underwear drawer.

Beside the king-size bed sat a family portrait of him and his parents. He was the spitting image of his father, but it was his mother's Blackness that had blessed him with his own warm skin tone. They stood smiling, all wearing denim jeans and bright white dress shirts against a background of lush greenery. There was so much love in the photo and pride that gleamed out of his mother's eyes.

A pang of jealousy trickled through Lizzy's insides. As she put the framed photo back on the nightstand, she couldn't help but think of her own mother and the family photos they had never been able to take.

After a midday lunch of grilled cheese and tomato soup, Ajay went back to his book while Lizzy rested her head in his lap and scrolled through her phone. Eventually, they ventured outside in the cold air to walk Pumpkin. A snowball fight ensued, and Lizzy pled the fifth about throwing the first handful of snow. Back inside, they watched a marathon of *The Walking Dead*. Dozing on and off, the two simply enjoyed the respite and the companionship. By the end of the last episode, it had grown dark out, and they were hungry again.

"Why don't we grab something to eat before I take you home?" Ajay asked.

Lizzy gripped the front of his T-shirt with two hands. She pressed her forehead to his chest. "I could always stay here," she whispered.

Ajay wrapped her in his arms and hugged her tightly. "I want to say yes, but you and I both know what will happen if you stay."

"You'll make wild, passionate, dirty love to me. How is that a bad thing?"

His laughter rang warmly through the room. "It wouldn't be a bad thing. Actually, it would probably be a very good thing, but we both know the timing's not right."

"Says who?" Lizzy snuggled closer against him.

"We both should be saying it, Lizzy. When I make love to you, nothing and no one will be able to keep us from our destiny. It'll be about our dreams and desires for each other. It'll be about planning for four boys and twin girls and the love we have for each other. There won't be any anxiety, doubts or need to explain ourselves. No one questioning why or whether or not we know what we're doing. But more importantly, there won't be one ounce of regret. No wondering if we've done the right thing. And right now, I think you'd be second-guessing your decision."

"I'd argue that the pleasure we would bring to each other would far exceed any second guesses either of us might have." Lizzy took a step back, her hands on both hips.

"You know better than I that pleasure is temporary. Regret can haunt you a lifetime." Ajay pressed a kiss to her forehead. "Any idea what you'd like for supper?" he asked, changing the subject.

Lizzy sighed. "Mama Jen made lasagna or some kind of pasta casserole. We can eat at the ranch, if that's okay with you."

"That works for me," he said.

They headed for the front door. "You do know I don't like being wrong, don't you?" Lizzy asked.

Ajay chuckled. "No one said you were wrong, Lizzy!"

"I'm just going to need you to let me win an argument every now and then."

"Only when you're right and I'm wrong."

"That's what I'm afraid of!" she said, giggling.

Ajay laughed. "You'll get used to it."

Despite his best efforts, Ajay found saying no to Lizzy virtually impossible. She was accustomed to having her own way, and in all honesty, there was little he wouldn't do for her.

Turning down her advances the previous day hadn't been easy because he had wanted her to stay as much as she had wanted to spend the night. His grandiose speech about the right timing and their destiny had just been him stalling in order to calm the rise of nature that had him sweating. Had he not talked fast, he had no doubt the first of their four sons would be arriving some nine months from now.

Not saying no to Lizzy was why he'd awakened an hour earlier than he had planned, Lizzy at his front door with fresh bagels and large cups of coffee from Hutch's Diner. Not saying no was why he was now standing beneath a cold shower, waiting for a raging erection to subside as Lizzy worked out in his home gym in the skimpiest pair of shorts and tank top she owned.

He could already see that their relationship was going to be a battle of wills. Lizzy was determined to best him every chance she could. What he found most amusing was that he was excited for the challenge. Lizzy kept him on his toes, and he hadn't realized how much he needed that.

He slathered himself with his favorite Oribe Côte d'Azur body wash. The soap was paradise in a bottle, a luxurious gel that left him smelling like a tropical explosion of starflower oils, meadowfoam and sweet almond with the barest notes of sandalwood. He tilted his face into the warm water as the suds cascaded over his chest and down his back. His hand stalled below his pubic line, the length of his manhood twitching for attention.

Before he could consider the possibilities, there was a knock on the bathroom door. Lizzy called to him from the other side.

"Yes, Lizzy?"

"Can I come in?"

"No."

"You scared?"

"No, Lizzy!"

"Then open the door. I promise I'll keep my hands to myself."

"That's not a good idea!"

"I just want to talk."

"We'll talk when I get out."

"Are you really going to turn me away?"

"Yes, I am. Now stop giving me a hard time."

"You don't mean that figuratively, do you?" she asked teasingly.

Ajay laughed. "I'm calling your brother. I think it's time you went home."

"But I just got here!"

"Then do me a favor, please, and go walk my dog. Pumpkin needs some quality one-on-one time with you."

"Only because it's Pumpkin."

"Thank you, Lizzy!"

She giggled. "You're welcome, Ajay!"

Chapter 14

The punch Ajay threw whizzed by Lizzy's head so close that it startled her. She blinked and ducked her face into her hands. Him teaching her self-defense tactics had seemed like a good idea when she first said yes. Now she wasn't so sure, and this was their fifth lesson.

"Hey!" she exclaimed. "This was supposed to be practice. Why are you trying to kill me on purpose?"

He shook his head. "You should have been ready. I told you, never underestimate your opponent. Even if he does love you." He threw another punch.

This time, Lizzy maneuvered left and swept his feet out from under him. Ajay landed on the ground with a loud thud.

"I didn't teach you that," he said as he gasped for air.

"Brothers!" Lizzy responded, her fists high in front of her face.

She danced about like a boxer in the center ring waiting for the count against her opponent. With a swiftness she didn't see coming, Ajay grabbed her ankle and threw her off-balance. He caught her before she hit the cushioned mat.

"Hey!"

"Always finish your opponent off," he said. "You should have followed up with a head-and-groin kick. You want to make certain your attacker doesn't get back up, or worse, pull you down to his level." He swiveled his body, flipping her onto her back. He pinned both her arms above her head, dropping his weight against her torso and pelvis. He sat above her, his knees on both sides of her legs. "Try to avoid getting into this position, but if it happens, you can get yourself out."

Lizzy took a deep breath. "Even if he's bigger than me?"

"Especially if he's bigger than you. You'll need to use a transition escape to get yourself out of that situation."

"Show me," Lizzy said.

"First, try to prevent yourself from losing full control. I've grabbed both of your arms, but I want you to bend your dominant hand like you're holding a mirror in it and looking at yourself. And it's all about the positioning of that arm."

Lizzy did as he instructed.

"Second, I want you to put your foot against my hip, on the same side as your bent arm. Once you've done that, you need to push me away with your leg and pull your arm up toward your head at the same time. This gives you control and takes my leverage away. With that free hand, you can then go for an eye gouge or an ear pull."

They practiced the move a few times until Lizzy felt comfortable with it. Ajay didn't give her any slack, using his full weight to subdue her. The last time she was able to get out, she followed with a pretend kick to his chin and another to his groin.

"Excellent!" Ajay exclaimed. "Follow-through is so important!"

Lizzy grinned. She was excited to be learning techniques that could potentially save her life. She wanted to discover more. "What if that doesn't work, and he does pin me down?"

Ajay nodded as she lay back down on the floor and positioned herself beneath him. "So, say your attacker has you by the wrists, and your hands are pinned by your ears. He's sitting above you with his knees on both sides of your legs.

I want you to bump your hips upward, and at the same time swing your arms down toward your ankles. This will throw me off-balance."

Lizzy did as he instructed.

"Now reach up and wrap your arms around my waist," he continued. "Hug me tight. That's it. In this position, I can't use my arms, and you want to regain your control. You're going to take your leg and swing it to trap my foot. At the same time, you grab my arm and roll."

Lizzy squealed excitedly. "That puts me back on top."

"It does, but you also need to be fast. Follow-through with a strike or two and then peel off and get out of there."

"Again," Lizzy said.

"No again," Ajay said, rolling onto his back. "You need to take a break. We've been at this all morning."

"I'm not tired."

"Well, then I need a break. You can play by yourself."

"That's no fun," Lizzy said as she rolled above him, pretending to pin him to the ground. She dropped her mouth to his and kissed him hungrily. Beneath her pelvis, she felt him tense, a rise of nature pressing firm and hard between his legs. Lizzy added fuel to the fire she ignited, grinding herself slowly against him.

With apt precision, Ajay flipped her over. He continued to kiss her for a brief moment before pulling himself away. "I'm headed to the shower," he said.

"I would think you'd have gotten tired of cold showers every morning," Lizzy said smugly.

"Cold showers are invigorating," Ajay said.

She laughed. "I hear great sex will do the same thing!"

Lizzy had been giving Ajay a hard time for days. She showed up at his home every opportunity she could, even on those days he and Pumpkin had to go to work. Her presence in his space was beginning to show in the decor that she'd added to make the home look lived in. Artwork now decorated the walls, and she'd introduced color in the throws and pillows. She'd also framed a selfie she'd taken of the two of them together, adding it to the photos in the master bedroom. With each addition, Ajay hadn't blinked an eye, seeming comfortable with her in his space.

She was genuinely awed by his willpower. She'd tried every trick in her book of tricks to try to seduce him, to no avail. He kept saying no, and she kept trying. She had immeasurable respect for his willpower.

But she knew he was right about them waiting. She wasn't ready, knowing a threat still existed. She wanted them being together to be special, not marred by her fears and the anxiety of knowing someone was still out to get her. She hated that the police were no closer to finding her attacker. But she was getting better about leaving the ranch. Even though she still needed someone in her family to be with her until she reached Ajay's side, her panic attacks had subsided. She was especially grateful that none of them gave her a difficult time about giving her a ride when she asked.

Now she enjoyed those moments of spontaneity when she could tease Ajay unmercifully. Because she knew one day, he would deem them ready, and he'd give in. The prospect of that day excited her.

So, until then she thought, she would keep teasing and flirting with him, because there wasn't an ounce of shame in her desire for the man.

"You really need to focus," Ajay said. Perspiration beaded across his brow and down his face. He and Lizzy had been working out, ramping up her self-defense training. He had just run ten miles on the treadmill while she lifted weights. For reasons he couldn't begin to explain, Lizzy kept staring off into space, her focus on everything but what she needed to be doing. "What's going on in that head of yours?" he questioned.

"What happens when this is all over? With us, I mean?"

"I'm sure we'll figure it out as we go along."

Lizzy drifted off into thought again. She blew out the softest sigh, just a faint gust of air easing past her lips.

Ajay eyed her intently. He swiped a towel across his brow and chest and moved to the workout bench to take a seat. "What's got you in a mood?"

"I was just thinking how I'm having such a good time when I'm with you, and there's some creep out here who wants to take that from us. It makes me angry!" Her voice rose ever so slightly.

"I understand it's frustrating," Ajay said, "but you can't give him so much control. The more he can keep you scared, the more control he has over you. You just need to focus on keeping your strength up so that you can defend yourself if you ever need to. And you want to practice so the moves become second nature. You'll be able to throw a punch or a kick without thinking about it."

Lizzy nodded. "I just…well…" she stammered. "I just want things between us to be good. I know we play around, and you're as big a flirt as I am, but I'd like us to keep that going. And I'd like for us to share more with each other when the timing is right."

Ajay smiled. "I hope that you consider yourself my friend. Because I do, and I like to think that I work very hard to maintain my friendships with people I care about."

Lizzy moved to where he'd taken a seat and dropped into his lap with a heavy thud.

"Ouch!" Ajay muttered. "If you keep that up, there won't be much of me left for anything more."

Lizzy eased up, then sat back against him with more grace than previously. She wrapped her arms around his neck. "So really, Ajay, how do you feel about me?" she asked.

"Are you really asking me that?" Ajay's brow lifted as he stared at her.

"Indulge me, please. My insecurities are kicking in. Sometimes I'll need your reassurance."

He shook his head. "I think it's obvious. I care about you very much. And it's important to me that you're safe."

"That sounds like love to me."

"It sounds like that to me, too."

"Well, although I appreciate you wanting to be my knight in shining armor, you're going to have to step your game up. I'm not going to make it easy for you to steal my heart."

"I don't steal, but I'm willing to put in whatever work is necessary to claim what belongs to me. Most especially your heart."

"I find your confidence very sexy, Ajay Wright."

"And I find your time-wasting tactics equally entertaining. Now, you need to get back to work, and you need to *focus*," he said, emphasizing the last word. He gently pushed her up and off his lap, tapping her bottom with a flat palm.

"Tease!" Lizzy exclaimed.

"Lazy," Ajay countered.

Lizzy feigned a pout and pretended to throw a punch at Ajay's head. He threw his head back to dodge her fist, then threw his own punch.

Lizzy was quick to adjust, moving swiftly from him as she danced on her toes. She laughed.

"You're not in a boxing ring, Lizzy," Ajay said. "The likelihood of you being able to outfight a man bigger than you is slim. You also risk breaking your hands, so don't think about boxing it out. Elbows, knees, front kicks, side and round kicks are best at close range. If you can't keep any distance between you, then the best chance you have is to draw him in close and then you crush him. If you hit him in the face, hit him with the palm of your hand or rake him across the eyes with your nails. Think tiger claw."

Lizzy nodded. "Tiger claw! Got it."

Ajay spun her around and moved against her backside. He leaned to whisper in her ear. "Now crush me!"

As he eased his arm around her neck, Lizzy dipped her chin to her chest to reduce the pressure he could get around her neck. She slipped a hand between his elbow and her neck and spun herself out and away.

"Good," Ajay said.

He reached out and grabbed her in a choke hold. Like Ajay had taught her, Lizzy tightened her neck muscles, ducked her head and spun herself below his elbows. Her moves were precise, quick and exactly as he'd taught her.

"Very nice," Ajay extolled, showering her with praise.

Lizzy swept her arms out and around and took a bow. Before she could catch herself, she was suddenly lying flat on her back, the wind knocked out of her lungs. Ajay stood above her, looking down at her as she worked to catch her breath.

"Don't forget to put distance between you and your attacker. A good run beats a bad stand each and every time. So run! Don't be dancing in the end zone. That just gives him another opportunity to come back at you."

"You don't fight fair," Lizzy finally gasped.

Easing himself above her, Ajay pressed his mouth to hers. He kissed her lips, the gesture an easy caress of skin against skin.

Closing her eyes, Lizzy allowed herself to drop into the

beauty of his touch, savoring the intensity of the moment. When he pulled away, she opened her eyes and smiled.

"Can we do that again?" Lizzy asked, biting down against her bottom lip.

Ajay grinned. "We should definitely practice you escaping choke holds until you're comfortable."

"As long as you kiss me like that every time," Lizzy said, "I'm good with that!"

Ajay laughed. "Just stay focused, please!"

"What are you looking for?" Vivian asked. "You haven't stopped fidgeting in your seat since Ajay dropped you off."

"Sorry," Lizzy said, reaching for her glass of orange pop. "I just thought I saw someone."

Vivian looked toward the large glass windows of Tap Out Brewery. Lizzy had called her out of the blue to meet for a midday lunch of burgers and beer like old times. They had only been seated a few minutes when Lizzy jumped, certain that she'd seen someone standing by the front door, watching her.

"Do you want to call Ajay?" Vivian questioned as she tried to see what Lizzy thought she saw.

Lizzy shook her head. "I'm always bothering Ajay. It's fine. I'm sure I'm just imagining things." She knew she didn't sound convincing as she took one last glance toward the door.

"So tell me something good," Vivian said, changing the subject. "How are you and Ajay doing?"

"He's so good to me," Lizzy gushed. "That man has the patience of Job!"

Vivian waved a dismissive hand. "How's the sex?" she asked.

Lizzy leaned in as if to share something decadent. Her friend leaned in closer as well. Lizzy's voice dropped to a polite whisper. "I don't know. We're waiting until things are settled down and that creep who grabbed me is captured."

Vivian sat back in her seat, dropping her hands into her lap. Her lashes batted rapidly. Finally, she said, "You're lying, right? This is a joke?"

Lizzy shook her head. "Nope! Ajay doesn't want us to do anything that I might regret later."

"Do you think you'll regret it?"

Lizzy felt her entire face lift into a bright smile. "I won't regret a single minute that I've been able to spend with Ajay Wright. I think making love to him would be the icing on some very sweet cake."

Vivian smiled. "You two are so funny!"

"Any changes on the dating front for you?"

"Let me make you laugh," Vivian said with an eye roll. "I have a new client, and he has a very nice-looking son."

"Nice-looking is good."

"The son invited me for coffee, so I agreed. We went over to Hutch's Diner."

"Good coffee."

"We're talking. I'm enjoying the conversation, and all of a sudden, he excuses himself from the table to go and speak with a woman who's sitting alone at the counter. I'm thinking, maybe it's someone he recognizes. He comes back a few minutes later and says to me, if she stops by the table on her way out, just roll with the conversation. 'I told her you were my sister.'"

Lizzy burst out laughing.

"This fool went to get her telephone number," Vivian continued, "and when she asked who I was, he said we were family. I was so over it!"

"What did you do?"

"I went to the register and paid my bill, and as I was leaving, I told the girl what a jerk he was. I am so done with men. They're all losers and fools."

"Not really," Lizzy said, her tone consoling. "You just haven't met your man yet."

"And I'm not going to. I'm not going on another date ever."

"I'm going to find you a man."

"Nope! Focus on your own problems."

Lizzy laughed.

"I'm serious," Vivian said. "What are you going to do if you and Ajay wait and then you discover he's really bad in bed? How are you going to come back from that?"

"I already know Ajay is not bad in bed. In fact, I can say with relative certainty that he will be the best I've ever had!"

"Well, I don't have your confidence," Vivian said, laughing heartily.

The two women paused as the waiter, a young man named Darryl, delivered two mushroom onion burgers, loaded French fries and mugs of their newest craft beer, a kettle sour brew blended with orange, pineapple and passionfruit.

"Bon appétit!" Lizzy exclaimed as she lifted her mug in salutation.

"That's good," Vivian said after their toast. "This one might become my new favorite."

"I don't know. I think I still prefer their milk stout. Especially the one that gets aged in the bourbon barrels. This is nice, though."

As they ate, the conversation shifted once again.

"How are things with the new siblings?" Vivian asked.

Lizzy sighed. "Okay, I guess. I've not been a good sister if I'm honest. I could probably reach out more or something."

"It's going to take time, I'm sure."

"Did I tell you Nate came to visit me in the hospital?"

"No! What's he like?"

"He's really a nice guy. Really nice. He actually came to help search for me. When he came to visit, he brought flowers and everything. But I could see how hard this is for him and his sister."

"And the sister…"

"Sarah. She's a teacher."

Vivian nodded. "Have you spoken to Sarah?"

"Not really. Like I said, I've not been a good sister."

"In your defense, you've had a lot going on," Vivian said. "I'm sure they understand."

"I really have no excuse," Lizzy said. "I could make the time. Don't encourage my bad behavior."

An hour later, after much laughter, the two women settled their tab and headed outside. There was a chill in the air, and Lizzy pulled her coat tighter around her torso.

"I can drop you off at the ranch," Vivian said. "Or do you need a ride someplace else?" She eyed Lizzy, her brow raised, a slight smirk on her face.

Lizzy laughed. "Thank you, but I am going to run down to the gift shop to see if I can find gifts for all the kids. I need to start my Christmas shopping. I texted Ajay, and he's going to meet me there and pick me up."

"Are you going to be okay?"

Lizzy nodded. "I am. I feel good." She glanced down the street one way and up the other way. "And clearly no one is standing around waiting to pounce on me, so I should be fine."

Vivian leaned to give her a hug. "Call me later so I know you're okay."

Lizzy watched as her friend hurried to her car. The chill in the air had become a cold wind, the kind that seeped into your bones and wreaked havoc through your entire body. She pulled up her hood and zipped her coat up to her chin.

Shoving both hands into her pockets, she began a leisurely stroll through the downtown area.

There was quaint charm about Owl Creek that always made Lizzy feel at home. There were no big-box stores or chain restaurants allowed within city limits. If she needed Macy's or Home Depot, she would need to drive to Conners or Boise. Tourists made the town interesting as they enjoyed the little mom-and-pop shops that added to Owl Creek's appeal. They came for the water in the summer and snow in the winter. Spring and fall were all about hiking the mountains and taking in the sights. Lizzy could never truly imagine herself living any place else.

She paused in front of an antique shop to stare in the window. There was an exquisite wall clock inside that would be perfect above Ajay's fireplace. She had just decided to go inside and inquire about it when a reflection in the glass caught her eye.

Lizzy felt her chest tighten, air escaping like helium from a popped balloon. She inhaled deeply, desperate to calm her nerves, the cold air burning her lungs. She turned slowly to stare across the street.

Standing on the sidewalk, staring back at her, was the man who'd been at the hospital. The same man with the mask who'd taken her hostage.

Lizzy gasped, and when he suddenly darted in her direction, moving too swiftly toward her, she turned and ran.

Chapter 15

Owl Creek's Main Street was beginning to settle down for the afternoon. Most of the storefronts would soon be closing and the number of places that would stay open past six o'clock were few and far between. As Ajay headed toward the gift shop to pick up Lizzy, he was excited that she'd spent the afternoon out on her own. Lunch with Vivian and shopping after would do her good, he thought. She needed to get back to the business of feeling normal and doing normal things that made her happy.

As he turned onto Main Street, he was not prepared for the police cars parked in front. A uniformed officer was talking to an older woman with a bouffant hairdo, who was pointing down the street and talking animatedly with her hands.

A large knot tightened in Ajay's midsection. He stole a quick glance at his cell phone to make sure he hadn't missed a call from Lizzy.

"Let's just hope it was a shoplifter," he said, talking to Pumpkin, who was also staring out the window. "Or a tourist who's intoxicated and needs to be cited for disorderly conduct. Just let it be anything else and not Lizzy."

Pumpkin barked.

Ajay pulled his Jeep into a parking spot on the other side of the street. As he approached, the uniformed officer gave him a look.

"Nothing to see here," the man said.

Ajay flashed his badge. "Lieutenant Wright. I'm just here to pick up a friend."

"Your friend have a name?" There was a hint of attitude in the officer's tone. Attitude that rubbed Ajay the wrong way.

"She does, but what's going on here, patrolman?"

The woman the officer was speaking with answered Ajay's question. "A young woman ran past my store screaming for help. There was a man chasing her. I came out to see what was going on. He came back past and got into a car and left, but I haven't seen the woman, and I'm worried he might have done something to her. I called 911 for them to come look, and this young man has been difficult about doing that. He says a crime needs to be committed before they can just go off searching for someone. For all we know, a crime may have been committed!" Her voice was filled with agitation.

The patrolman glared in Ajay's direction. "I was just taking her statement when you pulled up."

Ajay nodded. "Is there anyone in your shop right now?" he asked the woman.

She shook her head. "No. In fact, it's been very quiet today. Almost too quiet. No one's been since early this afternoon."

Ajay pulled his cell phone from his pocket. He tried to call Lizzy. Her phone rang and went straight to voice mail. "Ma'am, can you describe the woman?"

"Blonde, fair-skinned, petite. She was wearing a navy jacket and jeans, and she had her hood pulled up. I imagine because it's so cold out. But as she ran by, it blew off. That's how I know she was blond. And pretty. She was very pretty."

"What about the man?" Ajay asked.

"There was nothing pretty about him. He had on one of those full-face masks with the eyes and mouth cut out. It was black, and his clothes were black." The woman took a deep breath. "Oh, and she dropped this," she said, holding out a red knit scarf.

The knot in Ajay's stomach tightened as he recognized the scarf that Lizzy had proclaimed was her favorite. Mama Jen had crocheted it for her last Christmas, and Lizzy wore it often.

Taking the garment from the woman's hands, Ajay kneeled and held it out to Pumpkin. His dog had been sitting quietly at his side, seeming to take it all in. "Search, Pumpkin," Ajay commanded as Pumpkin took in Lizzy's scent. "Find Lizzy."

With the agility of a predator after prey, Pumpkin lowered her head and took off running. Ajay was right behind her, determined that they would find Lizzy and she would be safe and sound when they did.

Lizzy wanted to cry. And maybe she was crying, she thought, her face frozen from the cold. She was cowering behind a row of trees that bordered the property behind The Tides. The Tides was a high-end restaurant on the lakefront with a large open patio. Someone had gotten married, and from where she could see inside, the crowd gathered was having a good time.

Lizzy had cut across through the property, losing the masked man in the parking lot. Ducking down behind the cars, she'd practically crawled along the property's perimeter until she could dodge into the trees without him seeing her. Now she was too afraid to move, and somewhere along the way she'd lost her cell phone in the snow. It felt like déjà vu all over again.

"This is ridiculous," Lizzy muttered out loud. "Help is right there!"

She closed her eyes and took a deep breath. She couldn't believe she was too petrified to move, scared to death that man could find her, and embarrassed that she might disturb some newlywed couple's wedding reception.

Had she only made more of a scene in the center of Main Street, in front of the shops or inside one of the stores, that man could very well be in custody already. But the fear of him coming after her, and her not being able to defend herself the way Ajay had taught her, had sent her fleeing like a terrified mouse.

"I have to move," she said, still shaking in her boots. "Please, God, help me move!"

A loud noise sounded sharply to her left. Lizzy's head snapped in that direction, the rest of her prepared to run some more. Tears suddenly rained down her face, like a waterfall.

Pumpkin rushed toward her and jumped on her excitedly as Lizzy wrapped her arms around the pup and hugged her tightly. She cried into Pumpkin's fur, a wave of relief flooding through her.

Just a minute or two later, Ajay hurried to her side.

"Good girl, Pumpkin," he said, praising his four-legged friend for a job well done. He grabbed Lizzy by the shoulders and lifted her gently off the ground. Wrapping his arms around her, he drew her close. Her entire body melted against his. "It's okay," he whispered. "I've got you."

"I saw him again. And he was chasing me. I just ran. I didn't know what else to do!" Lizzy cried, feeling like a complete and total failure.

"You did good," he said softly. "You didn't put yourself at risk, and you got yourself to safety. There's no shame in that, Lizzy. No shame at all."

"But I didn't try to fight!" she cried out.

"You didn't put yourself in a situation that may have gotten you injured. You did the right thing."

He folded himself around her, wrapping her tightly in his

arms until she stopped shaking. He leaned to kiss the tears from her cheeks, pressing his mouth against hers sweetly. "Let's go home," Ajay said, as he guided her back toward the center of town, Pumpkin bobbing beside the two of them.

The next morning, after a pancake-and-bacon breakfast, Lizzy opted to forgo defense training. She was still feeling squirrelly after her encounter downtown and her inability to respond as she would have liked.

Ajay had let her spend the night, and he had slept on the couch in his own home, giving up his bed for her to get a good night's rest. Pancakes and bacon were the least she could do to show him her appreciation. After breakfast, he'd disappeared to the master bathroom, and she sat in the living room plotting additional changes to his home's decor.

An hour later, Ajay walked back into the living room, freshly showered and dressed. He had an appointment later that afternoon, and then he was having dinner with her brothers. Lizzy was thinking about meeting Vivian and their gang of girlfriends for an evening of ice skating. She didn't have the heart to tell Ajay or Vivian that she would have simply preferred to stay right where she was until he returned.

Ajay called her name, pulling her attention in his direction. "I have something for you," he said, a white box wrapped with a red satin bow in the palm of his hand.

At the sight of it, Lizzy grinned from ear to ear. Her rising excitement moved through the room like a drumline in the town parade. She jumped up and down elatedly, her entire being giddy with joy. "What is it? Because you know I *hate* surprises. But I do *love* a good present! Presents are everything! Can I open it?" she gushed with one big breath.

Ajay rolled his eyes skyward. "You know there's a contradiction in there, right? You hate surprises, but gifts are good."

Lizzy giggled, giving him a dismissive shoulder.

Ajay passed her the box, clearly enjoying her reaction.

Lizzy dropped to the leather recliner, tearing at the ribbon. She lifted the box top, glancing up at Ajay, her bright smile beaming, as she peeled back the tissue paper inside. She pulled a stunning beaded bracelet from inside the box.

"It's beautiful!" Lizzy gushed.

Ajay took it from her hands to clasp around her wrist. "It's also a tracking device," he said. "If anything happens, I'll be able to find you."

"How's that work?" she asked. She spun the beads with her fingers, admiring the range of colors against her skin.

"There is a small GPS chip and battery in two of the larger beads. It uses satellites to monitor your location. It's similar to the device they use for search-and-rescue dogs, and also Alzheimer's and dementia patients who might wander."

"Isn't that a little Big Brother-ish?" Lizzy asked sarcastically.

Ajay rolled his eyes. "I really want you to feel comfortable getting out more. You need to be able to go to town without an escort. Go have fun with your friends and visit your family. I don't want you to feel hampered by what might happen. And heaven forbid you get ambushed again and your defense training doesn't work, I'll still know where you are as long as you have that on."

Lizzy lifted her face to his. "Thank you," she said. "It's the best gift anyone's ever given me. And it really is beautiful!"

"I'm glad you like it. But think of it as another piece in your defense arsenal. Just like your mace, your switchblade and your training. It's one more element to keep you safe."

Ajay dipped his head to press his mouth to hers, savoring the sweetness of her lips. The touch was gentle and easy and joyful.

The doorbell suddenly chimed, ringing loudly through-out the room.

Pulling away, Ajay paused, tilting his head to listen.

"Are you expecting someone?" Lizzy questioned.

"No," Ajay responded. He grabbed his service pistol from the closet shelf in the foyer, tucking it into the holster beneath his arm.

The doorbell chimed a second time.

After peering through the peephole, he tossed Lizzy a quick glance over his shoulder, then he pulled the entrance open.

A uniformed delivery driver stood with a box in his hands. "Good morning. I have a package for Lizzy Colton," he said. He extended the box toward Ajay. "I'll just need you to sign here, please," he added as he proffered a digital signature pad.

Ajay took the stylus from the man's hand and scrawled his name across the line on the screen. As he closed the front door, Lizzy jumped from her seat and snatched the box from Ajay's hands.

"Another present! You're going to spoil me."

"Lizzy, stop!" Ajay shouted, his tone serious. "I didn't send that."

Her face dropped, her excitement deflating like a popped balloon. "Well, who did?"

"Who else knows you spend time here?"

"Besides my family, no one. And not even all of them know. I haven't even told Vivian."

"Would one of them send you a package here?"

She shook her head. "That's doubtful."

Ajay reached for his cell phone. "Do me a favor, please," he said as he dialed 911. "Put the box down and step away from it." He pointed his index finger to the floor, and then toward the kitchen.

Lizzy did as he instructed. She stepped back away from the box, grabbed Pumpkin by the collar, and the two withdrew to the other room. From where she stood in the kitchen, she could hear him asking for police backup.

Lizzy's heart began to race, the start of a panic attack beginning to rear its ugly head. She had wanted to believe that nothing bad was going to happen as long as she and Ajay were together, but even she couldn't pretend to be that naive. She wasn't safe anywhere, and wherever she was, she was putting other people in danger.

The detectives from the Owl Creek Police Department were huddled in conversation while Ajay and Lizzy looked on. The bomb squad had cleared the package, and when Ajay opened the box, the entire room gasped.

The dead bird inside had been crushed in the head with a rock. The rock lay beside the bird, a note wrapped with a rubber band around it.

They all had known what it said before reading it. The all-too-familiar mantra felt like a threat of magnanimous proportions. *We're coming for you.*

Lizzy stared down at the poor bird, wondering how depraved one's soul had to be to cause such harm. She could feel them all stealing glances in her direction, waiting to see if she would break. The attention was beginning to take its toll.

Max and Ajay stood together like deflated soldiers. At first, she thought they were arguing but soon realized they were coming to a consensus about their next steps.

"She needs to go back to the ranch," Max was saying. "She's safer there."

"I agree," Ajay said.

"The FBI's forensics team will start tracing that package. If they can tie it to their suspect, I'm sure they'll go pick him up right away. Finding him has been their biggest issue. With the prints from Lizzy's house and that cabin, this case should be a slam dunk."

"I say we don't wait. We need to pick him up now," Ajay murmured.

Lizzy stepped forward. "You have a suspect? You know who's doing this to me? How long have you known?"

Ajay and Max stared at each other, clearly deciding who was going to answer her questions first. Ajay lost that coin toss.

"Your brother has been following some leads we thought might pan out."

Max nodded. "Ajay suspected whoever broke into the house at the ranch was familiar with the property. That they used a key and knew exactly where your room was."

Lizzy's head snapped in Ajay's direction. "You think someone in my family would do this to me? My brothers would never hurt me. Neither would my cousins."

"I know, but even you said it would probably be easier to look at who didn't have a key than who did. And looking at the list of who did, opened up some questions we couldn't answer. Even your father acknowledged the possibility that…"

"No!" Lizzy shouted, cutting him off. She took a step back from him. "You think it's my mother, don't you?" She shot a look toward Max. "Do you think it's our mother?"

Max took a deep breath. "I think our mother may be involved with the man who is doing this. Yes. But we don't have enough proof yet…"

"How long? How long have you known this?" she questioned, her gaze shifting toward Ajay.

"For a minute now," he answered, contrition furrowing his brow. "We didn't want to say anything until we knew for certain."

Lizzy turned from them both, doubling over as she caught her breath. Her entire body was shaking, feeling like an explosion had gone off through every nerve ending.

Ajay reached out for her, and she shook him off angrily. She didn't want to be touched. She shot Max a look that could have melted stone, so he stepped away, obviously knowing she needed a minute to collect herself. He grabbed Ajay's arm and pulled him along. The two men followed the detectives to the front yard.

Della moved to Lizzy's side, wrapping a protective arm around her shoulders. "They were only trying to protect you, Lizzy. Don't be mad."

"I'm angry! Why is this happening?" Lizzy whispered. "What did I do to deserve this?"

"You didn't do anything. This guy just gets his jollies frightening people."

"But my mother might be involved. Why would she do this to me?"

"I can't answer that, honey."

"If only I knew what he wanted."

Della shook her head. "He wants you to be afraid. Monsters like him get off on seeing their victims be scared."

"Does my mother want me to be scared, too? Does she hate me that much?"

Della shrugged. She clearly didn't have an answer that would give Lizzy any comfort.

"I'm not going to be a victim," Lizzy said emphatically. "I refuse to be a victim!"

Della hugged her tightly. Max suddenly called her name, waving for her attention. "I'll be right back," Della said softly.

"I'll be fine," Lizzy said.

As she stood there, Lizzy realized there was no getting away. The threat was real, and not even the brief moments when she and Ajay could shut out the world would change that. Moving back into the living room, she grabbed her purse and headed out the door.

Max met her at the sidewalk. "The truck's running, and it's warm," he said. "Why don't you get in and wait for me? I just need to speak with one of my agents, and then we can leave."

She nodded. "Where's Ajay?"

"I think he's inside finishing up with his statement. I'll tell him where you are so he can come see you before we leave."

"Thank you," Lizzy said, her tone void of all emotion. She glanced one last time at all the activity buzzing in and out of the home. It wasn't lost on her that she had brought this drama to Ajay's front door.

Minutes later, Ajay and Max exited the house. Ajay tried to explain why he didn't want Lizzy to leave but Max clearly wasn't in agreement. Della moved toward them, and Ajay saw confusion wash over her face. "I thought you left," she said. Her eyes shifted from Max to Ajay and back.

"No," Max answered. "I'm still here."

"Where's Lizzy?" Ajay asked. Every muscle in his body suddenly tightened. He took a step, his gaze darting across the landscape.

Max said, "Where the hell is my truck?"

The trio exchanged looks, the revelation of what had just happened hitting them like a tidal wave.

Ajay swore. "Damn it, Lizzy!"

Chapter 16

They would soon be looking for her, Lizzy thought. And if they knew what she was planning, they would have done whatever they could to stop her. She couldn't begin to explain to anyone what was going on in her head. Because she didn't even have the words to make sense of the mess that had desecrated her life. One minute she was happy, feeling immensely loved, and the next minute it had all blown up, leaving her empty and hollow. If she felt broken before, it didn't hold a candle to how she was feeling now.

Lizzy still couldn't make sense of them suspecting her mother of being involved in the crimes against her. Jessie Colton was a lot of things. A horrible mother led the top of that list. But was it possible she wanted her eldest daughter harmed? Could she be involved with any man that would be so brutal toward her own child? Ajay didn't know anything about her family, but to have Max believe it cut deep. Or was Max just projecting because he resented Jessie so much?

Discovering that Ajay had suspicions that he kept from her felt all kinds of wrong. She was supposed to be able to trust him, and now she didn't know what to think. How could he have kept something like that from her? Tears began to rain from her eyes, and her heart felt like it might explode out of her chest. She took a deep breath and then another.

Her cell phone ringing startled her. She was about to turn it off when she saw it was Vivian on the phone. She pushed the talk button.

"Hello?" Lizzy's voice was raspy.

"Lizzy? What's wrong?" Vivian asked, concern flooding the connection. "What's going on? You don't sound good."

Lizzy began to hyperventilate, gasping for air. Her tears were starting to blind her view. She swiped her eyes with her hand. The truck veered left into the opposite lane and back. There was a squeal of brakes, and horns sounded loudly around her.

"Lizzy, are you driving? You need to pull over. Where are you? I will come and get you!"

Lizzy still couldn't catch her breath as she sobbed. Her body shook, and perspiration dampened her skin. She tried to speak, but her words wouldn't come, her tongue feeling like a wad of cotton in her mouth.

Pain shot through her torso, and Lizzy grabbed at her sweatshirt, letting go of the steering wheel. Suddenly everything went black, the sound of glass breaking and metal bending echoing against Vivian screaming her name in the distance.

"Where is she going with my damn truck?" Max snapped. "She has completely lost it!"

"I told you keeping that from her was not a good idea." Ajay was pushing buttons on his cell phone.

Della glared at the two of them. "She's not answering her new phone, and I spoke to Buck. He says she's not at the ranch, and they haven't heard from her. What were you two thinking?"

Max glared. "We were thinking it was a good idea to keep Lizzy safe. That's what we were thinking!"

"I might be able to find…" Ajay started, and then he cursed again. He tossed the other two a look and bolted for his front door. Max was on his heels with Della directly behind him. Inside, Ajay went from room to room calling Lizzy's name. He suddenly noticed Pumpkin lying on the sofa, her head tilted as she stared at him. He swore again.

"What?" Max questioned.

Ajay moved to Pumpkin's side, reaching for the collar around her neck. Hanging from it like a prized trophy was the bracelet he'd given Lizzy hours earlier.

"What's that?" Della asked.

"It's a tracking device I gave Lizzy. Clearly, she didn't want us to know where she's headed." He tossed the device to the table. He paused, then he asked Max. "Where can I find your mother?"

Max's brow lifted. "Why do you want to find my mother?"

"I think Lizzy might be headed there to talk to her."

Max scoffed. "None of us have anything to do with that woman. Lizzy would never go there."

"Do you know where she is or not?" Ajay asked, filled with frustration.

Della pressed a hand to the small of Max's back, caressing him gently. "Unless something has changed," she said softly, "she still has a home a few hours outside of Boise. I can make some calls and get you an address."

"Thank you," Ajay said. He grabbed his backpack and a leash for Pumpkin. "Text me when you get that information. And can you lock my house up when they're done, please?"

Della nodded. "No problem," she said. "Let us know what you find."

As he and Pumpkin hurried to his truck, Ajay shouted over his shoulder, "I will. And if you hear from Lizzy before I get back, call me!"

* * *

The home on Wildhorse Lane exceeded Ajay's expectations, and he really hadn't known what to expect. It was a custom home in a gated estate with acreage. It sat just outside the county seat with mountain views that stretched from the Owyhee Range to Oregon to the Boise Mountains. Expansive windows gave rise to dramatic views that could easily take one's breath away.

The only thing that surprised Ajay more was the woman who opened the door, eyeing him with reservation.

Jessie Colton was quite stunning and not shy about flaunting it. She wore a teal formfitting dress that hugged her thin, almost frail frame. Her chin-length bob was bottle blond, bright and free of any gray strands. She was immediately dismissive, ready to close the door in his face, until he flashed his badge and identified himself. After that, she was far more amenable to having a conversation.

"How can I be of assistance, Lieutenant Wright?" Jessie asked. "It must be serious for you to come all the way from Owl Creek." She batted lengthy lashes and gave him a bright smile. There was no missing the bright blue eyes that Lizzy had inherited.

"I'm here about your daughter. I was wondering when you last saw her?"

Jessie suddenly looked annoyed. "Has Sarah done something I need to be aware of? You raise your children to be upstanding citizens, but you never know what they do once they are out of your sight and your home."

"I'm here about Lizzy Colton," Ajay said.

The woman visibly bristled. "Why would you come here about Lizzy?"

"You are her mother, is that correct?"

She smiled again, seeming to think how she should answer. "Lizzy lives in Owl Creek with her father, Buck. I've not seen her in years. Divorce is so difficult for children, especially when one parent fights to keep the other away. Buck Colton was not the father some people think he was. He ripped those children from me when they were small and made it difficult for me to be a good mother to them. As you can see, I successfully moved on with my life. God has blessed me immensely."

Ajay nodded. "Are you acquainted with a man named Tiberius Wagner?" He studied her expression intently, noting the rise in her eyebrows and the slight quiver above her top lip.

She shook her head. "No. No. The name's not familiar."

"I understand he's affiliated with the Ever After Church. You are also a member, is that correct?"

She smiled brightly, the glaze in her eyes shifting. "Pastor Acker is a wonderful man of God. His ministry has many followers. I, personally, do not know them all. Now if you have no further questions, I need to prepare for Bible study."

"I appreciate your time," Ajay said. He passed her one of his business cards. "Should you hear from Lizzy, I'd appreciate if you'd give me a call please."

That smile pulled full one last time. "I don't anticipate hearing from her," the woman said sternly. She closed the door between them.

As she moved past the door's sidelights, Ajay watched her shred his business card into small pieces and drop them into a trash can.

Ajay blew a gust of stale air past his lips. He'd hit a dead end, but he was grateful to know that Lizzy hadn't reached her mother and that he'd been wrong. But he needed to find her in case she was still considering a family reunion. After meeting Jessie Colton, he could tell that such a get-together would not go well for Lizzy.

Now, he needed to find her more than ever.

When Lizzy opened her eyes, she didn't know where she was, how she'd got there or how long it had been. She vaguely recalled the car accident, being on the phone with Vivian and then blacking out as she tried to maneuver her brother's truck to the side of the road. She had no recall of anything after that.

It was cold and someone had taken her coat and shoes. Again. She suddenly had a déjà vu moment, memories of that cabin flashing before her like Polaroid pictures.

She struggled to sit upright, realizing her feet and hands had been bound with zip ties. Again. All that was missing was the rope that had tethered her to the floor. This time, though, she lay across a metal cot. Her hands were locked around the metal bed frame. The mattress smelled of urine and sweat. A wool blanket had been tossed across the foot of the cot, but she refused to let it touch her skin if she could avoid it. What looked like blood darkened one end, and dirt and filth soiled the other.

The room was small and smelled of dampness and mildew. Lizzy assumed it was a basement. There were no windows, and the concrete walls and floor were weathered and stained. A single lightbulb hung from the ceiling, casting more shadows than light around the room. There was a single steel door leading into and out of the space, and Lizzy was alone.

She slowly assessed her situation, reminding herself of everything Ajay had taught her. Although she was scared to death, she knew she needed to stay as calm as possible. She assumed the door was locked, and she would have to pay attention when someone entered or exited. There was a commode and sink in the corner, but nothing that could easily be used as a weapon.

Until she understood the severity of her situation, there was little she could do but sit and wait. She suddenly regretted the rage that had moved her to toss away the tracking bracelet. She only hoped Ajay wouldn't give up on her, because she needed to trust that he would go to hell and back to find her, whether he told her about it or not.

Ajay was coming. She just needed to be ready to fight if he didn't get there in time.

Ajay had almost made it home when his cell phone rang. He snatched it from the console, praying that Lizzy had listened to one of his many messages and was returning the call. But it was Max on the other end.

"Hey, where are you?" Max asked.

"About thirty minutes from Owl Creek. Have you heard from Lizzy?"

Max hesitated, and the sudden quiet put Ajay on edge.

"What's wrong?"

"There's still no sign of Lizzy, but they found my truck. It was involved in a single-vehicle accident about thirty miles from your house. Someone drove it into an embankment. The airbags deployed, but there was no sign of the driver. All signs indicate she walked away from the accident unscathed, but there might have been another car onsite. Tire tracks show one leaving the scene. We're pulling camera footage now to see if we can figure out what happened."

Ajay swallowed hard, fighting the sinking feeling in the pit of his stomach. "Do you have any idea where she might have gone, Max?"

"We checked the medical center and called the hospital in Conners. There's no record of her being admitted to either.

She was on the phone with Vivian when the accident happened, but Vivian didn't know where she was. She did say she heard someone talking to Lizzy before their phone line was disconnected. We've come up empty trying to identify who it might have been. The local cops have put patrol cars outside her house, your house and the ranch."

"Where the hell could she be?" Ajay muttered. He was worried before, but now he was genuinely scared for her safety.

"I'm here at the police station," Max said. "Swing by and pick me up."

"Where are we going?" Ajay asked.

Max hesitated one last time. "We need to find Wagner. Ring camera footage from one of your neighbors put him in the area at the time of her disappearance."

This time Ajay paused, pondering what they knew. It wasn't enough to get them to Lizzy before any harm could come to her. Time wasn't on their side. "I'm on my way," he said finally.

Lizzy woke with a start. This time both of her arms were free, and she was no longer tied to the bed frame. A metal chain had been wrapped around her ankle and latched tightly with an oversize lock. And she wasn't alone.

She sat up slowly, gauging the damage to her body. Although she felt bruised, she didn't think anything was broken. Her head still hurt, and she imagined her face slamming into the airbag had probably blackened both of her eyes and maybe even broken her nose. She probably wasn't pretty, she thought, but she could move when it was necessary.

The beady-eyed man stood in a corner by the door. He turned to give her a look, his smile twisted perversely. He wore no mask this time, no longer caring if she saw his face or not. Lizzy knew that didn't bode well for her in the long run.

A greasy bag of food rested on the floor beside her foot, and she knew without looking that it was more than likely a burger and fries.

She looked to the door that had been left open. It seemed to lead into a hallway or perhaps another basement room. She wondered if he would keep it locked and where he kept the key. There was still nothing that could be used as a weapon, and she shook her wrist to see if the bed frame might be easily loosened.

"Who are you, and why are you doing this?" she asked. She did her best to keep the hysteria out of her voice.

The man didn't respond. Instead, he stood staring at her. Time ticked by slowly, and then he moved out of the room, closing the door after himself.

Lizzy pulled her knees up and folded her body into a tight ball. She leaned against the concrete wall. The cold had taken on a life of its own, and it coursed down the length of her spine throughout her entire body. She was shivering, and she could already feel her chest starting to tighten.

If she knew nothing else, Lizzy thought, she definitely knew she was in trouble if Ajay didn't find her soon.

Chapter 17

Ajay and Max stood together in the situation room at the police station. Papers and files decorated the conference room table, and a team of detectives, patrol officers and FBI agents were poring through the entire lot.

"What do we know?" Ajay asked.

Max led the way to a big monitor connected to a computer. Ajay took a step closer as a video began rolling on the screen. The view was his home and the street he lived on. Police had rolled deep, patrol cars parked haphazardly in the road.

He watched as Lizzy sauntered to her brother's truck, her hand resting on the passenger-side door. There was a moment of hesitation, and then she seemed to change her mind. She walked around the front of the truck and paused a second time. She looked one last time toward the house before jumping into the driver's seat. After sitting for a good few minutes, she suddenly engaged the transmission and pulled off down the road.

Ajay glanced at Max, shooting him a look that mirrored her brother's frustration. He turned back to the monitor.

Almost immediately, an older model black Nissan pulled onto the road behind her. It was identical to the car Lizzy had described after her first kidnapping.

Max hit the pause button. "He was watching. He's been watching her for weeks. After sending her that dead bird, I'm sure he knew we would move her from your house to somewhere else. I don't think he anticipated she would be alone. We've also spotted the car on traffic cameras between your house and the accident. There's no way he missed what happened. For all we know, he may have run her off the road."

"What do we know about the car?"

"Nothing, other than there are one hundred and thirty-six cars identical to it registered in a one-hundred-mile radius of Owl Creek, and not one is registered to Wagner."

Ajay clasped both hands together over his head. He leaned back, trying to stretch the knot out of the center of his lower spine. "Do we have any idea where this man is right now?"

Max shook his head. "The FBI raided his home address an hour ago. The place is empty. Doesn't look like anyone has lived there for the past year." He took a deep breath. "I dropped the ball. I should have moved on him days ago, but I needed to know how my mother was involved."

Ajay ignored his comment, not needing to say he'd told him so. "Is it possible that car is registered to someone else close to him? Markus Acker, by chance?"

"We didn't get a hit on any of his known associates."

Ajay tried to consider other options. He suddenly turned and looked Max in the eyes. "See if there's a black Nissan Maxima registered to Jessie Colton at her current address."

Max frowned. "I don't think…"

Ajay stared at him. Understanding swept between them, a silent conversation conveying both men's fears.

Max looked over his shoulder. "Who's working on that Nissan?"

A young woman in uniform raised her hand. "I am, sir!"

"See what's registered to Jessie Colton." He gave the girl the address.

Ajay nodded. "It's a shot in the dark, but we need to take everyone we can. Lizzy's life may depend on it."

Max nodded.

Minutes later, the young woman rushed over and passed Max a sheet of paper. "There's a black Nissan Maxima that's been registered to Jessie Colton for the last two years. But it's registered at a different address."

Max snatched the paper from the woman's hands.

Ajay looked over his shoulder to read it. "Is the address familiar?"

"No, not at all."

"Let's go," Ajay said, rushing for the exit. He called out. "Someone wake up the judge and get me a warrant!"

"We need backup," Max yelled. "I want cars rolling now! And send a unit to pick up Jessie Colton. We need answers, and we need them now!"

Lizzy stared up at the ceiling, taking notice of a large spider and its web in the corner. She felt cold, but she was sweating profusely. She knew it had to be a fever. *Just my luck*, she thought, *first I get abducted, then I catch pneumonia again. If it's my time*, she mused, *let me die from this damn cold before that creep gets a chance to torture me.*

You're not going to die. I won't let you.

Lizzy's head snapped to the side, her eyes darting back and forth. She could hear Ajay's voice in her ear, and it surprised her so much that she actually started to laugh with joy. She whispered his name, hoping he would answer, and then she realized she'd been dreaming.

Damn, Lizzy thought. How was it possible that she was in this situation and how was she going to get herself out of it?

Stay focused.

You stay focused, Lizzy thought, a pout twisting her lips. *Always giving someone orders.*

She heard Ajay laugh, and then he kissed her. She liked his kisses. Butterfly wings fluttering against her lips. His touch was like silk passing over her skin. He was teasing her sensibilities. He liked to tease her, and he was good at it.

"Save me, Ajay," she whispered out loud.

I will, he answered. *But let me help you save yourself.*

A loud cough rumbled in her chest. It came and settled somewhere behind her breast.

I'll take care of you, Lizzy.

"Come get me, Ajay! Please?"

I'm here, Lizzy. Don't you worry.

"I have to tell you something," she said. She reached her hand out to press her fingers to his chest.

It's okay. I know.

"But I need to say it!" Lizzy could feel her muscles tightening. It was only three little words, and she couldn't remember if she had ever said them aloud. If Ajay had ever heard them roll off her tongue and past her lips. Just three little words.

Ajay laughed again. *I know. It's okay.*

"I'm dreaming, aren't I?"

Yes. This is a dream.

Lizzy opened her eyes. The room was dark, that one dim light bulb extinguished. Her arm was extended toward the ceiling as if she were reaching for the sky. She dropped her hand to her side and tightened her fingers into a fist. She took a slow, deep breath and then another.

I'm still here! Ajay called out to her. *I'm still here, Lizzy. I'm not going to leave you.*

So she closed her eyes, wanting to dream of Ajay one more time.

* * *

Block. Punch. Elbow. Drop. Punch.
Block. Punch. Elbow. Drop. Punch.
Block. Punch. Elbow. Drop. Punch.
Focus, Lizzy! Focus!

"My head hurts," Lizzy muttered. "I'll practice later."

You need to fight, Lizzy! Block. Punch. Elbow. Drop. Punch.

"I'm tired, Ajay. Please, come save me!"

I'm here. Just stay focused.

"Stay focused. I have to stay focused," she whispered out loud.

The door creaked, and Lizzy opened her eyes to see the beady-eyed man moving into the room. He was muttering under his breath.

She struggled to focus. She needed him to get closer. *Block, punch, elbow, drop, punch.* Ajay's voice had become a mantra, the words spinning over and over in her head. All she had to do was focus, she thought. Focus and run. She pulled herself upright, leaning back against the concrete wall. Focus and run, she thought.

"Please," she begged. "Can I have some water please?"

Draw him in close, she thought. *Then drop him hard.* "Please!"

The man turned and stared at her. Then without speaking, he backed out of the room and locked her inside.

"Next time," Lizzy muttered. "I'll be ready next time."

Something had changed between Ajay and Max. Max was now his brother, too, despite their differences. And his brother was hurting. He owed it to Lizzy to be there for Max as much as he would be there for her.

"I'm sorry," Ajay said, his car careening toward the address logged into his GPS.

Max tossed him a questioning look. "About what?"

"About your mother. I'm sorry for what you and your family have had to go through with her. What you are still going through. It's not fair."

Max turned to stare out the window at the landscape whizzing by. He didn't respond, as if he had no interest in the conversation.

Ajay continued, "I met Jessie. And you were right for wanting to shield Lizzy from her. Lizzy doesn't deserve that kind of hurt. But neither do you." He drove down the center of the road, his lights flashing. His sirens were silent, not wanting to forewarn anyone they were coming.

Max broke the silence. "I appreciate you being there for Lizzy."

"Always," Ajay replied. "She's my heart."

The two men punched fists in solidarity.

In front of them, the road narrowed as they began to climb the mountain, far from Blackbird Lake. The road suddenly turned right, still heading upward. Two quick turns and a lengthy driveway opened to a clearing in the woods. A small home sat centered on the lot, and parked in front was a Nissan.

Ajay had cut his lights one turn back, so everything was pitch-black, with the exception of a single light in a front window.

"Guns blazing?" Max asked.

"Shoot first, figure it out later," Ajay replied.

Max sat reading a message on his cell phone. "Backup is ten minutes away, and we got our search warrant."

"I'll knock on the front door," Ajay said.

Max nodded as the two men exited the vehicle. "I'll go around back," he whispered.

Pumpkin was glued to Ajay's leg, watching his every move in order to figure out her own. Approaching the home, he could see how dilapidated the structure was. It didn't appear that anyone had lived there for a long while, but a radio was playing loudly inside. The station was local. One of the Christian stations at the University of Idaho Boise.

At the front door, Ajay tested the handle, surprised when it turned and opened. He slowly pushed the door and stepped inside.

It took a quick minute for his eyes to adjust to the darkness. The home was devoid of furniture, nothing to impede his search. His service weapon was drawn, and he swung left and then right, stepping carefully as he checked for whomever was in the house.

A pot rattling in the kitchen led him in that direction. With the precision of a cat stalking prey, Ajay eased his way down a short hall and peered into the room.

Wagner stood over a small Bunsen burner, boiling a small pot of water. He was humming along with the radio, declaring his love for Jesus.

Ajay braced his body and announced himself. "Owl Creek Police! Tiberius Wagner, you are under arrest. Put your hands up!"

Wagner turned, surprise blanketing his face. He froze, his beady eyes shifting as he contemplated his next move. His gaze shifted from the pot of hot water to the large butcher knife resting against the table and then to the door. He wasn't prepared when Max moved in behind him and pressed his weapon against the back of his head.

"Give me a reason," Max said. "Get on your knees."

Wagner slowly lifted his hands in surrender. He dropped to his knees.

Ajay holstered his weapon. He moved behind the man and secured his hands. Then he lifted him back to his feet and pushed him into the only chair in the room. "Where's Lizzy Colton?" Ajay asked.

Wagner didn't reply. He dropped his head against his chest and closed his eyes. He began to pray, an invocation designed to give him absolution for his sins.

Max was racing from room to room, searching for his sister. When he came back into the kitchen, he shook his head, coming up empty.

"Where is she?" Ajay asked again.

Wagner opened his eyes to stare up at Ajay. "She is with our heavenly father. She is blessed."

Ajay felt his breath catch in his chest. "And where might your father be hanging out today?"

"How dare you mock our faith! You will never understand."

Max punched him. Hard. Sending the man back down to the floor.

Ajay knelt down to stare at him. "I understand that if you don't tell me where she is, you very well may meet your heavenly father sooner rather than later."

Wagner closed his eyes and began praying again.

Sirens sounded in the distance. The cavalry coming to render aid.

"You got this?" Ajay asked Max.

Max nodded.

A large flashlight lay on the counter, and Ajay picked it up and turned it on. The light was bright, illuminating a wide area of space.

Ajay whistled, and Pumpkin jumped, her stance tight. "Find Lizzy," he said. "Go get your girl!"

With her head down, Pumpkin raced through the home and returned to the kitchen. She scratched and barked at the back door. Ajay opened it and rushed behind her as she took off into the woods. He raced after her, passing two uniformed officers headed inside. "You two with me," Ajay yelled.

Pumpkin darted across the cleared expanse back to the tree line. She was determined as she led Ajay along a trail that had been recently cleared. Less than a mile ahead, Pumpkin came to a stop and sat down, barking once for Ajay's attention.

At the end of the trail was a concrete structure with a single door. Someone had built what appeared to be a bomb shelter, hidden behind piles of melting snow and stacks of lumber. There was a lock on the door, and Ajay fired his weapon, ripping into the metal. He snatched what remained of the lock away, tossing it to the ground.

Inside, steps led them down to another locked door. This time the lock was a dead bolt. Pumpkin had followed him, and she barked excitedly.

Opening the second door, Ajay was thrown off by the darkness. There was a single light and switch, but the bulb had blown. He pointed the flashlight inside, slowly moving it from one corner to the other, and then he called Lizzy's name.

She lay in the fetal position, her body curled tightly against a metal cot. Even in the dim light he could see that she wasn't well, every ounce of color drained from her face. She was shivering and all he could think was to get to her side and wrap himself around her. He suddenly realized that if anything happened to Lizzy, there would be hell to pay. No one and nothing could stop him from enacting revenge against whoever was involved in doing this to her. Even if one of those persons was Jessie Colton. He turned to the man behind him before rushing forward.

"I need an ambulance. Now!"

Lizzy couldn't imagine her dreams being any sweeter. Ajay held her hand and caressed her cheek. There were more kisses and gentle touches, and she knew that nothing could ever break their bond. Not even her own bad behavior. He was her friend first, and one day, he would be her lover and maybe even her husband and the father of her babies. One day when all this bad business was finished with. She could hear him in her ear, and she smiled.

You came!

I promised you I would.

Will you save me?

I'm right here.

We should name the twins Hope and Faith.

Hope and Faith.

Those are good names, right?

Very good names.

I was ready to save myself so I can be a good mother to your sons.

You will be a great mother. And I'm here now to save you.

You promise?

I promise!

Lizzy opened her eyes, the sweetest dream fading in the chilly air. She was being lifted onto a stretcher, warm blankets tucked around her body. Something licked her cheek, and she frowned. Then the softest whimper in her ear lifted her smile. She murmured, her voice barely a whisper, "Pumpkin!"

Ajay leaned down and kissed her forehead. "Hey, there! Everything's going to be okay. I'm right here, too!"

"Ajay!" Lizzy's smile widened. "I have something I need to tell you!" She gushed, happiness spilling over each word. "I love you!"

Ajay pressed his cheek to her cheek and whispered into her ear, "I love you, too!"

Chapter 18

Tiberius Wagner was arraigned at the Owl Creek courthouse on charges of kidnapping, stalking, assault and obstruction. Ajay testified before the grand jury to secure his indictment and would be there front and center when he went to trial.

Testifying in detail about all that had happened and sharing what had happened at his interview after Wagner's arrest only served to make Ajay angry. Reflecting back on it, he was once again ready to punch something.

"Why Lizzy Colton?" one of the detectives had asked.

Wagner's smile was arrogant and condescending. "I did as my Lord and Savior commanded."

"So God told you to terrorize and kidnap her?"

"She is a gift to he who is a true believer."

"And you are a true believer?"

"I am a man of faith. I honor the commands as they are given to me."

"Help me understand," the detective said as he scooted his seat up closer to Wagner. "You were commanded by God to kidnap a woman as a gift to yourself for being a believer?"

"My God is a kind and generous God. You have only to trust in his word and follow his law, and you, too, will be blessed abundantly."

Standing on the other side of the two-way mirror, Ajay and

Max had both been ready to go in and tear the man's head off. The questioning had continued, but when he was asked about Markus Acker and the Ever After Church, as nicely as he'd been ready to share before, Wagner shut down, refusing to utter another word. He had not spoken to anyone since, not even to his attorney to assist in his defense.

Markus Acker and the Ever After Church had disavowed any knowledge of Wagner's actions. They proclaimed him a once-loyal brother who had gone rogue. Pastor Acker had been eager to offer prayer for Lizzy and counsel for the family if they had need of his services.

Jessie Colton had also distanced herself from Wagner, proclaiming no knowledge of him using her property for any illicit dealings. Her car, her keys and that dilapidated building had been stolen with her having no knowledge of when or how. In fact, she was adamant that she had never met the man. Publicly, she asked for prayer for her daughter. Tears dampened a tissue when she gave a statement to the local media. Privately, she still hadn't bothered to check on Lizzy's well-being.

Ajay entered the hospital in Conners, meeting Malcolm and Max as they were making their exit. They both greeted him warmly.

"Lizzy said you pulled a double shift last night," Malcolm said.

He nodded. "Some hikers got lost on the trails leading to the other side of the mountain. It was a good rescue. How's my girl?" he asked.

"Mean!" Malcolm quipped.

Max laughed. "She's ready to be out of this place and home with you."

"I offered to stay at the ranch with her, but she's insisting she's not going back unless it's just for Sunday dinner."

"That's what she told us."

"We hate it for you," Malcolm teased.

"How's it going?" Ajay asked Max. "I heard you're leaving the FBI officially for the second time." He chuckled.

"I'm gone for good this time. No special assignments. No favors. Nada. Nothing. I'm past the point of being burned-out and I'm ready for a change. They have my badge, my gun, and I've signed all my pension papers. It doesn't get any more official than that."

"He's going to make furniture," Malcolm said as he rolled his eyes.

"And maybe I'll work an occasional search and rescue with my wife."

"Sign me up," Ajay said.

"Lizzy said you plan to take some time off when they release her?"

"I'm thinking the two of us could use a vacation. Maybe a tropical paradise somewhere warm."

"Don't tell, Della," Max said. "She's been aching for a beach trip somewhere since I met her."

Ajay laughed. "That's where I got the idea!"

The two brothers turned toward the hospital exit. "You take care," Max called out. "We'll talk soon."

"Christmas Day soon!" Malcolm interjected. "And don't forget to bring me a big present."

Ajay smiled as he moved on to Lizzy's room. At the door, laughter rang loudly into the hallway. Buck was telling one of his famous dad jokes, and Lizzy was giggling like a third grader.

"Whenever I try to eat healthy, a chocolate bar looks at me and Snickers."

Lizzy giggled. "Daddy, that is so bad."

"But you laughed, sweet girl!"

"I did!" Just then, Lizzy's eyes widened as she saw Ajay standing in the doorway. "Ajay! I was beginning to think you forgot about me."

"Not in this lifetime or any other," Ajay replied as he leaned to press his lips to hers. He shook hands with her father. "How are you doing today, Buck?"

"I'm doing good, son. Happy to see my baby girl happy. You need to keep up the good work."

Ajay grinned. "You can count on me, Buck! Where's Mama Jen? Did I miss her?"

"She's babysitting this evening. Greg and Briony are having a date night. I'm headed over to give her a hand. They like my jokes."

Lizzy giggled. "I like your jokes, too, Daddy!"

"We'll come check on you tomorrow, sweet girl!"

"I'll be at Ajay's house tomorrow," Lizzy said.

Ajay eyed her with a raised brow. "You will?"

Lizzy nodded. "They're releasing me. The doctor said I could go home as soon as my ride got here!"

Ajay and Buck laughed.

"I guess that's you, Uber Wright," Buck said with a hearty chuckle.

"I guess it is, sir! I guess it is!"

Buck said his goodbyes, promising to run by Ajay's house to make certain she was settled. Visiting hours were coming to an end, and Lizzy was getting restless waiting for her discharge papers.

"Are you certain you don't want to go to the ranch?" Ajay asked.

"I'm positive. Unless you'd prefer I not impose on you?"

"It's not an imposition. You know how much I want you there. It makes it easier for me to keep an eye on you."

"How did things go in court?" Lizzy asked, her tone losing that joyful lilt.

"Bail was denied. He is never going to set foot outside of a jail cell ever again."

She blew out a sigh of relief. "I started therapy today, and I really like my therapist."

"That's great! The healing process is going to require a lot of work on your part, but it's nothing you can't handle."

Lizzy smiled. She twisted the beaded bracelet on her arm, feeling safe with it on and having vowed to never take it off as she had done weeks earlier. "I think we should go home and celebrate."

"Anything in particular you think we should do to celebrate?"

She lifted her eyebrows suggestively, and Ajay laughed. "Something tells me you're going to be insatiable," he said as he eased into the hospital bed beside her.

"I'm a lot to handle, but I think you'll do just fine."

They shared a kiss, melting slowly into the moment like freshly lit candles. Ajay's hands danced across her back and settled against the curve of her buttocks. His fingers burned hot against her skin, the warmth spreading throughout her entire body.

Lizzy suddenly pulled herself away from him. "I had the most interesting dreams about you," she said, matter-of-fact.

His smile lifted his eyes, his gaze dancing over her face. "The doctors said it was the fever."

She nodded. "If you say so."

"I do."

"I've been thinking about our future babies."

He laughed again. "Four sons and twin daughters, correct?"

"I was thinking about names."

Ajay shook his head. "That was definitely the fever," he said teasingly.

"Maybe, but out of curiosity, what names would you give our twin girls?"

"Really, Lizzy?"

"Play along, Ajay. It's therapeutic for me."

He sat back against the bed pillows and contemplated her question. Finally, he answered, "I think Hope and Faith would be great names for twin girls."

Lizzy grinned. "Hope and Faith?"

"And since it's almost Christmas we could save the names Rudolph, Donner, Dasher, and Blitzen for those four boys!"

Lizzy laughed until tears rained out of her eyes. "I don't think so," she said.

Ajay shrugged. "Then let's go with Matthew, Mark, Luke and John."

Lizzy wrapped her arms around his neck and pressed her lips to his. "Hope and Faith," she repeated. "Those names sound like something I might have dreamed."

"It was a good dream then."

"It was about you."

He kissed her again. "Then it was a dream come true."

"Yes, you are, Ajay Wright! Yes, you are!"

He smiled. "I love you, too, Lizzy Colton! I love you, too!"

* * * * *

Chapter 1

Special task force.

Those words swirled through Gavin Hayes's mind as he prepared himself for a morning in the waters around New York City.

He stared up at the beautiful stretch of the majestic Verrazzano-Narrows Bridge as his police boat moved through the tidal strait that separated Brooklyn and Staten Island on their way toward the Statue of Liberty. The bridge's arches speared toward the bright blue early spring sky, a testament to man's ingenuity and sheer prowess at building over, around and *through* nature.

He was on a patrol shift, and while they had no overt mission at the moment, he had no doubt something would come in before the day was out. He'd worked two recovery jobs yesterday and had done structural checks the day before that. So it was a nice change of pace to just be out on the water, focused on the city that rose up as majestically as the bridge.

The quiet moments were also just low-key enough that he had plenty of time to think through Captain Reed's invitation to join a special task force in collaboration with the Feds, the Coast Guard and the DA's office.

It was a welcome change from the endlessly roiling thoughts that hadn't left him since welcoming in the new year with a gorgeous redhead who'd fled on New Year's Day never to be seen or heard from again.

Put it in the past, Hayes. Firmly in the past.

There were bigger challenges ahead. Ones that he had some control over. Unlike the reality of being left all alone around three in the afternoon after the most incredible sex of his life.

Which was only a small portion of the problem. The bigger issue was that the sex—amazing as it was—had only been the physical outcome of the most extraordinary eighteen hours he'd ever spent with another person.

Sera.

He could still feel her name on his lips and could still picture the way a lock of her deep auburn hair lay over her cheek as she slept.

Damn, he needed to let this go.

Because all he had were the memories of those eighteen hours and her first name.

He caught the light spray of water as it foamed up from the boat's wake and imagined it as a cool slap in the face.

Let.

It.

Go.

It was time. He had an exciting new opportunity in front of him and recognized it would be a challenge. A task force full of large governmental entities was a big deal. But the moment you mixed local and federal jurisdictions, things could get sticky quickly.

As much as that was true, he also recognized that New York was different. And while everyone liked returning to their own corners at the end of the day, everyone also understood that governance and security in the largest city in America was unique.

Which only added to his excitement. He'd worked his tail off to make the Harbor team, and he loved what he did in the water, but he also saw it as a path toward his future. The men and women who worked the Harbor team might have expertise in diving, but they were NYPD cops, and as such, he wanted to make detective and continue his progression up the ranks.

The task force would go a long way toward supporting those ambitions.

It was also an opportunity to show what Harbor could do. While he'd felt respected from day one, the uniqueness of his job and the work they did wasn't as well understood by outsiders. Joining a team with federal as well as local government resources would give him an opportunity to raise the profile of their diving work, too.

While there was a lot of overlap between the Coast Guard's responsibilities and the Harbor team's, there were significant differences as well. The Coast Guard's remit was far broader, including search and rescue, marine safety and fisheries law enforcement. Gavin and his team supported search and rescue in extreme circumstances, but their work was far more narrowly defined in the realm of public safety and police work, and specific to the waters surrounding the city.

As such, there was clear sharing of jurisdiction in a way that provided minimal friction and maximum benefit to the city of New York.

Especially because once a problem hit Atlantic waters, the Coast Guard took over.

He understood it, Gavin thought as he looked out over the harbor, the Statue of Liberty growing larger as they narrowed the distance. The work. The jurisdictions. Even the politics.

And when you understood something, you could influence the good and help support change of the not-so-good.

"Gav!"

He turned to find their dive lead for the day, Detective Wyatt Trumball. Wyatt had been a force for change on the Harbor team, leading several cases over the past few years that had been both high-profile and well-executed to ultimately help reduce crime in the city.

It had also led him to his new wife, Marlowe McCoy. Granddaughter of one of the 86th Precinct's most respected detectives, Anderson McCoy, Marlowe was practically a legend in her own right in their Sunset Bay neighborhood. She was the precinct's favorite lock-and-vault technician and was frequently pulled in on jobs to help open recovered items in the course of casework.

A series of safes, strapped to bodies, that Gavin and Wyatt had pulled up early last fall had been a huge case for the Harbor team.

One that had also created the unexpected proximity for Marlowe and Wyatt to fall in love. Sadly, the case also brought the disturbing news that her grandfather had used his well-respected position of authority in the precinct to hide Marlowe's father's misdeeds decades ago.

They'd all reeled from that unsettling revelation, and the lingering fallout hadn't fully subsided, but Wyatt had held up well under it and so had his new wife. Anderson had come clean and, while not fully exonerated, had been able to avoid jail time due to his overarchingly positive contribution to the NYPD. Now working off his remaining debt in volunteer service, the man was doing some great things with an at-risk youth program several days a week.

Was it justice?

Gavin knew there were several around the 86th who didn't

think so. But others who had already seen some improvements in those at-risk youth thought the tradeoffs were more than fair.

"Hey." They shook hands in greeting.

Wyatt had already been in the wheelhouse when Gavin boarded, so they'd missed initial hellos as they'd started their shift. Wyatt settled in against the rail as the boat steadily navigated through the harbor.

"Heard the good news about the task force."

"Word travels fast."

Wyatt smiled before shrugging. "When the captain asked for recommendations, there was no one else who came to my mind. I couldn't put you forward fast enough."

Although they'd always had a good relationship, the endorsement went a long way.

"Thank you."

"You're going to knock this one out of the park."

"It'll reduce my time on Harbor for the next few months."

It was the only fly in the ointment of the opportunity, and Gavin had weighed that aspect when Captain Reed first approached him.

"Which will be a loss for us," Wyatt acknowledged, "—but you have to do this. The opportunity's too big, and frankly, it's time to spread your wings a bit. Good things happen here, but the only way we keep getting better is to expand perspective and grow our talent."

This mindset was a key element of Wyatt's management. Even bigger than that, it was the ethos of the entire 86th Precinct they were part of in Brooklyn. Under Captain Dwayne Reed's leadership, those who showed promise were given opportunity.

And, in a virtuous cycle, because people knew there was

opportunity, they worked harder and smarter and more collaboratively for it.

"I do think I can make a difference." Gavin said it because he believed it. Way down deep.

"I know you can."

"Speaking of different, how's married life treating you?"

Wyatt had only returned from his honeymoon a few weeks before. "Married life is amazing. Marlowe is incredible. And she proved just how awesome she is by indulging me in a honeymoon full of diving in Grand Cayman."

It was good to see his friend so happy. More, Gavin admitted, it was encouraging to see him come out the other side. The case that had pulled him and Marlowe together had been difficult, for the work itself, the impact on the precinct and the fact that Marlowe's father was murdered in the process.

He was well aware that sort of grief didn't just vanish, but it was good to see people he cared about showing signs of moving past it with the right partner to make it through.

Sometimes the right people did find each other.

It was a sobering thought, especially when all it did was bring to his own mind images of deep blue eyes and lush auburn hair.

Shaking it off, Gavin gave Wyatt a hearty slap on the back. "So you spent two weeks with an amazing woman and crystal-blue water, and now you're back here."

He and Wyatt turned to look over the other side of the railing. Although the Hudson had improved considerably over the past decade, the river still surrounded a major city, in a shade of blue that bordered on gray. Along with the less-than-appealing color, they regularly dived through all manner of undesirable things.

Wyatt nodded, his grin broad and most definitely sincere. "A dream all its own."

Gavin recognized those words for truth just as a shout went out from the wheelhouse. They were heading up toward the George Washington Bridge for evidence recovery after an accident.

And as he slipped into the cold, late March water under the bridge ten minutes later, clad head-to-toe in his gear, Gavin couldn't help but grin. He really was living the dream. Wide awake, full of the sweetest adrenaline, every damn day.

Now if he could only get a certain redhead out of his nighttime ones.

Serafina Forte reached for the clean tissue she'd had the foresight to stuff into her suit jacket pocket and wiped her mouth as she got up from the floor beside the toilet. She'd gotten lucky this afternoon. The ladies' room at the courthouse was empty, and she hadn't had to worry about being overheard.

A fate she had failed to escape several times over the past few months. A woman could only claim a winter stomach bug or a "touch of food poisoning" so many times.

The only upside to her daily visit to the ladies' room— and really, what idiot called it *morning* sickness when her visits could happen at any time?—was that she hadn't put on much weight. Her body was still changing, though, and she could see that in the fit of her work suits.

A fate that was going to catch up with her before she knew it.

With a sigh, she laid her head against the cool tiles of the wall, grateful she'd chosen the last stall so she could give the misery in her stomach time to settle a bit.

What was she going to do?

The question had been her constant companion for the past two months since she'd discovered her pregnancy and, as of yet, she hadn't come up with much beyond *take it one day at a time*.

Perhaps the advice she should have taken was *don't have amazing sex with a man you've known five hours as a way to ring in the new year*.

It seemed sound and eminently smart now, but was nowhere near as loud as the clanging voice in her head—one that had echoed through her body—on New Year's Eve. That night, all she wanted to do was get as close to Gavin as possible.

Gavin.

That was all she knew. His name was Gavin, and he was a cop. They'd met at a local bar in Brooklyn and had struck up a conversation so engrossing it had taken a while for them to realize their friends had moved on to another party down the street.

Neither one of them had cared.

They'd agreed to only discuss who they were in broad strokes, which is why she'd only told him she was a lawyer, not an ADA with the city. And all she knew was that he was a cop. Since the NYPD employed roughly 36,000 people, it was a bit of a needle in a haystack.

Even if he'd wanted to get a hold of her, she hadn't made that easy, fleeing his apartment after a bout of lovemaking that had left her breathless.

And scared.

Because people didn't feel this way about each other— or have this sort of reaction to one another—that quickly after meeting.

Hadn't she learned that young?

And hadn't she been paying the price ever since?

Since that thought only produced profound misery, pregnant or not, Sera shook it off and pondered, yet again, how she could have played this differently.

They'd gone to his apartment, and it had been full of boxes. When she'd teased him on his decorating skills, he'd confirmed that he was moving in a few weeks. It was the perfect segue into a congenial conversation about why he was moving and did he like his building and where was he going?

Only their need for each other had taken over and they'd ended up kissing against said boxes, evaporating any questions she might have asked about where he was moving *to*.

Which now only left her with one dead end and absolutely zero lines to tug.

She had no last name. No cell phone. No known address.

And she was pregnant with his child.

On a sigh, she pushed off the wall and fixed her skirt. She slipped a breath mint out of the package she'd taken to carrying in her other jacket pocket and smoothed her hair.

Between her crushing workload, her random acts of morning sickness and her endless mooning over Gavin, she'd sort of drifted through her days—and nights. She needed to get her head back in the game.

Today's case was big, and it meant they could get a solid handful of thugs out of the local drug trade. She'd prepped well, and she had a strong case. It was time to put her focus back on that and *off* her memories.

Off her worries.

Off her stupidity.

After all, crime in the city didn't stop. And she'd be damned if she was going to let her current lapse in judgment stop her from her work.

She would figure this out. And while it wasn't what she'd planned, in a relatively few short months, she'd have a child. One she was already beyond excited to meet. That was her reality, and her child needed to be her full focus.

Not the child's father.

And not the way she'd become pregnant.

Even if she did look for him every time she walked the neighborhood. She'd even tried going back to their bar a few times, although once she'd realized she was pregnant, she'd switched to club soda instead of her usual wine spritzer as she'd sat alone in the bar, her breath catching in her throat each time the door opened.

But to no avail.

Gavin was a memory, and whether she liked it or not, he was going to stay there.

Their child was her future.

Gathering her things along with her renewed focus, Sera headed for the door and the waiting courtroom. Which made the presence of her boss in the hallway something of a surprise.

"Sera?"

"David. Hello."

David Esposito was a formidable presence in the Brooklyn courts, their district attorney as adept at his job as he was at working the media. Tall and dashing, he had just the right amount of gray in his dark hair to make people feel he had the necessary gravitas to prosecute the criminals of the city and his broad shoulders filled out his suits to perfection. The media loved him, and lucky for her, his ADAs loved him, too.

He had an agile, exemplary legal mind, *and* he was a champion of his people. She loved working for him.

"Do you have a minute?"

"Of course." She moved to take a seat on one of the benches that lined the hallway, but he gestured toward a small meeting room.

"Let's go in there. I want to discuss something with you."

"About the Landers case?"

He smiled as he waited for her to enter the room before him. "I read your brief. You've got it more than well in hand."

Although she appreciated the compliment, it only added to her confusion. But he was the boss, which gave him the right to be a bit mysterious. Resolved to let him tell her in his own time, she took a seat at the small table that filled most of the room.

"I know how hard you've been working, Sera."

"It's the job." She gave a light shrug, knowing that for the truth. "And I love the work."

"Which is what I want to talk to you about."

Although all lawyers were subject to scrutiny and the highest of expectations as to their behavior, the bar was set infinitely higher for the district attorney's office. They were scrutinized, evaluated and, ultimately, held to a standard that was beyond the beyond. She'd always believed herself up to the task, but she knew there would be raised eyebrows as her pregnancy became widely known. She wouldn't be fired for it—she had full confidence on that front—but she would get knowing glances. A fact that would only be further exacerbated by the reality that she wasn't dating anyone.

Was that why David had pulled her into this discussion? Had her bathroom retch sessions somehow tipped someone off?

Her mind raced, and she nearly missed his words until she finally keyed back into what he was saying.

"I'm proud of all my ADAs, but you have to know, Sera, just how much your work stands out. Your dedication and your passion for the law is something to see. Our city is better for it, and my office is better for it."

"Thank you."

"It's why I'm willing to give you time away to take advantage of this opportunity."

"Away?"

He smiled at that, his expression lighting his normally serious face. "I've put you in for a borough-wide task force. It'll be members from my office, the NYPD, the Coast Guard and several federal agencies."

"A task force on what?"

"The drug trade is out of control. The governor and the mayor have been in talks with the Feds, and we want to put a team together to evaluate what can be done with the situation."

"But I'm not a cop. I have no real knowledge of how to apprehend or take down criminals."

"That's why your contributions are so valuable. This is a problem we want to attack from every angle. From the jurisdiction to those running the ops to the way we prosecute. We need every mind on this and all the effort we can muster to get ahead of the enterprising criminals who make New York their home."

It was a huge ask, and her pregnancy flashed quickly through her thoughts as a reason to decline. In fact, she nearly came out with it before Sera stopped herself.

Why say no?

What example did that set for her child? More, what did it say to herself? She was pregnant, not dead. And motherhood aside, she fully expected to have a long career in front of her.

Now would be the worst time to say no.

"I feel like I should ask you a few more questions, but you know I'm in, David."

"I hoped so. Which is why you need to be at the 86th bright and early Monday morning." David leaned forward and laid a hand over the back of hers folded on the table. "I'm going to miss having you in the office, but we'll get your caseload redistributed. I want to keep you on the Landers case as well as the discovery on the Nicholson murders, but everything else will be shared out."

Sera mentally calculated the workload. While both of those were huge cases, the reprieve from her other work would be welcome.

"It's an amazing opportunity, David. I won't let you down."

He gave her hand a quick squeeze before he stood up, effectively ending their meeting. "That thought never crossed my mind."

Sera walked the last few blocks from the subway, her umbrella up, albeit ineffectively, against the howling spring rain overhead. April had come in with a vengeance, and the city felt like it was practically underwater as she dodged puddles and what looked like a small lake at the intersection just shy of the 86th Precinct.

She'd opted for one of her pantsuits, but the thick rain boots pulled up over her calves, her slacks firmly tucked inside, were the height of frump. A fact she'd willingly overlooked as she anticipated dry feet for the day. The boots could be stowed in a corner of whatever conference room they'd be stuffed in this morning, so the fashion faux pas wasn't permanent.

She hadn't spent much time at the 86th, but she'd been here before. Captain Dwayne Reed ran an outstanding team, and she always enjoyed working with his officers when it was necessary for a case.

Captain Reed's style of leadership—and his belief in his people—had caught on, and there had been clear winds of change blowing through the other neighborhoods in an effort to emulate the precinct.

We need every mind on this and all the effort we can mus-

ter to get ahead of the enterprising criminals who make New York their home.

David's pitch for the task force had lingered in her mind all weekend as she prepared for this morning. She wanted to start off strong and make a good impression, meeting the other professionals she'd work with for the next several months.

Could they get ahead of the criminal element?

While she wasn't an inherently negative person, she would admit to moments of frustration and disillusionment with the system. Too many criminals flooding the streets. Too few people to catch them and ultimately prosecute them. And a bad life for the ones who were caught, locked up in a system that, while often full of well-intentioned people, was home to many who weren't.

She'd always understood it but had also believed the work she did to serve the goal of justice would result in good outcomes. Even if her pregnancy had made her start to question some of those things and the reality of the world she was bringing her child into.

Her parents had never set a very good example, and she'd had to forge a path forward on her own. It was only recently that she'd begun to wonder if her dogged pursuit of justice was more because of them than in spite of them.

"Sera!"

Saved from her own maudlin musings by the loud shout, she glanced up to see a former law school classmate waving to her from down the hall. Picking up her pace, Sera headed his way.

"Sam, how are you?" They quickly exchanged hugs. "It's great to see you, but what are the odds we're here on the same day?"

"Pretty good if we're both on the new task force starting up this morning."

"You're a part of it?"

He smiled before pointing toward the conference room a few feet away. "I am and will confess to getting here early *and* seeing your name badge on the sideboard. I'm glad we're working together again. I'm representing the local FBI office."

"I'd heard the Feds snapped you up. Lucky for them."

"Lucky for me, too. I love the work."

Although she'd always known she wanted the DA's office, Sera was happy for him. His agile mind and love of complex cases likely made him a huge asset to the government.

"I love it, too, but I do have to say I'm disappointed in us."

"Oh?" His blue eyes widened.

"We're both guilty of that dreaded post-law school sin of spending most of our waking hours together for three years and then abandoning one another for the work after getting out."

"Proof they didn't lie about the work."

She shook her head but couldn't hold back the smile. "I wouldn't have it any other way."

"Me, either."

They found seats at the table and, after settling their things, wandered over to the sideboard to pick up their badges and get some breakfast. Sera eyed the pastries with a bit of caution but was pleased to also see a selection of hard-boiled eggs and some dry toast waiting for toppings.

She hadn't been able to stomach anything that morning but recognized the breakfast foods as a gift of fate. The protein from the egg and the bland toast with a bit of honey on top would go a long way toward keeping her level throughout the introductory meeting. A bit of tepid tea and she'd have a breakfast trifecta that would hopefully stave off morning sickness.

"You always were a healthy eater," Sam whispered, leaning in conspiratorially.

"Not everyone can eat sugared cereals and donuts for breakfast." She eyed his plate, a match for her own. "What happened?"

Although he'd always been a good-natured person, even in the throes of the most difficult exam periods, Sam lit up in a way she'd never seen before. "I'm a man with a fitness plan. And a wedding in three months."

"Sam! That's wonderful." Sera put her plate down and pulled him in for a hug. "Tell me all about her."

"Her name's Alexandra. Alex." He smiled, his gaze going hazy with love. "We met at the Bureau, my second week on the job. She held out for a long time, saying we shouldn't mix personal with work and that it was a bad idea."

Although it wasn't forbidden in the Bureau, Sera could understand the reticence. But she also knew Sam Baxter and figured the woman was a goner when faced with such an earnest and truly wonderful man.

"Is she a lawyer, too?"

"Nope, a field agent. Which puts us in the same office but not working directly together most of the time."

His happiness was electric, and Sera tried to tamp down the small shot of sadness that filled her as she pictured Gavin's face in her mind's eye.

Would it ever fade?

Even as she considered it, she knew the truth. Did she want it to?

And then she pushed it all away and gave Sam another hug. She could be sad in her own time, but there was no call for anything but joy in the face of such good news for a friend.

Which made the hard cough and rough "excuse me" a bit jarring as she pulled back from Sam's embrace.

And turned to find the one man she hadn't been able to forget standing two feet away.

Chapter 2

*S*era.

She was here—actually *here*—with her arms full of another man.

As he tried to maneuver around the hugging couple, Gavin wasn't sure what was more embarrassing. That his heart was exploding in his chest or something worse.

Something that felt a lot like jealousy.

It's just a hug.

With some dude who looked like he'd walked out of the pages of a men's magazine in his perfect suit, crisp red tie and artfully sculpted hair.

Bastard.

Especially since Gavin had forgotten an umbrella and currently felt like a wet junkyard dog after the run from the subway to the precinct entrance.

The perfect specimen of law and order turned and extended a hand. "Hello. I'm Sam Baxter. Local FBI bureau."

"Gavin Hayes. NYPD." He then turned to Sera, his expression carefully neutral. "I'm Gavin."

"Serafina Forte. Brooklyn DA's office."

Her hand slipped into his, and while it was a cordial handshake, he immediately had the memory of their fingers linking together on New Year's Eve as they walked to his apartment.

Something raw and elemental sparked between them, and Gavin purposely pushed it down. Whatever sparks had flared between them three months ago—and obviously still flashed and burned now based on their touch—had no place here. This was his shot. His appointment to the task force was an essential step in matching his ambitions to the outcomes he wanted at work. And in a span of two minutes, he'd raced through jealousy, envy and embarrassment.

Not the way he'd envisioned his first day on this all-important next step in his career. Yet here they were.

While he'd known she was a lawyer, he hadn't known she was with the district attorney's office. They'd avoided talk of what they did beyond the basics. It had seemed intriguing at the time, the "who do you know" and "what do you do" conversations too mundane for them. Too pedestrian to interfere with the passion that arced between them.

It was only now, face-to-face, that he realized a bit more conversation might have helped in the months that had passed since.

If he'd known she was in the DA's office, he could have…

Could have what?

Gone after her?

Tried to talk to her?

Asked her why she left him?

None of those questions led to good outcomes. Especially because of one, outstanding truth: if she'd wanted to see him again, she'd have found a way.

And she hadn't.

Even with that disappointment, he couldn't fight the bonedeep interest that filled him. That vivid color of her hair was even richer in person than his memories. The sweep of her heavy lower lip still intrigued him, leaving him with the raw, damn near elemental need to draw it between his teeth.

And those eyes.

It was idiotically poetic, but those liquid blue eyes were fathoms deep, full of knowledge and secrets and something that looked a lot like forever.

Which only added to the bad mood that punched holes in his gut.

He'd wondered about her every damn day since the first of the year, and now she showed up on the most important morning of his professional life?

"We were just getting some breakfast." Sera gestured toward the table along the wall lined with breakfast and coffee carafes. "Please, help yourself."

Her voice was low, professional and incredibly polite. Something in it made Gavin wish he could smudge a little bit of that perfection that had gotten under his skin and made him ache.

It was hardly rational. Or fair.

But what about this situation was fair?

Before he had a chance to consider it further, the room was brought to attention, and they were all instructed to get breakfast, pick up their badges and find a spot at the conference room table.

"Looks like the bell for round one," Sam said with a chuckle.

Sera's answering laugh had Gavin crumpling the edge of the notebook he'd grabbed from his locker on the way in, but it *was* enough to pull him out of his thoughts.

Time to get coffee and take a seat as far away from *Serafina Forte* as he could. He had his future to focus on.

And he needed to get his mind the hell off his tempting past.

Gavin was here.

In the room. In the building. And *on* her freaking task force.

Gavin *Hayes.*

He was a cop, and in a twist that she should have seen coming, he worked in the precinct that covered her Brooklyn neighborhood.

What were the odds?

Even as that question drifted in and out of her mind, she had to admit, they were pretty darn good. They had met at a local bar, after all. On some level it was a bit of surprise she hadn't seen him sooner.

Only...

He was here. Now. Back in her life as she embarked on one of the most important opportunities of her career. A three-month task force, the lead had told them during introductory remarks, with a possible extension to a fourth month.

And she was pregnant with Gavin's child.

She'd complete the work, of that she had no doubt. But there was no way she'd complete it without everyone knowing she was pregnant.

Which meant Gavin would know.

Hadn't she wanted that?

She'd gone to their bar several times in hopes of seeing him so she could tell him the news. So she could...

Could what?

Apologize for running out? Apologize for getting scared because she didn't do relationships and she wasn't cut out for the emotional commitment required to be with another person? Even as she'd thought, more than a few times, that emotional commitment might be worth the risk with Gavin.

"The purpose of this task force is to ensure cooperation and collaboration." The moderator's voice cut back into her thoughts, and Sera knew she needed to focus.

She could obsess over next steps later. Right now she had to pay attention and find a way forward.

"We're fortunate in a city this size that there's a strong base of support across federal, state and local agencies, but it needs to be stronger. Tighter. It's the only way we'll maximize our strengths. One and one will make three."

Sera nearly choked on the small sip of herbal tea she'd taken as the moderator's words hung over the room. Unbidden, her gaze drifted to Gavin. He'd taken a seat at the opposite end of the room, but since he was on the other side of the table, she could still see him easily enough.

His dark gaze seemed to see through her, and she had the most absurd impulse to laugh.

Because one and one *had* made three.

The moderator pointed toward a screen at the front of the room and a slideshow presentation she'd used to frame the launch meeting. As the woman flipped to a new slide, Sera directed her attention back to her words.

The first week of the task force would focus on getting to know one another and creating an action plan. Every team would build out ideas on how to address crime, expand a plan for social services and address the legal ins and outs of their ideas. One team would be fully local, one fully federal and then two would be a mix, having one federal team member and one local member. It was, their moderator explained, a chance to collectively review how collaborations could grow and how they would look different with varied perspectives.

Sera had already begun to envision the work she could do if she was paired with Sam. They knew each other and had worked well together all the way through law school, and she had every confidence their collaboration would be strong. She was doing this work so she could improve her relationships with federal jurisdictions in the region. Wasn't that the whole point?

"Serafina Forte, DA's office. Gavin Hayes, NYPD Harbor. You're a team."

Of course we are.

The urge to drop her head to the table was strong, but she kept her gaze straight ahead and didn't dare glance Gavin's way again. Just like she wouldn't lift a fist to the sky and rant and rail that this was all some cosmic mistake.

She did offer a small smile and nod for the moderator in a show of gratitude for the assignment.

Nothing in her life had been normal or usual for three months now. Why should that change?

She jotted down the conference room where she and Gavin would be paired for the day to begin work on their project before gathering her things from where she'd stowed them beneath the table.

But as she glanced down and saw the thick rain boots still wrapped around her calves and her slacks, Sera was sorely tempted to lift that fist.

Could she look any worse?

Since the room was already in motion, there was no time to slip them off and change into the heels buried at the bottom of her bag, so she picked up her things and proceeded toward the door.

Gavin waited for her just outside, and she lifted a hand in a small waving motion. "Let's go, local team."

"Sure."

Ooooh-kay.

What was that joke Sam had made about the bell for round one?

She followed Gavin down the hall and toward an elevator. Several other task force members were with them and their nervous small talk to the others ensured she could avoid talking to Gavin for a few more minutes.

Until they were the only ones left, heading toward the top floor of the precinct.

"Serafina, is it?"

"Sera. I mean, I go by Sera." Damn it, she would *not* stammer before this man. "Serafina is my given name, but I go by Sera." When he only nodded, she pressed for a bit more from him. "And you're on Harbor patrol? Diving?"

The elevator stopped, the doors swishing open on a quiet floor. "That's what I do."

"But you're a cop?"

"Yep."

He was already heading down the hall, and she clomped behind him in the damn boots, each step a sort of squeaky *thwap* on the ground.

Irritation spiked at the quick dismissal and the feeling of following him. They hadn't followed each other three months ago. Instead, there'd been a sort of *entwining*. An equal footing that had engaged them both and pulled them forward with an elemental tug she'd never felt before.

But this?

He had a cold, almost military demeanor. His back was so straight and his gaze deliberately held straight ahead.

Well, fine. She could give as good as she got.

Even as she nearly slipped over her squeaky boots when a terrible, awful thought filled her.

What if he didn't remember her?

Gavin caught her just as she reached out to grip the doorframe to their small conference room. She straightened herself, unwilling to read too much into the fire radiating up and down her arm where he'd held her, firm yet gentle, just above the elbow.

"Thank you."

He dropped his hand and just nodded.

God, why did she feel so clumsy? And so off her game?

She hadn't felt this way three months ago. Sure, she'd been a bit nervous, but their time together had seemed to melt away any nerves or concerns. They'd just been Sera and Gavin, and it had been...

Well, it had been wonderful.

And now they were here, and they both had to make the best of it.

But how had she managed to forget just how good he smelled? And exactly how broad his shoulders were? And...

And she needed to get her damn head in the game because there was no way she was going to let a single bit of whatever happened to them three months ago ruin this. She was highly competent, and this task force was a shot at her future.

Mooning over Gavin was *not* the way to start it off right.

So she marched into the room, her head held high, her bearing damn near regal.

She could *do* this, she thought, a fierce sort of righteousness welling up inside of her. She *would* do this.

The conference room might be roughly the size of a broom closet, but she deliberately selected a spot on the far side, settling her things on the scarred table. Gavin still stood by the door, his gaze on her when she finally glanced up after carefully placing each of her personal items.

"Serafina?"

"I told you, I go by Sera."

"Fine. Sera."

"Is this room okay?"

"It'll do just fine."

She stared at him, suddenly realizing her mistake in taking the far corner. The windows might be at her back, but she suddenly felt her lack of escape. Or, more to the point, the need to move past him in order to escape.

One more sign she was flustered and off her game. Worse, that she suddenly felt like his quarry, his deep brown gaze seeming to size her up.

Where was that man she'd met on New Year's? The one with the kind eyes and broad smile and caring touch? Had he been an illusion?

She'd lived with the reality of her momentary lapse in judgment for three months now, but she'd never felt that she'd shared herself with a jerk.

A stranger, maybe. But never a jerk.

Resolving to worry about it later, she tapped the folder she'd settled on the desk, on top of the legal pad she'd used to make notes during the initial briefing. "Let's get down to it. We're the local team. Between the police perspective you bring and the legal perspective I bring, we should be able to put together a solid plan of local cross-collaboration."

"I'm sure we will."

Heat filled that dark gaze at her reference to collaboration, but Sera ignored it and soldiered on. "We've all seen the challenges to both our teams with budget allocations, staffing constraints and the overall volume of what runs the streets of the city." She realized her potential misstep and added, "Or fills the waters around it."

"Day in and day out."

"So where should we start?"

He finally took a seat but never touched the folder that had been handed to them during the briefing. Instead, his attention was fully focused on her, nearly pinning her to her seat. "I think the first place we start is with the past."

"Oh?" She dimly sensed a trap closing around her but had no idea why. The city had a legacy of crime—that sort of underbelly was impossible to separate from a place so large—but so much work had been done over the years to make New York not only livable but a truly thriving, positive place to live for its ever-growing population.

"The city does have a history," she agreed. "But this task force really is about the future."

"The task force is, sure. But I'm talking about you and me. And why you walked out on New Year's Day without so much as a good-bye."

Gavin took the slightest measure of satisfaction at the way Sera's throat worked around whatever words she was trying to come up with.

What he couldn't figure out was why the satisfaction was so short-lived. And why this desperate need to question her seemed to live inside of him like some wide open, gaping maw. They were here—as she'd said—to focus on the future. Why tread through a past that had happened months ago and realistically should mean nothing to him?

He wasn't generally interested in one-night stands, but he could hardly say he'd never had sex with a woman he didn't know well. And since his life up to now had been suspiciously devoid of successful long-term relationships, he couldn't understand the weird, swirling emotions this woman churned up in him.

And yet, she did. From the unceasing thoughts of her these past several months to the spears of jealousy at seeing her hug another man, he clearly hadn't moved on the way he should have.

The way he *needed* to.

So maybe just putting it all out on the table would help him get past it.

"Why I walked out?"

"Yes. We had a pretty amazing night. I don't think I gave

any suggestion you needed to leave so quickly, but if I did, I'm sorry."

His apology clearly flustered her, her hand coming up to smooth her blouse.

"We were two consenting adults who welcomed the year in, Gavin. It was great, but all good things have to come to an end, right?"

If he weren't looking so hard, he'd have taken her words at face value. He'd likely have believed her, too.

But the heavy pulse at her throat was evident, as was the barely-there quaver in her voice.

"And now?" he finally asked.

"Now what?"

"Now we're working together. So our good thing hasn't actually come to an end after all."

"Are you suggesting we pick up where we left off?"

She might have been flustered, but he'd give her credit, she could turn on the freeze when she needed to. While something sharp and needy filled him, he was more than aware this task force was a huge opportunity for him. For both of them, no doubt.

Was he even remotely considering muddying the waters with sex?

His body screamed a resounding yes, but the control he was known for somehow managed to prevail at the last minute.

"I'm suggesting we both deserve to go into this partnership fully acknowledging what came before. This is a major step in my career. I have to believe it is for you, too. Not addressing the past is foolish in the extreme." He leaned forward slightly over the table, the incredibly small space ensuring he could see her as clearly as if she were sitting beside him. "Don't you agree?"

That flutter of pulse at her throat never faded, and if he were a fanciful man, he'd say he could practically hear her heartbeat.

But he wasn't given to whimsy. And he had zero illusions about life anymore.

What he didn't expect was her to capitulate so easily. He figured her for a bit more bravado. Maybe even a few excuses. Not the warming of her freeze ray. Or a raw sort of truth that settled hard in his gut.

"We had a lovely night together, Gavin. One I don't regret in any way. But the new day had dawned." She shook her head. "The new *year* had dawned, and it suddenly struck me that sitting around the apartment of my one-night stand wasn't a good look. For either of us, but certainly not for me."

He was tempted to ask again if he'd given her any hint she needed to leave but opted for a slightly different tack. "Did you want to leave?"

"It was time for me to leave."

It was hardly an answer, but it was the one she was willing to give. He could keep pressing and probing, in hopes he'd get a different reply, but why? Worse, why was he hoping for a different answer?

The knock on the door pulled him out of the question without an actual answer, and he turned to find Wyatt Trumball in the doorway.

"Detective." Gavin nodded as he stood. "How are you?"

"Good. I wanted to talk to you about the dive tomorrow morning. I'm sorry I'm interrupting." Wyatt glanced over at Sera, his smile broad. "The task force started today."

"It did."

Wyatt stepped into the small conference room, extending a hand toward Sera who'd already stood to say hello. "Wyatt Trumball, NYPD."

"Sera Forte. I'm with the DA's office."

"So you two are representing the local team."

Since there was little that got past the seasoned detective, Gavin shouldn't have been surprised by the man's ready knowledge of the work, but it still stunned him how much Wyatt actually *knew*.

"We are. We'll present solutions on how the city's resources can work together," Sera said. "I know everyone thinks the solution to this is working with the Feds, and I don't think that's wrong, but I am excited to show what we can do right here, too."

"Everyone thinks bigger's better. But some of the best work I've ever seen has been local teams who know their neighborhoods, working together to get it done."

"Fewer egos?" Gavin asked, his sole intention to make a joke.

Which made it a surprise when Wyatt's demeanor changed. "The Feds have a lot to offer, but they get in the way, too. They think we're rubes who can't see past the end of the block, or they want to run the show."

Coming from a man who was a quintessential team player, Wyatt's words struck hard. But if he were being fair, Gavin had already seen a bit of that posturing that morning. Hell, they were all posturing, trying to prove their worth to be a part of the team. But that tension was there, all the same.

"We'll be sure to keep our guard up," Sera cut in smoothly. "I happen to like my block quite a bit. I think I've got a rather sophisticated approach to the work, too."

Wyatt's smile returned, his grin broad. "Then I say, go get 'em. I know you two will do great. Let me know if you need anything from me."

Gavin nearly let Wyatt walk away before he remembered. "And tomorrow's dive?"

"I just came to give you the oh-so-happy news that we're diving up at Hell Gate tomorrow."

Gavin sensed Sera's attention to the matter but didn't want to give Wyatt any indication anything was off. So he went with his usual good-natured humor. "Lucky us. With all this rain, it'll be sure to be churned up and extra gross."

"Which is why the team can't dive it today. Weather's expected to clear up tonight, and we should have a grand time running evidence recovery. Criminals really do love tossing weapons off the city's bridges."

"Only trains run over Hell Gate," Gavin said. "Someone was dumb enough to try to cross electrified train tracks on foot?"

"Not quite that bad but not much better. Someone ran across the RFK Bridge on foot."

"In the middle of traffic?"

"Yep. Slammed on the brakes when he realized the cops in pursuit were getting close. He jumped out of his car, then raced through traffic to the first break in fencing he could find. Tossed the weapon as hard as he could north." Wyatt smiled, his hands up in the air in a what-can-you-do gesture. "We're the ones who get to go find it."

Wyatt made his good-byes, and it was only as Gavin took his seat again that he caught Sera's gaze.

"It's really called Hell Gate?" she asked, a small furrow lining her otherwise smooth brow.

"Yep. The upper portion of the East River. We'll be in the area underneath the RFK Bridge and a little farther north probably."

"Wow. I—"

"What?"

"It sounds dangerous, is all."

"It's one of the tougher waterways, but that's why we dive

in pairs and have a team working around us, also keeping close watch."

"Sure. Of course. It's just that I…" She stopped again, seeming to gather her thoughts. "I didn't realize just how difficult your job was. Anyone who works in law enforcement has a challenging job with obvious risks. But this sounds like a whole other level."

Although he appreciated the concern and her obvious bother at the work, he wasn't entirely clear where it was coming from. "It's a job I'm trained for. And something I continue to train for regularly. We don't rest on our laurels or ignore our conditioning."

"No, of course not."

"Wow. Be careful there." He gave the warning as he opened his folder, pulling out the briefing sheet they would work against for the next week. He nearly cursed himself for saying anything, but now that it was out, he realized his emotions had about as much finesse as that criminal who'd run out in the middle of traffic.

Emotions he had no business even having.

Way to be an ass, Hayes. You might as well see it through now.

"Be careful of what?"

"All that concern. You keep talking like that, and I might start to think you care."

Chapter 3

I might start to think you care.

That rather dismissive brush-off had remained in the back of her mind all day, through her walk home and on through the preparation of dinner.

And damn it—Sera tossed a potholder on the counter after dumping a pot of cooked pasta and boiling water into a waiting colander in her sink—he'd gotten to her. Yes, it was unexpected to walk into the conference room that morning and see him. And yes, she was fully aware that she was nervous and off her game when the two of them had broken off for their committee work.

But that line? Seriously?

I might start to think you care.

Start to?

What an ass.

Only he wasn't. Despite the tense working conditions and the subtle threads of irritation he wove around her all day, he wasn't a jerk.

She would bet quite a lot on that fact.

The man she'd spent the night with wasn't a jerk. The man the NYPD had selected to represent them on a multi-jurisdictional task force wasn't a jerk. The man who'd *fathered her child* wasn't a jerk.

Unable to pivot well with her reentry into his life? Yeah,

she'd give him that one. But he wasn't a bad person. No amount of conference-room bravado was going to change her mind on that point.

Which meant she needed to double down. Leave her irritation at home and focus on the good that would come of working together.

And oh yeah…tell him she was pregnant with his child.

But how?

While it was incredibly easy to put their night together firmly in the column of sexual attraction, part of why it had been so incendiary had nothing to do with the sex. It had been the connection between them.

They'd spoken freely and easily after meeting in the bar. It was the only way she'd have actually gone home with him, if she were honest. She needed that connection in order to feel it was worth taking things further.

And oh, they had a connection.

She'd laughed easily, and they'd talked of so many things. Their work in broad strokes, yes, but more *why* they were drawn to what they did. How they'd found their paths in life. And what drove them as people.

It had been wonderful to speak freely about her ambition and not feel it was either being judged as too work-focused or worse, threatening somehow that she had goals for herself. Instead, he'd asked her questions and seemed genuinely interested in her answers.

And for her, Sera knew, there was no greater aphrodisiac.

She shook the colander of any excess water before scooping out a portion for herself and the waiting sauce she'd made for it. Although she still struggled with food, especially in the morning, by the time dinner rolled around, she was always hungry and had seemingly gotten rid of that day's roiling stomach acid.

Pasta had been one of her steady cravings over the past few weeks, so she'd taken to making extra and preparing a cold salad with it for the next day's lunch. It wasn't perfect, but it seemed to be working, and her doctor hadn't felt the food was problematic, especially when she'd assured her OB-GYN that she was adding vegetables to the mix.

With dinner in hand, she headed for the small kitchen nook to eat just as a heavy knock came on her front door.

Sera set her plate down on the drop-leaf table nestled in the corner of her kitchen and headed for the foyer. Her apartment wasn't huge, but she had some space in her oversize one-bedroom corner unit, courtesy of an uncle who owned the building and had given her a good deal since she'd graduated from college.

Anyone defending my city deserves to live in a good, safe space while doing it, Uncle Enzo had intoned as he handed over her rental contract.

She half expected it would be him and Aunt Robin at the door, their occasional drop-ins always welcome.

Only to find Gavin on the other side.

"Hi."

He stood there in her doorway, his shoulders set, and her stomach gave an involuntary flip. Damn, why was he so attractive? Tall, broad and extremely fit from the work he did.

All of which was appealing but had nothing on the smile that lifted the edges of his lips. A small bouquet filled his hands, and despite his solid bearing, she could see the slightest hint of nerves in the way his foot tapped lightly on the ground.

"Hey." She fought the small smile of her own that threatened to undermine her attempts at being aloof.

"I'm sorry to bother you."

"It's no bother." She stepped back, extending a hand to allow him in. "Though I am curious how you found me. I work for the DA's office. I don't keep my address in public databases."

"I live in the eternally up-to-date database that is Sunset Bay, Brooklyn." When she must have given him a curious look, Gavin added, "Once I knew your last name, I put two and two together. Your uncle, Enzo Forte, is my landlord. I saw him coming into my building this evening with your aunt and some of their friends and mentioned we were working together."

"My uncle gave you my address?"

"I told him I was a pompous jerk during our first meeting, and I owed you an apology. Your aunt couldn't rush fast enough to give me your address." He held out a hand. "She told me you like Gerbera daisies, too."

"I do."

She took the bouquet—a solid peace offering yet not so large as to appear pompous or as if the flowers could solve everything—and gestured toward the kitchen. "I was about to eat some dinner. Would you care to join me?"

"You don't mind?"

Since she'd already invited him, she just shot him a look and headed for the kitchen and the small pitcher she kept on her windowsill. In a matter of minutes, she had the colorful daisies in the pitcher, settled on the edge of the table where they sat across from each other.

He'd taken the portion of pasta she was going to use for tomorrow's lunch, and as she saw him settle his napkin on his lap, Sera had to admit to herself she didn't mind.

She didn't mind at all.

The pasta wasn't much, but Gavin dug into it like a starving man. If she expected him to complain that her vegetable and herb-filled sauce was missing meat, she soon realized she wasn't going to get it.

Instead, she got the opposite.

"This is really good."

"Thanks." She took a sip of her club soda before returning to their earlier topic. "My aunt and uncle really told you where I live?"

"I'll admit to some surprise on that front as well, but I guess I ooze trust." He grinned at her, that bright flash broad and wide. "It also helps I rented right out of the academy in their building over on Eleventh. They have my credit score, my phone number *and* my address. You know, basically it's like they know how to hunt me down."

"I suppose they could."

And while she did get the local connection, it was clear she needed to give her Aunt Robin a bit of a drubbing on sharing personal information like that.

"The moment I saw them I made the connection with their last name. And then once I mentioned us working together on the task force, that clinched the deal."

Since Sera could also imagine the twinkle that no doubt had lit up her aunt's eyes, she opted to shift the conversation.

"Is your pasta hot enough?"

Although she'd intended the question as a kindness, all it really served to do was show her extreme nerves at his presence in her kitchen. One that had felt a heck of a lot larger before he arrived than it did now.

"The temperature is fine. It's not really why I'm here, though I'll never turn down dinner with a beautiful woman."

"Flattery?"

"Is it working?"

She didn't want to be flattered by the compliment. Even worse, she didn't want to be caught up in him again or the cute banter that was stamped full of notes of appreciation and…*notice*.

Wasn't that how all this had started? That compelling gaze and ability to make her feel as if she was the only woman in the world?

"I also didn't come here to give you a line," he continued, smoothly shifting gears. "I came to give you the apology you most definitely deserve."

"Oh."

"I wasn't the best version of myself today. I knew it, even as it was happening, but I couldn't seem to see past myself, and I am sorry." He set down his fork. "I'm truly sorry for it."

For all that the apology was a surprise, Sera had to admit it fit the man she remembered. What she'd sensed of his character, even after only spending less than a day together. And with that memory came a resolution of her own.

"If we're being honest..." her gaze drifted to the small bouquet "...I'm not above saying the flowers weren't a smooth touch."

"I'm glad you like them."

"But I wasn't my best self, either. I was surprised to see you this morning. And then we were put together for the duration of the task force and—" She couldn't fully hold back the sigh. "It was like my personal life slammed right into my professional life, and I didn't like it."

"Same."

"This task force is an important step in my career growth. I'm sure it's equally important for you."

"It is," he agreed.

"Then we're going to have to find a way to put what happened between us at the holidays firmly in the past."

"Is it?"

His comment sort of hung there between them, like a pulsing question mark hovering over them in blinking neon.

"Is it what?"

"Is it behind us?"

The irrational urge to laugh hysterically at his question suddenly gripped her and she had one terrifying moment where she thought she actually might break down in laughter. Because that night might be over, but nothing about it was behind them. In fact, in six more months the consequence of their choice would be right there in *front* of them.

She'd had their one night together expressly for the lack of strings. Attachments. Or any consequence other than pure, unadulterated need. She wasn't particularly well-versed in doing that, and it had felt good—better than good, actually—to take something just for herself.

Her life had been about studying and remaining focused and living with a strict, almost rigid, code of behavior. She wasn't going to be her mother. And she had no interest in throwing her life away to listlessness or to excess.

And yet, Gavin had somehow found a way beneath that. In the moment, he'd felt like impulse but never excess.

So she took a long, deliberate moment to stare at her fork before lifting it to toy with a few pieces of pasta. "It's all behind us. Of course it is."

"Things ended a bit abruptly."

Whatever distraction her dinner had provided faded as she stared at him head on. "We had a one-night stand, Gavin. By their very definition, they have a short shelf life. A point I've thought was pretty clear based on how neither of us has found the other these past several months."

"Did you try to find me?"

Just like that morning, it was a neat, verbal trap and one she'd walked straight into. Yet even as a part of her wanted to wrap herself up in emotional tinfoil, deflecting the truth with all that she was, she found she couldn't.

"I went to that bar several evenings in hopes I'd see you

again. When you never showed, I figured I wasn't meant to see you."

A series of emotions flashed across his face, telling in that he obviously felt *something* but maddening in that she couldn't actually read a damn thing.

Did he think her needy? Hopeful? Was he glad she'd tried to find him? Or was it more proof what they'd had was only meant to last a few hours?

Which made his quiet, scratchy tone a bit of a surprise when he finally spoke. "If you wanted to see me again, why'd you leave?"

Had she been wrong?

Since there was no way of knowing, she pressed on, willing him to understand her explanation.

"Again, Gavin. New Year's Day. One-night stand. Two strangers. It's sort of the exact definition of awkward."

"It didn't feel awkward."

"No, it didn't."

And when his dark gaze met hers, she had to admit that even now, it still wasn't awkward at all. It was freeing. This strange connection between them that had no reason for existing yet did all the same.

"I wanted to see you again, Sera. I looked for you every time I went out. Each time I walked the neighborhood. Each time I got on the subway."

He'd looked for her? Hoped to see her again?

All those lonely moments, practically willing him to show up at the bar hadn't actually been for naught. Even if they really didn't have a shot at a future, there was a special sort of joy in knowing that he hadn't been unaffected.

And with that knowledge, she couldn't hold back the small smile that she suspected held the slightest notes of sorrow for what could have been. "And here all you really needed to do was call my aunt and uncle. Keep that in mind next time you go hunting for a one-night stand."

"Why would I go hunt for anyone else?"

Whatever humor had pulled at her faded, and something sharp speared through her at the earnest expression that set his face in serious lines.

"This can't go anywhere," Sera finally said, even if she wished she were wrong. "Especially with the task force. It's a conflict now."

"How?"

Whatever outcome he was considering wasn't readily apparent, but the fact he was considering any outcome other than the path they'd been on—going their separate ways—needed to be squelched.

"What do you mean, how? We're partnered on an important work project."

"One that won't last forever. We don't work in the same department. We don't even work for the same entity. Last time I checked, employees of the City of New York can date each other."

"We're not—" She stopped abruptly, catching herself before trying again. "What we had isn't dating. Let's not pretend there's more between us then there actually is."

Sera wasn't quite sure who she was trying to convince, but knew she needed to hold her ground. Because she *had* wanted to see him again. And once she'd gotten over the shock of seeing him again that morning, it had felt so good to be in his presence once more. To look across the table and see that face that had been emblazoned on her mind as if every feature had been captured in indelible ink.

But she couldn't give into this.

Nor could she delude herself into thinking somehow this all had a happy ending. They'd come together in a heated rush and had proceeded to go on with their lives. Only now there was a very large secret between them. One that she knew she had to share.

One that he *deserved* to know.

Yet no matter how she spun it in her mind, she couldn't seem to find the words to tell him the truth.

"But there is something between us, Sera."

Whatever Gavin might question about his feelings and the odd way they'd come in and out of each other's lives— twice now—there was something there.

Wasn't this very conversation proof of that?

Sure, things had had gotten very personal, very fast. That had been true between them from the start. But at the moment, things had also gotten much too serious. So with his dual police *and* dive training in the forefront of his mind, Gavin did what he knew how to do best.

Pivot and attack the situation from a new angle.

"Let's go get some ice cream."

"Now?"

"You ever heard of dessert, Forte?"

"Well, yeah, but—"

He stared pointedly down at his empty plate before looking back up at her. "Do you have ice cream in your freezer?"

"No."

He shook his head and let out a small *tsk* for good measure. "A crime against nature, but we'll address that later. Let's go get some ice cream."

Based on her initial resistance, Gavin figured she'd put up more of a fight, so it was a welcome surprise to find themselves walking into the Sunset Bay pharmacy and heading for their soda counter twenty minutes later.

"Best ice cream sundaes in Brooklyn." Gavin breathed

in deeply of the mixed scents of sugar, cream and chocolate as they took two stools at the counter.

Sera slipped onto the stool next to him, and he took her coat as she shrugged out of it, walking it down to the small coatrack at the end of the bar before returning to her.

"Thanks."

"You're welcome."

As he settled himself on his stool, he couldn't help but notice the two of them reflected in the big mirror that stretched along the back of the soda fountain. Although they didn't touch, they looked like they were on a date, the light tension arcing between them evident even in the old mirror with desilvering in small splotches up and down the length of it.

"This place has seen a lot." He said after a quick glance at his menu.

"It was the heart of Sunset Bay while I was growing up. And even more so for the generation before us. Aunt Robin still talks about how Uncle Enzo brought her here when they were dating."

It was interesting. She'd spoken of her aunt and uncle several times throughout the evening, but still nothing about her parents. Were they absent? Dead? Gavin wondered.

He was about to ask, but a skinny, bored teenager came up to them to take their orders.

"What'll you have?" the kid asked Sera.

"Scoop of chocolate with some peanut butter sauce."

"Banana split for me."

The bored teen trotted off, leaving them to their conversation at the mostly empty counter. It was the distinct lack of people that had him drifting straight back to their unfinished dinner conversation.

"So about this something more between us."

She was in the middle of settling her purse on hooks beneath the counter, her attention focused elsewhere, but Gavin didn't miss the wary lines on her face.

Whatever had gripped her in that moment was gone when she gave him her full focus. Her spine was rail-straight as she sat on the backless stool, and her voice held what he assumed was a match for the formidable tones she'd use in the courtroom.

"There isn't something more."

"Sure there is."

"A single night of passion? And while I won't say it's nothing, it shouldn't stand in the way of what each of us wants to accomplish."

"Why are you so insistent on relating the two things at all?"

"Oh, come on, Gavin. Of course those two things are entwined. They're intimately entwined." She leaned closer before seeming to catch herself. "We've seen each other naked."

While he assumed she'd brought up that enticing fact to make a point, he couldn't help but needle her a bit. "We most certainly did."

"Be serious."

"I'm certainly not laughing. In fact, I'm remembering a few things in rather vivid detail."

"You're impossible."

"And you're combining two things together like they somehow cancel each other out. I'd like to know why."

"My work is important to me."

"As mine is to me."

"We slept together. Do you think anyone on that task force is going to take us seriously if we suddenly start up an affair?"

Although there was a thread of irritation starting to simmer in his blood at her continued pushback, he fought to maintain the steady, easy, nearly carefree notes in his voice. If she didn't want to go out with him, he could live with that. But her arguments centered around what others would think or why they couldn't have a shot at something, *not* basic disinterest.

He just couldn't let it go.

"Two single people having a relationship isn't an affair."

"It is when they're paired up on a work project and keeping it a secret."

"So make it public." As he said the words, Gavin realized them for solid truth. "To my earlier point, it's not a crime if the city's employees date each other."

"That won't keep people from talking."

"So let them talk."

Their ice cream arrived, cutting into the argument that was steadily building between them. He wasn't going to get anywhere in this conversation behaving like a petulant child. And he certainly wasn't looking to date someone who didn't want to be with him.

So why was he pushing this?

He'd never put that much stock in the romance dance. You saw someone. You liked them. You spent some time with them. Was it simplistic? Sure. But he'd always had far more important priorities in his life, and no one had ever made him see a reason to change them.

Until Sera.

Something in that time they spent with each other—less than twenty-four hours of his life—had wrecked him. He hated the vulnerability, but more, he hated the idea that what they did for a living needed to dictate their private moments.

Sera had already taken a few small bites of her ice cream and he opted to dig into his banana split, hoping the mix of sugar and heavy cream would cool their conversation off a bit.

"Can we maybe chalk it all up to a complicated situation that we don't have to decide right now?" she finally asked.

"Yeah. We can do that."

And he could. While he wasn't ready to fully back off, Gavin could appreciate that a lot had been thrown at both of them and a bit of time to figure it out would go a long way.

"How's your ice cream?" He asked, their heated conversation fading. He'd brought her here to take her out for a treat and it was actually quite nice to sit and enjoy her company.

"Delicious. I haven't been here in a while. Dessert was a good idea."

"Sugar usually solves most problems. Or at least makes them seem less fraught."

"As someone who solves problems for a living, I'd like to say we're more evolved as a species, but—" She stared down at her ice cream, tapping the side of the small metal dish with her spoon. "It's hard to argue with sugar therapy."

Their dessert seemed to diffuse the tension that had spiked when he'd brought up their relationship status, and they sank back into that easy conversation that had been there between them from the first.

It ebbed and flowed, until they both looked down and realized they hadn't just finished their dessert, but their dishes had long been whisked away by the bored server.

With dessert completed, Gavin collected their coats once more, and then they were weaving their way back out into the early spring night.

"Thanks for the ice cream."

"My pleasure."

Gavin fought the suddenly desperate desire to lay a hand low on her back and shoved his hands into his pockets as they headed back in the direction of her apartment. The lights of the pharmacy spilled back onto the sidewalk and illuminated the deep red tones of her hair.

The rain that had dogged them for days had faded, and

in its place was a cool breeze that promised spring, even if winter hadn't quite relinquished its cold grip.

"I still think your lack of ice cream in the home is a crime against nature, but I'll do my best to reserve further judgment."

"Maybe I just prefer eating ice cream with others."

That breeze kicked up once more as they passed by the alley between the pharmacy and the old shoe store that was its neighbor. The same kid who'd waited on them had obviously been put on closing duty, and he carried two big black bags in his hand to the curb, the distinct scent of the aging garbage filling the air.

"Maybe we'll—" He broke off as a dire look came over her face, the color instantly draining from her cheeks. "Sera?"

But she'd already bolted, heading straight for a city garbage can at the corner. The distinct sounds of misery rose up into the night air as she lost the remnants of her meal, and he made it just in time to hold her shoulders when a second, wracking jolt ripped through her.

"Oh God!" Her choked sob ripped at his heart, but it was the distinct words that followed that robbed him of breath. "I thought I was past this."

Don't miss
Threats in the Deep
by Addison Fox,
available wherever Harlequin Romantic Suspense
books and ebooks are sold.

www.Harlequin.com